THE TRUTH ABOUT DEATH

The Confessions of Frances Godwin
Snakewoman of Little Egypt
The Italian Lover
Philosophy Made Simple
Blues Lessons
The Fall of a Sparrow
The Sixteen Pleasures

THE TRUTH ABOUT DEATH

And Other Stories

ROBERT HELLENGA

BLOOMSBURY
NEW YORK · LONDON · OXFORD · NEW DELHI · SYDNEY

Bloomsbury USA
An imprint of Bloomsbury Publishing Plc

1385 Broadway	50 Bedford Square
New York	London
NY 10018	WC1B 3DP
USA	UK

www.bloomsbury.com

BLOOMSBURY and the Diana logo are trademarks of Bloomsbury Publishing Plc

First published 2016

© Robert Hellenga 2016

ISBN: HB: 978-1-63286-291-4
       ePub: 978-1-63286-292-1

LIBRARY OF CONGRESS CATALOGING-IN-PUBLICATION DATA.

Hellenga, Robert, 1941–
[Short stories. Selections]
The truth about death : and other stories / by Robert Hellenga.
pages ; cm
ISBN 978-1-63286-291-4 (hardback) — ISBN 978-1-63286-292-1 (ePub)
I. Title.
PS3558.E4753A6 2016
813'.54—dc23
2015031690

2 4 6 8 10 9 7 5 3 1

Typeset by RefineCatch Limited, Bungay, Suffolk
Printed and bound in the U.S.A. by Berryville Graphics Inc., Berryville, Virginia

To find out more about our authors and books visit www.bloomsbury.com. Here you will find extracts, author interviews, details of forthcoming events and the option to sign up for our newsletters.

Bloomsbury books may be purchased for business or promotional use. For information on bulk purchases please contact Macmillan Corporate and Premium Sales Department at specialmarkets@macmillan.com.

To Simone,
and in memoriam,
Heathcliff,
Saskia,
Maya,
Mishka

CONTENTS

THE TRUTH ABOUT DEATH

CHAPTER I: THE REMOVAL

PART I: SIMON

In the prep room Simon Oldfield studied his daughter, Hildegard—Hildi—as she slipped on a pair of disposable gloves and adjusted the strings of a shiny, disposable gray apron. He could see her mother in her stance—back straight, hip cocked, weight on one foot; he could see her mother in her long legs and long red hair—a splash of color in the pearly gray windowless room—and in her easy smile and her careless physical confidence; and he could see himself in her small-town, open, Midwestern face, though she'd just moved back from four years on the West Coast.

"You need to tie your hair back," he said, "before we get started."

"You got any of those curiously strong mints you used to give me?"

He laughed and shook his head.

1

The man stretched out on the steel embalming table, head propped up on a head block, as if he were peeking at his toes, was Simon's father—Bartemaeus Oldfield. He was naked, but his genitals were covered with a towel. Simon had already inserted the eye caps and set the features.

"You can shake his hand," he said. "He won't mind. Not anymore. I've already given him a bath."

"You're sure he's dead?"

"He'd better be." Simon put his hand on his father's chest.

"I guess sometimes you've got to joke around," she said.

"You're sure you're up for this?"

"Pop." She gave the word two syllables—"Pah-ahp"—and adjusted her granny glasses. Simon didn't know if they were fashionable or just old-fashioned. They made her look serious.

"You're glad he's dead, aren't you?" she said.

"Well, relieved."

Simon sutured the mouth shut, and then inserted a cannula into his father's carotid artery and a drainage hose into the jugular vein. He hooked up the embalming machine, and while the machine pumped a diluted mixture of formaldehyde and glutaraldehyde into the artery, forcing the blood out through the drainage hose, he massaged his father's right hand. "You take the left hand," he shouted over the loud hum of the machine, "and just work your way up. You want to loosen up the rigor and massage the blood out and work the embalming fluid in." Hildi didn't hesitate. She took her grandfather's hand in her own and began to massage it.

"You're right," he said in a loud voice. "I am glad. He made life miserable for your grandmother at the end. He made life miserable for everyone. He and that fake priest. All those e-mails."

"I got them too," she said. "Josh thought they were hysterical."

Josh was Hildi's soon-to-be ex-husband.

The fake priest, Father Axline, had persuaded Bart, and quite a few others, that the End Times were near. The signs were unmistakable: 9/11, the massing of a great army in the Far East, the wars in the Middle East, Hurricane Katrina, the proliferation of false teachings and of homosexuality, a Muslim representing Illinois in the United States Senate. These were wake-up calls, reminders that there was work to be done. Father Axline had persuaded Bart to write several large checks to his Holy Rosary Abbey, and Bart would have written more if the bank hadn't called Louisa, Simon's mother, who then got their lawyer to get a court order giving her financial power of attorney over all Bart's affairs.

"There was a long article about Father Axline in the *Register-Mail*," Simon said. "Your grandmother clipped it. He's just been indicted for swindling two old women out of half a million dollars."

Once the body was sufficiently infused with embalming fluid, which had given it a little color, Simon disconnected the embalming machine, tied off the veins and arteries, sutured up the incisions, and attached a rubber hose to the back of a suction trocar. The other end of the trocar was attached to a hydroaspirator. "Two inches above and two inches to the left," he said, indicating his father's navel with the tip of the trocar.

"Why left?"

"Because otherwise you'll get jammed up in the liver."

"You *want* to do this, don't you?" Hildi said. "I mean, why not let Gilbert do it?"

Gilbert was Simon's embalmer.

3

"It's a family tradition," Simon said. "Your grandfather and your great-uncle Aaron took their kits and flew down to Florida to embalm their father, your great-great-grandfather Jethro."

"Did Jethro embalm *his* father?"

"That I don't know. You're sure *you* want to do this?"

Hildi nodded. "I'm not squeamish. Besides, I'd better get used to it."

"You're really serious? About coming home?"

"I'm tired of making my life up one day at a time. I want a sense of direction, a sense of moving forward."

"Good idea," Simon said. "Establish some good habits and then you don't have to reinvent each day." She'd always been a free spirit, full of mischief. A good pal too. There was nothing small or mean about her, and she didn't have an ironic bone in her body. He liked to picture her holding a sick child or pinning up a clean diaper. Harder to picture her holding a suction trocar.

Twenty-five years old, she was coming off a bad marriage. He didn't know how bad. Not yet. She'd only been back two days. At least she and her husband, Josh, hadn't accumulated any children, or property. She'd been working at Cody's Bookstore on Telegraph Avenue in Berkeley when it closed. She'd worked at Elliot Bay, too, in Seattle and at Powell's in Portland. She'd always fit in everywhere. Josh had never fit in anywhere.

She's lost, he thought. *She's lost her way.* Unlike her brother, Jack, who confronted the world head-on, shaped it to his will, Hildi let the world flow through her.

Her plan was to enroll in the new mortuary science program at the community college, so she could live at home and then go into the business. Oldfield and Daughter, Funeral

Directors. He'd have to change the sign, which still read OLDFIELD AND SON. He hoped it was the right thing. There were a lot of things to discuss, but like a lawyer, he hesitated to ask questions to which he didn't know the answers.

Simon plunged the sharp trocar into his father's stomach. "You move the tip of the trocar around," he said, "to pierce the organs and aspirate the stomach fluid. If you look quickly you'll see his last supper passing through the glass connector."

By the time they'd packed up the orifices and cleaned the trocar, it was time to join the family in the living room, though Hildi's brother and his wife wouldn't be arriving till tomorrow.

What had just happened? Simon studied his daughter's face as they were washing up, looking for a clue. She tipped her head to one side, quick and alert like a bird in the grass, and smiled. Her smiles were always a pleasure. He wanted to tell her how much he loved her, wanted to tell her that he would keep her safe, at least for a little while. But he wanted to warn her too.

"It's not a job for the faint of heart," he said. "You're always on call. When the phone rings at three o'clock in the morning you've got to put on your undertaker duds and go. You're always dealing with people who are emotionally distressed. You've got your accidents, your children, your jaundice, your AIDS, your organ donors, your floaters, your autopsies, your suicides. You've got no personal boundaries, and you've got to have a strong stomach."

"Pop," she said, "it's not like I don't know what you've been doing every day ever since I can remember."

"Some people don't want to sit next to you," he said. "Even when I was in 'Nam. Nobody wanted to sit at the same table with the guys from Mortuary Affairs. They called it 'Graves

Registration' then. Here you're expected to join the Lions Club and the Rotary. You're expected to be a pillar of the community.

"When you show up for a removal, you're the only one dressed up, the only one whose face isn't tearstained. Everything is on hold for the people in the room. Time has stopped for them. You've got to join them. You're not the main character in this drama, but everyone's looking at you, waiting for you to enter their story, tell them what has to be done."

"You *are* a pillar of the community," Hildi said. "I mean, what would people do without you? Look at how many people you've helped."

Simon thought it was time to move on. "You know what Father Cochrane says at the beginning of every funeral?"

She shook her head.

"'Behold, I show unto you a mystery,'" Simon said. And then he put his hand on his father's forehead and said it again: "Behold, I show unto you a mystery."

They maneuvered Grandpa Bart onto a gurney, rolled him into the cooler, turned out the lights, and closed the door behind themselves.

PART II: LOUISA

Louisa, Simon's mother, tried to suppress her anger as she slammed down the phone in the upstairs hallway, stormed into the living room, and bore down on her family. It was a large comfortable room. Two faded Oriental rugs, deep red but with different designs, partially covered a darkened hard-wood floor. A row of windows looked out on what had once been a paddock. Someone had lowered the old-fashioned venetian blinds, but she could see strips of sky through the wide slats. Simon was in his chair at the bay window, next to an ancient hibiscus with two deep red flowers; Hildi and her mother, Elizabeth, were sitting next to each other on the old red sofa with weak springs; and Louisa's son-in-law Morris—who taught psychology at the University of Chicago and lectured all over the country, all over the world, on memory and cognition—was striking a pose in front of the fireplace, hands behind his back, his belt denting his substantial stomach. He was married to Simon's younger sister, Alexandra, who was taking a nap in one of the upstairs bedrooms.

"You look like you're about to launch into an adventure story," Louisa said to him, "about your trip to Africa."

"I was lecturing at the University of Ghana," he said, "not looking for Dr. Livingstone in the Congo. Or was it Dr. Stanley? I forget who was looking for whom."

"Livingstone," Louisa said. "How could you forget that? Stanley was looking for Livingstone."

Julia, Simon's older sister, would be coming later with her husband, Curtis, and their three children. Curtis owned an appliance store in Winnetka and was president of the Rotary Club. Julia managed an independent bookstore called Open Books.

Drinks were ready to be poured. Glasses were waiting on a silver tray on the coffee table next to a stack of *New Yorker*s: three Waterford tumblers, some French bistro glasses (the kind that don't break), and some wineglasses from Target. White wine for Simon and Elizabeth and a bottle of Irish whiskey too. Bushmills, for Louisa and Morris. A loaf of bread and a chunk of Gorgonzola on a wooden plate. Ice cubes melting in a mixing bowl.

"That man," Louisa said, tugging at her gold earrings and tweaking her silk blouse till it sat comfortably on her shoulders. "That man. I've been on the phone for half an hour." She shook her head and gave her blouse another tweak. "He wants to have the funeral at his Holy Rosary Abbey. He says that's what Bart wanted. And he wants a copy of the will ASAP. He says Bart made a new will and left a lot of money to the Abbey."

"Father Axline?" Morris said. "The one who's been charged with 'deceptive practices'?"

"And 'financial exploitation of elderly persons,'" Louisa said. "I sent you that article, didn't I? Bart said the charges were all nonsense, but he's been denounced by the Church too. Every Sunday Father Cochrane has something to say about him and his fake abbey. We've all been warned. Catholics are not supposed to have anything to do with him."

"Bart didn't make a new will, did he?" Morris asked.

"You can relax, Morris. He wanted to, but he couldn't do it. Everything's in both our names. I wouldn't sign the papers. Arthur—that's our lawyer—told Bart he was crazy, but Bart wouldn't listen to him, so Arthur drew up some phony papers, but I wouldn't even sign *phony* papers. You should have heard him."

"The lawyer?"

"No. Bart."

"Louisa," Morris said, "you shouldn't have to deal with this. Let Simon handle it. He's the funeral director."

"But I'm the widow," she said, "and the will was just the tip of the iceberg." She looked around at her family. "I'm going to help myself to some old Bushmills. Why is everyone so quiet anyway? You're waiting for me to cast the first stone. Well, consider it cast. Now it's somebody else's turn. Don't stand on ceremony.

Nil nisi bonum doesn't apply today. I need to sit down." Elizabeth stood up to make a place for her mother-in-law.

They all started casting stones at the dead man in the downstairs refrigerator: the drinking, the bullying, the abuse, the anger, the threats, the crazy political e-mails: *Why is it that "American" and "Republican" both end in "I can," but "Democrats" ends in "rats"?*

"*The American Way of Death*," Louisa said. "Bart was never the same after they reissued that book. And then when he got the cancer and the doctors told him there was nothing they could do, he tried to bribe Father Cochrane to promise him a miracle, and then he threatened him, and when that didn't work he finally went to see that fake priest."

"Hardening of the arteries," Simon said. "You lose some mental functioning. Maybe Alzheimer's."

"It was the opposite of Alzheimer's," Louisa said. "He started remembering things he should have forgotten years ago: old grudges, old arguments. And he never forgave a thing, or if he had, then later he'd take back his forgiveness."

"Neural plasticity," Morris said. "Be interesting to see if he had an enlarged hippocampus like a London cabdriver." Morris surveyed his audience and started to explain: "Because they have to remember so many street addresses. Their hippocampi become enlarged."

"He unforgave people?" Alexandra interrupted, rubbing sleep out of her eyes as she entered the room. "I didn't know you could do that."

"Bart could do anything," Louisa said. "He could unforgive you for things you did forty years ago." She was thinking of her Italian professor at the college. Love had lifted her up like a big wave and had left her stranded on the shore. Where Bart had been waiting for her. Her professor Gianluigi Bevilacqua had gone back to Rome after he'd been kicked out of the college, and she'd never seen him again. Bart, who'd met Louisa through Father Arnie at the Newman Center, had been so much in love with her at the time that Gianluigi Bevilacqua hadn't mattered; but forty years later it had mattered, and he'd sat in his Barcalounger in front of the TV and had called her a whore and accused her of running around. Sometimes he hadn't let her stay in the room with him to watch *Seinfeld*.

Louisa lifted the tumbler of Bushmills to her lips and swallowed. "I think I'll go to Rome," she said. "Hildi can come with me."

"Rome?" Hildi asked.

"Bart promised to take me, but he was always too busy. People kept dying."

"Why Rome?"

Louisa emptied her glass and sucked on an ice cube, thinking. "I want to see all the Caravaggios."

"Rome's the right place," Elizabeth said. "But I never knew you were keen on Caravaggio."

In fact Louisa wasn't particularly keen on Caravaggio, but she was reading a mystery novel set in Rome, in which the detective has to analyze some of Caravaggio's paintings in order to solve the crime, and she'd just said the first thing that popped into her head. She didn't want to mention Gianluigi Bevilacqua, and she couldn't remember the name of the mystery novel; so she said, "You lectured on Caravaggio in your art history survey." Elizabeth was an art historian. Louisa had sat in on her introductory course at the college. "I want to see *The Calling of Saint Matthew*. What would it be like to be *called* like that? There you are in a gambling den with a bunch of lowlifes and this strange figure comes. 'Follow me . . .'"

"It's in the French church," Elizabeth said. "San Luigi dei Francesi. And it's a customhouse, not a gambling den. Caravaggios can be very intimidating, you know."

Before they could pursue the subject of Caravaggio, the phone rang. They stopped talking and listened while Simon took the call in the hallway. Anders Johansen had died. Simon would have to go out on a removal.

"Johansen," Louisa said before Simon was even off the phone. "He's prepaid. He's one of the last prepaids I handled before they started putting everything on the computer."

"Isn't he the one who sold Grandpa Bart the horses?" Hildi asked. "Stormy and Salty? For the Amish funeral?" And the conversation took a sudden turn.

"You couldn't have been more than seven years old," Louisa said to Hildi, counting backward on her fingers.

What had happened was that an Amish family had been stranded in Galesburg. The husband had died on the train— a massive heart attack—between Burlington and Galesburg, and the train crew had put him in the baggage car. They'd wanted the body off the train at the next stop.

"He'd been ostracized," Louisa said, "and they were on their way from somewhere in Iowa to Kewanee, where they had family. Shunning, they called it. No one would talk to any of them. The whole family. It was okay for them to take the train, but not to ride in a motorcar, so Bart borrowed a horse from Anders Johansen. Anders hitched it up to an old buggy and Bart drove it into town."

"It was Salty," Hildi said.

"That was right after Van Gogh's *Irises* sold for fifty million dollars," Elizabeth said.

"Yeah," Morris said. "Right after the stock market collapsed."

Salty was a small-boned, flat-footed Tennessee Walker. Bart had bought her after the Amish funeral, and then Hildi'd thought she'd be lonely, so she talked her grandfather into buying the second horse, Stormy, a broken-down quarter horse. He'd made a paddock in the lot in back, which had since been turned into a parking lot, and when the city had sent him a notice that he couldn't keep horses in town, he'd said it was part of the business, that he needed the horses for Amish funerals. So he'd been granted a variance.

"It was sad," Louisa said. "Bart and a couple of the conductors got the body into the buggy and Bart brought it back here, and then he went back to the station to get the rest of the family, a wife and two little girls. He brought *them* back here too. They didn't have anyplace else to go. I fixed sandwiches, and we all ate in the kitchen, and they slept on the floor up in Simon's tower. They held themselves together."

"The Amish don't make a big fuss about death," Simon said. He was standing in the doorway. "It was like a Jewish funeral. Plain box. No embalming."

"They must feel something."

"Yes, but it's different. We're all trying to *find* ourselves," Simon said. "The Amish are trying to *lose* themselves."

"I'm coming with you," Hildi said, struggling to get up off the sofa.

"Don't be silly," Elizabeth said. She turned to Simon. "Can't you call Gilbert? He could take Henry with him." Henry operated the crematory and sometimes worked as a greeter. But Simon shook his head. "Or wait for Able to get here." Able, Simon's younger brother, was a funeral director in Kewanee.

"He won't be here till eight o'clock," Simon said.

"Or take Morris," she said. "It might be an interesting experience for him, something to remember."

"Whoa," Morris said.

"At least let me finish the story," Louisa said. "We had the funeral the next day. Bart took the body to Hope Cemetery in the buggy, and then came back for the family. He let you drive," she said to Hildi. "I remember. That was the first time you ever drove a horse and buggy. Probably the last time too. That night they got on the train to Kewanee. Bart never charged them."

Bart hadn't charged them for the funeral, and Louisa remembered all the unpaid invoices she'd found in his desk when she'd started doing the books, and she began to cry. She didn't think she had any tears in her for Bart, not after the last couple of years, but now they began to dribble down her cheeks. Elizabeth brought a box of Kleenex and sat down next to her on the sofa and put her arms around her. After a few minutes she freshened Louisa's drink and then poured some white wine for herself.

PART III: ELIZABETH

Whom would I commission to paint this scene? Elizabeth asked herself. There wasn't anything especially dramatic or picturesque about it—her mother-in-law's tears catching the light as she sipped her whiskey, her husband and her daughter standing next to each other in the wide doorway that opened into the upstairs hall, Morris still posing in front of the fireplace, Alexandra patting her husband's arm before sinking down into Hildi's place on the sofa, a pair of Waterford tumblers sparkling on a silver tray—so it wouldn't be Caravaggio or

Rembrandt. Not Leonardo. It would have to be a Dutch genre painting, a cozy living room with a memento mori—a skull sitting on top of one of the bookcases. Not that this family needed to be reminded of death! They lived and breathed death. At times it was exhilarating. Made Elizabeth think about what she was doing. But it was hard, too. She didn't want her husband to go on a removal just as she was about to put on the potatoes, didn't want her daughter to go with him, didn't like the way that Death trumped everything. There was Gilbert, of course, always ready to step in. Loyal to a fault. But there was something cold about Gilbert. He would never have let the Amish family get away without paying. Simon, like his father, let people get away with it—hard times in Galesburg after the Maytag closing—but at least he wrote the losses off on their taxes.

Maybe De Kooning, she thought. *Wouldn't that be something!*

Elizabeth had come to Galesburg from Princeton University, where she'd studied iconography with Kurt Weitzmann, and like a lot of new faculty in her cohort, she hadn't been planning to stay in the Midwest once she'd published her dissertation, hadn't been planning to marry one of her students, hadn't been planning to marry a funeral director. But then she'd met Simon, who'd swaggered into her classroom in the Fine Arts Center in his combat fatigues. He'd been twenty-three, older than most of the students, and she'd been twenty-seven, younger than most of the faculty. He was going to school on the GI Bill and working for his father. He'd been a "mortuary specialist" in Vietnam, and he wrote a paper about the failure of Art to stand up to the things he'd seen in the mortuary in Da Nang, in order to erase the images that he couldn't stop seeing in his dreams. Beauty itself was impotent, he argued, and so were the attempts of Art to confront Truth: the *Isenheim Altarpiece*, Goya's *Third of May*, Michelangelo's *Rondanini Pietà* . . . they couldn't shock you or numb you like a box of putrid body parts or a face covered with mold and crawling with maggots, the skin slipping off. Day after day. They'd been equipped to process 350 bodies a month, and they were getting almost a hundred a day. It was the only job in the army, he'd told her, that you could quit! But Simon hadn't quit.

And she hadn't quit either, had never lost her faith in the healing power of great art, and years later she'd decorated his hideaway up in the octagonal tower, which she called a belvedere, with good quality prints—Lascaux, Caravaggio, Rembrandt, Vermeer, Monet, Renoir, Pollock, De Kooning, and even a painting done by an elephant—so Simon would have something beautiful to look at when he wanted to get away from his work. She'd wanted him to see what she saw when she looked at Rembrandt's *Side of Beef* or Pollock's *Alchemy*, or a still life by Morandi, and she had wanted him to learn from Chardin to see the beauty all around us, to feel the emotional impact of colored pigments.

She'd stopped short of framing them, but she had labeled each one with the painter's name and dates. There wasn't much wall space, just room for twenty-four prints, in columns of three, between the eight pairs of high windows.

Now she was fifty-six years old, still attractive. One of her colleagues, a man Elizabeth had always admired, had propositioned her only last week. She hadn't been tempted. She and Simon had been lucky in love. And lucky in their vocations. She was preparing a paper on a series of odd figures—figures that didn't belong—in medieval and early Renaissance iconography, and would be presenting her paper at the CAA conference at

New York University in the spring. And Simon—well, people kept dying. The phone kept ringing. And like Hermes, the Greek god of transitions and boundaries, Simon kept on conducting the souls of the dead from this world to the next.

She had a pork roast in the oven. All she needed to do was boil some baby potatoes and make a salad. Without Simon and Hildi there'd be nine—she counted on her fingers— including the kids. Eleven, if Simon's brother Able and his wife, Marilyn, showed up.

There'd be enough left over for sandwiches tomorrow. Elizabeth and Simon's son, Jack, and Jack's wife, Sally, would be coming from New York in the morning. They were going to rent a car at the airport in Peoria. She went upstairs to speak to Hildi.

PART IV: HILDI

Hildi was looking out her bedroom window, trying to picture the parking lot as a paddock, trying to remember Salty and Stormy, when her mother snapped a picture with a new digital camera. When Hildi heard the camera click, she turned around and smiled. She'd been rummaging through a suitcase, which was open on the bed, looking for something to wear on the removal.

"You don't have to do this, you know," her mother said. "You've only been here two days. There's no reason Morris can't go."

"Uncle Morrie?" Hildi laughed. "Right."

Her mother handed her the camera so she could look at the image on the tiny screen. "You're too nice," her mother said. "You need to be tougher, stronger."

"I am strong," Hildi said, flexing her muscles. "I don't know why you don't want me to go."

"I just don't. That's all. It's not right."

"Uncle Morrie wouldn't pick up a dead body in a million years," she said. "Besides, it's Mr. Johansen. Anders. He's the one who sold Grandpa Bart the horses."

"I know about the horses. That doesn't mean *you* have to pick up his dead body. Your brother never went on removals."

"Mah-ahm," Hildi protested.

"What are you going to do if he weighs three hundred pounds?"

"He can't weigh that much. Pop said he had cancer. Besides, Pop's got the new Med Sled. He showed me this afternoon. It's got a stairwell braking system, so you can attach it to something at the top of the stairway and just slide the body down without worrying that it's going to get away from you."

"That's wonderful, Sweetie. Now put on some dark slacks and a white blouse." Her mother started to look through the clothes that had been piled up on the bed. "You need to look respectable. Like you know what you're doing."

"I do know what I'm doing," Hildi said.

"I hope so."

"Maybe I'll take some of your shortbread. Do you think that would be a good idea?"

"Shortbread's always a good idea. I'll make up a tin."

Hildi tossed the Med Sled into the back of the van. She was eager to get started on her new life. She thought of the Oldfield funeral home as a place where the important questions got asked, if not answered. A place where people were forced to confront the great contingencies of human existence. At least one of them. She thought of it as a place where the spirit was forced to confront the mechanics of death—the embalming machine humming on the floor, like one of the little robots you see in the Hammacher Schlemmer catalogs, aspirating blood and body fluids into a drain that looked like a urinal attached to the wall. It was her first removal, and she was excited, though she tried not to show it. She was not afraid of the dead, and she didn't think she was afraid of grief, didn't think she'd be afraid of the grieving widow. She imagined herself taking Mrs. Johansen's hand, touching her arm, reminding her of Stormy and Salty and the Amish funeral.

The Johansen farm was five miles east of town, on old Illinois 34. Her father cranked up the air-conditioning—it was the end of August, high of ninety-three that afternoon—and put a cassette into the player, and they listened to Floyd Cramer as they drove. Hildi had never heard of Floyd Cramer.

"Your grandfather loved Floyd Cramer," Simon said. "He always kept two or three Floyd Cramer cassettes in the glove compartment. 'On the Rebound,' 'San Antonio Rose.' He was Elvis Presley's piano player." The notes bounced out of the speaker. Hildi'd never heard anything like it.

"It's called slip-note piano," her father said.

Hildi was just a little bit nervous as her father knocked on the Johansens' side door. Mrs. Johansen opened the door and a big dog burst out of the house and put his feet up on Hildi's shoulders.

"Don't mind Charlie," Mrs. Johansen shouted.

"What kind of dog is he?" Hildi asked, pushing him down and bending to kiss the top of his head.

"Just a plain old farm dog," Mrs. Johansen said. The dog sniffed Hildi's shoes and then raised his leg on a pot of impatiens.

The simple unreconstructed farmhouse kitchen was hot. There was no air-conditioning. The floor was faded linoleum and a box fan had been duct-taped into an open window. Mrs. Johansen hadn't called the coroner, so there was no death certificate. The dog circled around and then curled up on a quilt.

"I'm going to need a death certificate," her father explained.

While her father made the call to Sam Martin, the coroner, Hildi helped Mrs. Johansen make coffee—filled the carafe with water while Mrs. Johansen eyeballed the coffee into the paper filter—and got three white china mugs down out of a cupboard. "Get one for Sam too," Mrs. Johansen said.

They sat down at the table. *It's going to be a while. What will we talk about?* "Would you like a piece of shortbread?" Hildi asked, taking the tin out of her bag and setting it on the table.

"That would be nice," Mrs. Johansen said.

Hildi opened the tin. The pieces of shortbread were stacked like dominoes. Mrs. Johansen helped herself to a piece. "Real butter," she said after the first bite.

"My mother makes it," Hildi said.

Mrs. Johansen sat with her legs slightly apart, leaning forward and putting her hands on the table. She slapped her leg and Charlie came over and put his head on her knee. She put a hand on Charlie's head. Hildi put *her* hand on Mrs. Johansen's *other* hand, which was flat on the table. After about thirty seconds Mrs. Johansen pulled her hand away. "There's a bottle of bourbon under the sink," she said, motioning with her arm. "Would you get it out, and then pour me some coffee? It'll be ready in a minute."

"These mugs are just like the ones we have at home," Hildi said, setting the whiskey down on the table.

"How about a game of pinochle?" Mrs. Johansen asked. "To pass the time."

Simon, still on the phone, nodded.

"I've never played pinochle," Hildi said.

"It's easy," Mrs. Johansen said, shuffling the cards. "You can pick it up in no time. You play with a forty-eight-card deck. In each suit you've got two aces, two tens, two kings, two queens, two jacks, and two nines. The tens outrank everything except the aces. You just have to get used to that. Just think of the queen of spades in hearts. Or just say 'ace, ten, king' over and over. Your aces, tens, and kings are counters. You get points for them. You can win tricks with queens, jacks, and nines, but you don't get any points. But let's play a practice hand and you'll soon catch on. You play euchre? You know what a 'bower' is?"

Hildi shook her head. She got up to pour the coffee.

"Never mind," Mrs. Johansen said.

Mrs. Johansen held her cards in one hand and kept the other on the dog's head, except when she took a trick or laid down her cards. When she finished her coffee she poured some bourbon into the cup. She looked at Simon and Hildi, but they shook their heads.

They played for fifty cents a game and twenty-five cents a set. At first Hildi kept reneging, but by the time the coroner arrived she was laying down her melds with a flourish and gathering in tricks right and left. She was almost sorry they had to quit.

The coroner, Sam Martin, didn't bother to knock. He came through the screen door, looked around, leaned over to pat the dog, which sniffed at his crotch. "Haven't seen *you* in a while," he said to Hildi, pushing the dog away. Mrs. Johansen asked him if he wanted to play.

"Not tonight, Alice," he said. "I'll just step upstairs."

"I already cleaned him up a little."

The coroner put his hand on Mrs. Johansen's head. "You didn't need to do that, Alice. That's what you're paying Simon for."

"It's all right," she said. "It's what he would've wanted. Keep the door at the bottom of the stairs closed or Charlie'll be up there in a jiff. I had to leash him to pull him out of the bedroom."

The coroner went upstairs. Mrs. Johansen dealt another hand, but they didn't play it. They just let the cards lie. Mrs. Johansen poured a little more bourbon into her cup and passed the bottle around. Hildi didn't mind Scotch, but she didn't see how anybody could drink bourbon. But she poured a splash into her cup anyway, on top of an inch of cold coffee.

The coroner came down and sat with Mrs. Johansen while Hildi went upstairs with her father. Mr. Johansen's neck and fingers and ankles were rigid, but his shoulders and thighs were flaccid, and they had no trouble wrapping him in a sheet and rolling him onto the Med Sled and strapping him in. He was wearing blue flannel pajamas and his hair had been combed. His was the second dead body she'd touched that day. *What is it like to touch a dead body?* She couldn't say. *Just an empty shell?* She didn't think so, and she knew her father didn't think so either. He didn't have to say it, but a dead body was something holy. Otherwise you might as well just put it out with the trash. *Does the spirit of the dead person hang out for a while to see what's happening?* She didn't believe that either. But she thought about it, picturing Mr. Johansen's spirit up in a corner of the ceiling, looking down. It was a large room with a braided rug on the floor, the edges worn where Anders Johansen had put his feet down when he got out of bed in the morning.

They slid the Med Sled down a narrow hallway and around a sharp corner to the top of the stairs. "Piece of cake," her father said. He locked the stairwell braking system at the foot of the Med Sled to a newel post so it wouldn't get away from them as they slid it gently down the stairs. "Easier than carrying him," her father said. Mrs. Johansen had put the leash on Charlie and held him with both hands while they pulled the body through the kitchen, out to the van, and onto the lift.

They went back into the kitchen and sat down with the coroner and Mrs. Johansen to take care of the paperwork. The cards from the last hand of pinochle were still facedown on the table.

"You going to be all right here all alone?" Hildi asked.

"My sister's coming from Peoria," she said. "But I'll be all right. Thank you for asking."

It was now almost midnight. Halfway home her father turned off Floyd Cramer and started to sing. "'You are my sunshine, my only sunshine.'" Hildi was a little self-conscious. But when her father sang the first verse a second time, she sang along with him. Softly at first, then with more confidence. "'You'll never know, dear, how much I love you. Please don't take my sunshine away.'"

They sang "Home on the Range," "Camptown Races"— "'Doo-dah, doo-dah'"—and "Show Me the Way to Go Home," and Simon pulled the van into a spot on Cherry Street in front of Duffy's Tap, an old-fashioned bar with a hand-lettered sign in the window that said HOME OF THE POOR AND UNKNOWN. Simon rolled the windows down. In the bar they both ordered drafts and took their glasses to a booth, where they sat across from each other.

"I always used to stop here with your grandfather," her father said.

"It smells good," Hildi said. "If you like the smell of stale beer." She lifted her glass. "Which I do." The beer tasted fresh and clean after the bourbon-coffee mix. "I've been wondering," she said, "if you could have a funeral that tells the truth about death? Something not based on lies and fairy tales. I reread *Anna Karenina* earlier this year. When Josh and I were splitting up. It's such a wonderful novel, but Levin just can't come to terms with death at the end. Or Tolstoy can't. Can't leave it alone. Keeps clamoring for a fairy tale, and when he gets one, it doesn't ring true. Not compared to Anna's suicide."

"What's the truth we should be telling?"

"I'm not sure it's something you *tell*. Maybe I just mean, there are things we could do differently."

"For example?"

"You know what we should do, Pop? We should get a dog, a big dog."

"A dog?"

"You know, like Charlie. The kind they take to old people's homes now. A therapy dog. They're specially trained."

"You mean so they don't bite the old people?"

"No, Pop. I'm not joking. Don't you think dogs are comforting in a really deep, uncomplicated way? A dog would go right to the person who's grieving hardest. Look at Charlie. He could be a therapy dog. There must be a school for therapy dogs in Peoria or the Quad Cities."

"I'll take it under advisement."

"If there's a dog in the frame, it's a better frame, don't you think? And we could get some different pictures too. Get rid of the clichés, all the sunsets and sunrises. Bring in some works by local artists. Maybe turn the visitation room into a gallery. I'll bet the Civic Art Center would be glad to cooperate. Get some bright colors in there and in the hallways. Josh and I went to a funeral home in Berkeley where they had a regular gallery, a place for local artists to sell their paintings."

"This isn't California, Hildi. It's the Midwest. The middle of the Midwest."

"Oh, poo. We could set a new trend."

"Trends are always new."

"I guess I mean something about a funeral being a celebration of the dead person's life."

"You couldn't get more trendy. 'We are here to celebrate the life of . . .' The latest thing is the tableau. You know, for somebody who liked to go to the beach and drink beer: you prop the body up on a beach chair and pour a lot of sand on the floor, get a cooler full of beer, hire a comedian to make beer jokes. Or prop the body up on a motorcycle, as if it's going sixty miles an hour. It's being done. Drive-through viewings too."

"That's *so* California," she said, "but it's true, isn't it? I mean about a funeral being a celebration of a person's life."

"Yes, it's true. But it's not the whole truth, and it's not wholly true. It's too simple. Death is a mystery, not an excuse for a party. There's a time to weep and a time to laugh, a time to mourn and a time to dance, and you don't want to get them mixed up. You don't want people grieving at a baptism, do you?"

"I agree, Pop, but don't you think there's more we could do? Make it possible for the families to help prep the body, for example."

"Let me explain something to you, darling daughter. People don't want to help prep dead bodies. They want dead bodies out of the house. Why do you think they pay me to collect dead bodies and prep them? Why do they call in the middle of the night instead of waiting till a decent hour?"

"I know, Pop. But what I'm feeling right now . . . close to Grandpa Bart. Mr. Johansen too. Something important has happened, and we're part of it. Not just spectators. Didn't the family used to wash the body in the old days?"

"Very old days. They had cooling boards too and gravity embalming. You'd have to carry buckets of blood out to the outhouse."

"Don't you think it's important? Don't you think people would . . . I don't know . . . feel it's important? Don't you think there's a kind of communal memory about this sort of hands-on experience? Look at Mrs. Johansen. She wanted to clean up her husband, at least a little. She wanted to touch him, she wanted to put her hands on him."

"It's messy," Simon said. "Dead bodies don't last very long. The insides . . . Never mind."

"I know it's messy. That's why it's important. Life is messy. That's why it's better to get your hands dirty than to post a Facebook photo of the dead person for people to 'like.'"

"You'd put us out of business in a year! You want to bring someone who's grieving into the prep room and hand them a suction trocar and say 'Have at it'?"

"Pop, you know that's not what I mean. I mean help wash the body—that's all. Touch it with their hands. Not be afraid of the dead. Help dress them. Embalming's not really neces-sary anyway, is it? I mean Jews don't get embalmed, do they? The Amish man didn't get embalmed. Why not just let them help wash the body?"

"And pack the orifices so they don't leak?"

"That too," she said. "What did they used to do?"

"The women took care of it."

"Figures."

Simon finished his beer. "How much did you win?" he asked.

"About three dollars," she said. "I forgot to remind Mrs. Johansen about Stormy and Salty. I wanted to tell her how Grandpa Bart and I used to ride them around the paddock. Or just sit on them and talk to each other."

"You'll have another chance to talk to her."

"Do you think Nana will go to Rome?"

"No idea. Do you want to go with her if she does?"

"I want to stay here with you," she said. "I just want to sit here and have another beer."

"We've got to get Mr. Johansen into the cooler."

"He'll keep for a while, won't he? One more beer?"

"He'll keep for a while, but not too long, not in this heat."

CHAPTER II: HILDI IN LOVE

Hildi had been anxious to get on with her new life. Her new vocation. She'd been anxious to strengthen the bonds that bound her to her father and her mother, that bound her to a place where she'd been happy—the whole family living together in the funeral home. Two apartments. Upstairs divided. Grandpa Bart and Nana and her mother and father, and her brother too. A beautiful old house with seven working fireplaces. Now three working fireplaces. A carriage house in the back that had been converted into a garage. A paddock, not a parking lot, where she'd looked after Stormy and Salty. She remembered the way Stormy had scratched her head against the two-by-four that Bart had nailed up to stabilize the gate, and how Salty had liked to have her fore-lock braided.

For the first time in a long time, if ever, she'd experienced a sense of a larger purpose. Not large enough to overwhelm, but large enough to give her a sense of direction, a sense that her life might matter to someone other than herself and her parents—and her grandmother, of course.

But then she went to Rome with her grandmother, and Rome took her by surprise. She fell in love with Rome and felt something happening inside her, as if she'd become preg-nant and a new and different kind of happiness was growing inside her.

She worried at first about Nana's sore throat and persistent cough, but she was reassured by the doctor at the *guardia medica* on Viale Trastevere who listened to Nana's back to check for pneumonia, and to Hildi's back too, just in case. He took Nana's temperature and prescribed Ciproxin. The medical care at the *guardia medica* was free, but Nana would have to pay for the Ciproxin.

Hildi didn't expect to see the doctor again, but he stopped by their apartment the next morning at the end of his shift to check on Nana. He took her temperature and listened to her back again and left a big fat Italian thermometer with Hildi and told her to call if Nana's fever went up. And then he went to Bar Belli with Hildi to get a *dolce* and a cappuccino for Nana's breakfast.

Every morning Hildi and Nana went out to see a Caravaggio or two. Afternoons Nana stayed in bed with a slight fever. Hildi liked being in charge, liked taking care of Nana, who had taken care of her so many times. Liked figuring out the bus routes, liked keeping them supplied with tickets, liked reading to Nana in the afternoons, taking her temperature with the big fat Italian thermometer. Nana's fever was never more than one degree centigrade above normal, just enough so she could relax and not feel guilty about staying in bed. Hildi knew the feeling from when she was a child and didn't want to go to school, how nice it was to stay in bed with a book and have someone bring you tea with honey.

She liked shopping with Marcella, the nosy neighbor, who wanted to practice her English and who enjoyed introducing Hildi to all the shopkeepers: at Antica Cacciara, where she bought salami and cheese, olives and wine; at the *macelleria* across the street from Antica Cacciara, where she'd buy a couple of chicken thighs or a couple of pork chops; at the bakery on Via della Lungaretta where she bought two little round loaves of bread every day; and at their last stop, the Antica Frutteria on the corner of Via della Luce, where she bought fruit and vegetables.

And she liked having tea or coffee with Marcella, and not just with Marcella, but with Roberto from the rental agency; and with the Russian woman Anastasia, who came to clean the apartment; and with a Dutch woman—Griet, an opera singer—who'd asked her for directions at the foot of Ponte Palatino.

All these new friends thought she needed help, instruction. They were all eager to teach her about Italy, about Rome: Why the food was better in Rome than in Florence or Bologna, and the importance of certain unwritten rules: don't cut spaghetti up with your knife and fork (like an English tourist); don't put Parmesan cheese on *spaghetti alle vongole*; don't ask for a cappuccino in the afternoon.

Hildi was grateful for this kind of instruction. She had a sense that she'd never get it quite right, but that was okay because there was always someone there to correct her.

And there was the doctor, of course, Dottore Francesco Tonarelli, who had stopped by on Wednesday and then again on Friday to check on Nana. Both times he'd gone to Bar Belli with Hildi. He was the only one who didn't seem to think she needed tweaking, didn't need a course in how to behave in Italy, and so Hildi was happy, even excited, to go out to dinner with him on Wednesday night, the middle of their second week in Rome. She spent some of the money her father had given her on a new outfit—new shoes and the kind of long sweater that everyone was wearing over tights, that looked like a *very* short dress. She'd given Nana her Ciproxin and tucked her in with *Anna Karenina*—on Hildi's e-reader, a Nook—and was admiring herself in the glass doors of one of the bookcases in the living room when she heard Nana shuffling down the hall.

"What on earth ... ?" Nana was looking at her watch, which she held in her hand.

"I'm going out for a while," Hildi said.

"It's almost nine o'clock."

"That's early in Rome."

"But where are you going?"

"Just out. I need to get out for a while."

"But we went out this morning. Doria Pamphilj. We saw *Mary Magdalene Penitent* and *Rest on the Flight into Egypt* and the Breughels. And you went out this afternoon. You did the shopping."

"And now I'm going out tonight. I won't be late."

"But where will you go?"

"I'm going to meet a man, okay?"

"But how did you meet a man?"

"He's the mysterious passenger who got on the train in the middle of the night, like Count Vronsky."

"I hope his intentions are better than Count Vronsky's."

"I'm twenty-five years old, Nana, and I'm going out. Do you want me to help you find your place on the Nook? Levin and Oblonsky are having dinner in a French restaurant."

"I'm not senile. At least Anna's back in St. Petersburg." She sat down on the sofa that opened into the bed that Hildi slept on.

"There you are. Do you want me to leave my *telefonino*?"

"If your *telefonino* is here, then I can't call *you*, can I? Besides, I don't know how to work it anyway."

"I'm glad you're starting to feel better," Hildi said.

"I'm *not* feeling better," Nana said.

"I'm going to meet the doctor," Hildi said. "Dottore Tonarelli—Francesco, or Checco—at a restaurant on Via della Lungaretta. *He* has a cell phone. You could always call *him*."

"I see," Nana said, and shuffled back to bed, and Hildi tried to imagine her grandmother young and in love with her Italian professor, a shadowy ghost that haunted the family archives.

Via della Lungaretta was definitely touristy, but there weren't that many tourists in November. Hildi stopped, as she always did, to read all the menus posted outside the restaurants, which were mostly empty. Maybe it was too early. Or maybe it was too late. She wasn't sure. Not yet.

Sometimes she wished she knew Italian, but she liked not knowing it too. Liked relying on other senses. Sights, sounds, smells: Christmas lights up over Via della Lungaretta, chestnuts roasting on a street corner, the lights of the little parachutes that the children launched high into the air above the piazza with a sort of slingshot, the cello player in the piazza, water gurgling in the fountain, every little corner a thing of beauty. Well, most little corners.

She studied the menu outside Carlo Menta while she waited for Checco. It was more or less the same as all the other menus, except that it was very inexpensive. Through the window she could see that it was full of people—including children of all ages—eating and drinking, talking and laughing, the way a restaurant should be. She checked herself for nerves. None. Only a little sadness, as if she were starting down a familiar road and wasn't sure about her own intentions. She didn't really need another adventure.

Checco arrived, and a girl who didn't seem to know Italian very well—probably Albanian—showed them to a table. They ate some bread and drank some wine. Hildi told him she was going to be an undertaker.

"An *impresario funebre*," he said, and he told her that he worked one twenty-four-hour shift a week at the *guardia medica* but that his real specialty was a rare pathology—*linfomi cutanei*—a kind of skin cancer.

"Corpses and skin cancer," she said. "We make quite a pair." And she told him her ideas about changes she wanted to introduce in her family's funeral home—get a dog, put up works of art by local artists, hire local musicians, bring in members of the deceased's family to help prepare the body. And she was surprised to learn that there were no funeral homes in Italy. Just those little offices like the one she walked by every morning on the other side of Piazza San Cosimato when she went shopping with their neighbor. The *impresario*—that's the undertaker—goes to the deceased's house or to the hospital to prepare the body.

Hildi liked this idea and thought she'd suggest it to her father. "I suppose it doesn't matter where the body is prepared," she said to Checco. "The important thing is that the dead body forces you to confront the big questions."

"And these big questions are?"

"Oh, you know, about the meaning of life, about love, death."

"Oh," he said, "those questions."

"Well, it's more than that. You have to ask yourself about courage and fortitude; you have to ask yourself about hope and love. And the interesting thing is," she said, "that these questions change. At least the answers do. If you were dying fifty years ago—maybe a hundred years—you'd be afraid of going to hell because you'd lost your faith or had fallen into despair, or just had too many sins on your conscience. But I think that if you're dying today, you're more likely to be afraid that you haven't really lived your life at all, afraid that you've just been passing the time, afraid that life itself—not just your own life, but *life*—is meaningless."

"And you? Are you just passing the time?"

"Right now? Probably. Waiting to go home. Get to work. Step into my new life."

"In general?"

She shook her head. "Not anymore."

The waiter came to take their order. He and Checco seemed to be old friends, but Hildi couldn't be sure. Maybe all Italian waiters acted like old friends.

Checco described his own work. His research group—International Extranodal Lymphoma Study Group (IELSG 11)—was working on a prognostic model to improve the therapeutic approach to two different lymphomas. The prognostic model was built to fit a Cox proportional hazard model, which he explained also. The results would be published in the *Annals of Hematology*.

She asked if *linfomi cutanei* was genetic, and why did genes want to screw up people's lives? How did skin cancer help genes increase and multiply? And he said that it probably wasn't genetic, though there was some evidence to suggest that non-Hodgkins lymphoma might have a genetic component, and that genes didn't "want" anything. They just occasionally misfired.

He told her that one day a week he worked as a *medico scolastico*. It took a while for her to figure out that a *medico scolastico* was a school nurse. Once a week he drove to a little town north of the city and vaccinated the children, screened them for hepatitis B and other infectious diseases, and talked to them about hygiene.

"What about head lice?"

"Ah, yes," he said. *"Pidocchi del capo."*

"I had head lice when I was in fifth grade," she said. "I had to put Vaseline on my hair. It was horrible."

"Yes," he said. "Ordinary shampoo doesn't work at all."

"You must be a good person."

"It's part of my vocation. 'Vocation' means 'calling,' you know. Not just a job . . ."

"I know what 'vocation' means," she said. "I've got one too."

They ate a Roman dish, *cacio e pepe*—spaghetti with pepper and Pecorino Romano.

"Why not Parmesan?" she asked.

"Not enough bite."

Hildi held her fork vertically and twirled a little bundle of spaghetti strands from the edges of her bowl, working her way in toward the center, the way Marcella had taught her. They ate without talking, and when they'd finished she wiped her plate clean with a piece of bread.

They both ordered stuffed squid for a second course. And a salad.

He told her that his father owned a Stearman biplane and

that his father had gone to Galesburg with his girlfriend two years ago to the Stearman Fly-In.

Hildi wasn't sure whether to believe him or not.

"You'll see," he said, and he began to speak of members of his family as if she already knew them, as if she were a part of this world: "Don't be put off by Cousin Gianni . . . Ask my aunt Lotte about the time she went to New York . . . Don't mention my mother to my father and his girlfriend. She's living in Milan now. My mother, that is . . . You'll like my sister. You can pet her Seeing Eye dog, but ask first."

"She's blind?"

"That's why she has a Seeing Eye dog."

"I get it."

"She went to a special school for the blind, but you don't get a dog till you're eleven or twelve. She's a singer. We could go to hear her sometime. She's going to be at Club Dante next week, on Vicolo del Piede, behind the piazza. She has a new voice coach now, and she's sending out demos, but the competition is fierce. Today you can hook your computer up to a synthesizer and all you have to do is hum along."

Hildi excused herself to go to the bathroom, and when she came back the waiter had brought their squid and their salads. When they had finished they each had a bowl of fruit—called a *macedonia* because the fruit is chopped up like Macedonia— and then they went for ice cream. They ate their little cups of ice cream in front of a mask store, Maddelena Atelier, with a NO FOTOS sign in the window. Checco knew the owner, Salvatore, and his daughter, Maddelena. He would be happy to introduce them. "Salvatore is very famous. He exhibits in Venice at Carnevale—all over the world—masks for Carnevale, for the theater, for collectors. But they're very expensive." And Checco pointed out masks modeled after

Maddelena's face. "Maddelena's very beautiful, but not in a conventional way."

"Nobody's beautiful in a conventional way anymore," Hildi said. "Why is that? Why can't a woman be 'conventionally beautiful,' and if she's not, why does she have to have a 'special something'? I mean . . . isn't it enough just to be what you are?"

"You're expecting me to say something about you?" Checco put his hand on her arm.

"Yes," she said. "Something nice."

"You know," he said, "a little makeup really can make a woman more beautiful. When you were in the bathroom . . . you did something . . . nice."

"It's just a little blusher," she said, "and I freshened up my lipstick." She pointed at a double mask in the window. "That's your face too, isn't it?" she said. "You and Maddelena." The two faces were turned toward each other, red lips almost touching. "Can two people wear the mask at the same time?"

"Just one," he said.

"You and Maddelena," Hildi said. "You were lovers."

He didn't say no right away, and she knew she was right.

"In my new life," she said, "I'm not going to say I'm going to do something if I'm not going to do it; I'm not going to tell a man I love him if I don't, not even if we're having sex, and I'm not going to pretend that a one-night stand is anything but a one-night stand. And I'm never going to put Parmesan cheese on *spaghetti alle vongole*." (She wagged her finger the way Marcella wagged *her* finger.)

"Is that what you call 'a warning shot across the bow'?"

"Something like that. But across my bow, not yours." When he didn't say anything, she said, "'Tutored by bitter experience.' It's a line from Chekhov. Josh used to say it all the time.

My ex-husband." She paused. "Except he never seemed to learn anything from his bitter experiences." She paused again. "But then, maybe I didn't learn anything either."

She liked the fact that he didn't try to argue with her, didn't insist that she was too young to talk like that, that she had her whole life ahead of her, and so on, and she started to laugh at herself.

Hildi didn't want anything to change. She'd stepped outside of ordinary linear time and was standing at the center, where she could feel the world revolving around her: Bar Belli, the museums and galleries, the shops, tea or coffee with Marcella or Roberto or Griet or the Russian cleaning lady, Carlo Menta with Checco. But when Nana reminded her that the next day, November fifteenth, was the halfway point of their trip, linear time started up again, rolling down a straight track, unstoppable. She got out Nana's camera and skimmed through the manual. She'd refused to carry the camera earlier because she hadn't wanted to look like a tourist, but now she didn't care. Maybe because she didn't feel like a tourist and maybe because she wanted to capture everything, starting with the mask store—Maddelena Atelier.

She got up very early one morning to take pictures. On Via della Lungaretta metal gates were rumbling open. The street was being transformed. She wanted to send some photos to her father, wanted to persuade him to buy masks for the funeral home. The NO FOTOS sign was on the inside of the window, so she couldn't move it. The store itself was dark like a cave. She couldn't see very far into it. And the sun reflected off the glass, making it difficult to see anything but her own reflection. She wanted a shot of the Caravaggio Medusa mask for Nana, of the light reflecting off the gray-and-black backs of the snakes.

The original was in Florence, not Rome, so they wouldn't get to see it, but maybe this was better.

She was looking for just the right angle when a woman called to her in English: "No *fotos*. Can't you see the sign?"

"I'm not hurting anything," Hildi said, and then she added, "You're Maddelena. It's very early. It's not even seven o'clock."

"It's my shop. I can come and go as I please."

"I want to send some pictures to my father," she said. "I'd like to buy some masks for our funeral home."

"Ah. You're Checco's friend, the one who's going to be an *impresario funebre*."

"Right."

"Funny, you look like an ordinary American tourist."

"I suppose I am. But I want something for the visitation room—where everyone gathers to look at the body and say good-bye."

"You mean a *camera ardente*—a burning room, an ardent room, a passion room?"

"I suppose. Something that tells the truth about death. Right now my father's got sentimental sunsets and inspiring sunrises. Don't you think the masks tell the truth about death? Some kind of truth, anyway. Some kind of recalibrated reality. They're not lugubrious, not Victorian, but they're not a stupid 'celebration of life' either. They're something else. I'll have to figure it out. Whatever they are, they speak to me. Are they expensive?"

"Recalibrated?"

"Transformed."

Maddelena nodded. "Some of the half masks that just cover your eyes—fifty euros. The bigger ones—two, three, four hundred euros. But you're in love with Checco? He'll buy one for you. It's wonderful, isn't it? Love. Till you get to know each other. I give it about six weeks."

""I'll be gone by then," Hildi said. "But tell me about the Caravaggio Medusa mask. My grandmother wants to see all the Caravaggios in Rome."

"Caravaggio's *Medusa*'s in Florence," she said. "And my Medusa mask is four hundred euros."

Hildi put her camera back in its case. "You're joking."

Maddelena laughed. "About the mask? No. About love? No. How long are you going to be in Rome?"

"Another two weeks."

"Perfect. You'll be fine. And you'll be looking for a nice present for Checco. How about a mask of your face?"

"I'm hoping my father will buy a lot of masks."

"Maybe he won't. But he'll buy one modeled after you for sure, and you can buy one for Checco so he'll be able to remember you, at least for a little while." She took out a large ring of keys from her large purse and unlocked the door. Three locks.

"It's like Aladdin's cave," Hildi said. "A place where you might run into magicians or maybe a genie. But wasn't Aladdin's cave booby-trapped?" Maddelena didn't know the expression, and Hildi had to explain. "But you're okay if you have a magic ring."

"That's always a problem, isn't it, the magic ring?"

Hildi looked around at the masks. Masks covered the walls; masks hung from the ceiling; masks were propped up on tables.

"These aren't empty symbols, you know," Maddelena said. "They have power; they confer authority; they change you. They can hide you, or they can reveal your true self."

"Is that why they're so expensive?" Hildi didn't think her father would be too enthusiastic, and she didn't know about Nana's credit line on the credit card, and didn't really want to ask.

"They're so expensive because they're beautiful, and they're a lot of work. You want to try one?" She took the Medusa mask off the table and handed it to Hildi. Hildi put it on and tied the strings behind her head.

"Can you feel the difference? Look in the mirror."

Hildi had trouble seeing through the little eyeholes, but finally managed to locate her reflection.

"How strong you are, how much power you have."

Hildi made a noise.

"No, no. You've got to accept your power. You're Medusa. You've gotten a bad deal—a 'bad rap,' don't you say? You've been mistreated, misunderstood all along. Look at this man Checco. You shouldn't be afraid of him. You think you're afraid of him, but in fact . . ."

"I'm *not* afraid of him."

"No? Did he tell you how he goes to the school and checks the little children for head lice? He tells all his girlfriends what a nice man he is, how kind to the little children."

"He *is* kind."

"You shouldn't be afraid of him, because I can tell you that he's afraid of you. You terrify this man. Look at him." Hildi started to look around. "No, no. Not here. But you need to be careful too. Italian men can't imagine a strong woman who isn't a monster—or their mother. Don't let that happen to you. You don't need to explain yourself. You turn them to stone because they're afraid, because they refuse to look into your eyes. Tell him not to be afraid. Tell him that if he looks into your eyes, it will be like looking into a lake. He'll see himself drowning. Or swimming."

Hildi could feel a surge of power as Maddelena talked to her, but she was a little bit angry too. "You know something, Maddelena?" she said. "You're just like all the Italian women

I've met. You're very nice, very confident, and very helpful, but you think I need to be tweaked. Checco's the only person I've met in Italy who thinks I'm okay just as I am."

"Tweaked?"

"Made better, improved."

"*Ottimizzato,*" she said. "Optimized. Good. I see you're not afraid of me either." She laughed—a nice, rich, dirty laugh.

Two days later Maddelena made a plaster cast of Hildi's face. Salvatore himself was there but only stayed long enough to ask Hildi a few questions. He spoke in Italian, and Checco translated while Maddelena mixed the plaster.

"Are you afraid of the dark?"

"No."

"Claustrophobic?"

"No," she said, though she was a little claustrophobic.

"*Hai mai avuto una risonanza magnetica?*" asked Salvatore.

"An MRI," Checco said.

"No, but my brother and my cousin shut me in a coffin once in the room over the garage. They banged on the lid and wouldn't let me out. It was horrible, and I was glad that my grandfather whipped them both with a strap."

"But you want to go ahead?"

She nodded.

They were not in Maddelena Atelier but in a nearby workshop behind one of the restaurants in the piazza. It was a real workshop: sculpting tools of all kinds on pegboards, buckets full of slushy liquids and sacks of plaster on the floor, jars of Vaseline. Cans of paint on a worktable. Hildi was lying on her back on a long table with a couple of blankets on it.

Checco was there, partly because Hildi didn't trust

Maddelena, and partly because she wanted him to take pictures with her camera to capture everything.

"'If you start to panic,'" Checco translated for Salvatore, "'just wave your arms and Maddelena will stop. Do you understand?'"

"*Sì.*"

"It's just like getting a haircut," Checco said.

"It's not like that at all," Maddelena said. "It's not 'Do you want it long or short?' It's not 'Do you want it feathered in the back?' It's not a question of curling the sections away so you don't box in a round face." She shook her head.

"Her face isn't round," Checco said.

"It's a little round."

"It's not round at all."

Maddelena translated for her father, who said to Hildi, "'You don't have a cold? Allergies? Anything to interfere with your breathing?'"

"No."

And he said to Maddelena, as he was leaving: "Don't let any plaster get in her nostrils."

"*Papà,*" she said, exasperated, "I've done this before, you know."

Checco translated.

"Pull this stocking over your head," Maddelena said to Hildi. "Pull it down just to your hairline. Then I'm going to rub your eyebrows with Vaseline so the plaster won't pull them off—I've mixed it thicker than usual—and then I'm going to put a piece of foam covered with a sheet of plastic around your face."

Hildi pulled the stocking over her head, and then Maddelena ladled the plaster over her face, adding layers, using a palette knife to spread it.

Hildi was afraid it would run in her nostrils but Maddelena always caught it just in time with the palette knife. Hildi could feel the knife smoothing and scraping. She experienced some panic but kept it under control.

What she didn't like was waiting for the plaster to set. She couldn't see, couldn't open her eyes, couldn't open her mouth to speak, but she could hear Maddelena and Checco talking in Italian. Were they talking about her? Was her face too round? Not round enough? She couldn't understand. Or was Maddelena asking Checco about his intentions? Or was she recalling the times they'd made love? Was she touching him? Were they going to kill her? Was she going crazy?

She couldn't open her eyes, but she could see the masks staring at her. Unfinished masks in the workshop. Not the beautifully finished ones in the shop. Unpainted. Corpselike. Looking down at her. Demons, elves, clowns, bird heads, the plague doctor, Dante Alighieri. Maddelena's face was everywhere, crowned with leaves or fruit, shining like the moon, sporting a clown nose, kissing, winking, laughing. She imagined them in bed and started to get aroused. She *could* move her hand, *wanted* to move it to her crotch. She had to *struggle* to keep it at her side, to ignore this arousal and also the itch that was starting to burn her neck like a single fresh mosquito bite. She tried to think about the horses, Stormy and Salty, but they galloped away, carrying Maddelena and Checco on their backs. She let them go, and the itch resolved itself into a drop of warm oil and then disappeared entirely.

She was startled by Maddelena's hand on her shoulder. She'd been asleep. "Just lie still," Maddelena said. "I'm going to ease the cast off your face. You'll feel it pull on your eyebrows, but it won't pull them off."

In five minutes she was able to open her eyes, and when she did, she was almost blinded by the light. She was on the edge of tears.

"What were you talking about?"

Maddelena and Checco looked at each other.

"When I had the plaster on my face."

"I was saying how beautiful you are," Maddelena said, brushing her face, scraping off bits of plaster. "I was asking him if he took you to his school where he checks all the little children for head lice."

"No, but I'd like to go."

"I told you he takes all his girlfriends there. To show them what a good person he is."

"He is a good person."

"How about flying? Has he taken you flying yet?"

"We're going to go on Saturday—"

"Maddelena finds goodness offensive," Checco interrupted.

"That's only because I'm jealous. Bad people are always jealous of good people, don't you think? They always are wanting to bring them down. But now I'm going to stop all that nonsense and just be happy for you."

On Saturday they drove out to a little airport in Ostia, near Fiumicino. Checco was going to take her up in his father's Stearman.

"Did you take Maddelena flying?" she asked.

"In another life," he said.

They were going to meet Checco's father, Enzo, and his girlfriend, Chiara, in the flight club, and Checco's sister too. The narrow city streets, crowded with restaurants and bars, apartment buildings, and small shops, gave way to flat, open spaces. The sky was gray, closed. Checco was driving sensibly, but she took a deep breath as they passed an isolated Lottomatica, where you could buy lottery tickets or bet on a horse race or buy minutes for your cell phone.

"You're not driving like a real Italian," Hildi said.

"Sorry. You want me to speed up?"

"Yes," she said. "Sort of. You know, you don't have to take me flying just to get me to go to bed with you."

"What do I have to do?"

"You could just ask."

"What about your rules?"

"The rule is that I'm not going to tell you I love you."

He laughed. "You're being a bad girl now."

"I know I'm being a bad girl," she said. "If I had a cigarette I'd light it now. But I can't help myself. A girl doesn't like to be alone all the time. No one touching her. I feel like I've been here before. It's all familiar. Desire. Loneliness. Need. All the things I was going to put behind me."

"Why do you want to put them behind you?"

"I don't like feeling that I've disappointed everyone, that I've deceived myself and everyone else. I didn't finish college. I didn't finish my marriage."

He looked at her.

"Watch where you're going."

"I am watching."

The flight club, a little building at the end of the runway, reminded Hildi of the little airport in Galesburg. Nondescript. It had started to sprinkle, and they got wet walking from the car. Checco's sister, Marina, was there too in the flight club lounge, wearing dark glasses. And with her dog, Bruno. They'd gone to hear her twice at Club Dante, near the piazza, where the dog had sat on the stage with her. A cello player—the same one who sometimes played in the piazza—put a floor under her rich alto voice, warm and bluesy. She'd finished the first set with a couple of songs in English—"Summertime" and Elton John's "Georgia"—without a trace of an accent, though she didn't speak English.

"You sing beautifully," Hildi said, sitting down next to Marina on an old sofa. She waited for Checco to translate. It was awkward, having to ask someone to translate, but Hildi didn't care.

"'My manager told me I have to sing without hunching my shoulders,'" Checco translated for Marina.

"Pensi che incurvo le spalle quando canto?" she asked, turning to Hildi, and Hildi could almost understand her without waiting for Checco to translate.

"I don't think you hunch your shoulders at all," Hildi said. She felt comfortable right away in the flight club lounge. "You sing beautifully," she said again, and Checco translated.

"Oh, va' avanti," Marina said, and laughed.

"She says you can pet the dog," Checco said.

Hildi kissed Bruno on the top of his head and inhaled his nice rich doggy smell. She passed Marina a plate of the sandwiches—prosciutto and rucola—that Chiara had brought. Checco was edgy because of the weather and didn't want anything. He stood at the window.

It wasn't exactly a rich man's club, but a club for men of a certain class who understood how to wear expensive old clothes. The tables were covered with flight magazines, books, and calendars, and taped on one wall was the front page of the *Galesburg Register-Mail*, with a picture of Enzo and Chiara at the airport. An antique rug on the floor had seen better days and so had the comfortable chairs that were arranged around it, but everyone was beautiful: Checco's father, Chiara, Marina, Bruno.

"So you really did go to Galesburg," Hildi said to Enzo. "All the way from Rome."

"Just like you come all the way to Rome from Galesburg. In Galesburg we're eating at the Landmark and Chez Willy's," he said, "and the Coney Island. Now will you believe me?"

"Did you fly over in your Stearman?"

He shook his head in disbelief. "There are only four Stearmans in Lazio," he said, "the area around Rome. And there are lots in England. But you don't fly a Stearman across the Atlantic Ocean."

"How did they get them to Italy?"

"By ship."

The blue-and-yellow Stearman, visible on the runway through a large window, was beautiful too. At two o'clock Checco went out and walked around the plane, looking up at the sky. When he came back in he wasn't happy.

"You can't fly today," his father said. "It's already raining. I want you to take a look at this mole."

"I want to show Hildi the plane first."

"Okay, but then I want you to take a look."

It had been a U.S. Army plane. Built in 1942. Then a mail plane, then converted for crop dusting, and then converted again to a sports plane. Checco showed her the welds where the plane had been refitted with a larger engine.

They couldn't fly because of the weather, but they climbed up into the two cockpits anyway. Hildi stepped onto the large lower wing, reached up and grabbed hold of the handles on the trailing edge of the top wing, stepped in to the rear cockpit, and took her seat. Checco strapped her into a four-way harness and put on her headset before climbing into the forward cockpit.

They sat on the runway and talked to each other through

the headsets, and after a while it seemed to Hildi, as she listened to Checco talking, as if they *were* flying—flying in the old way with a compass and charts only, climbing to three thousand meters to clear a mountain, shuddering as they exceeded the stall angle, picking up a low wing with the rudder, and coming in for a full-stall landing. It was as if she were inside him, seeing what he saw, and she liked this.

No planes were going in and out at the small airport, but they could see the big planes from Leonardo da Vinci disappearing into the cloud cover. Afterward, as they stood next to each other, she wanted him to touch her the way he was touching the plane, as if it were a spirited horse that needed calming.

"You could stay here, you know," he said. "At least till Christmas. At least till Maddelena finishes the mask. I could help you find a room. Or you could live with Marina. We could—we could go flying. When the weather's better."

She had trouble saying no. She didn't want to surrender to this feeling, not because it was strange, but because it was familiar. She'd been down this road before.

"It's hard for me to say no," she said. "I've always been a yes kind of girl. It's been a problem." But she said no.

Back inside they talked more about Galesburg with his father and his girlfriend. Everyone was so friendly. Marina was beautiful too, and she loved to fly. "With my brother, of course. Sometimes he lets me take the controls!'" Checco translated.

"You can do that?"

"'With Checco there, yes.'"

"What about the dog?"

"'He stays with *Papà*.'"

Hildi couldn't keep her hands off Bruno.

Enzo kept mentioning names, people he'd met in Galesburg, till they finally found a mutual acquaintance—a woman who worked at the Civic Art Center and who brought a little dog to the center with her. Enzo and Chiara hardly knew her—Hildi hardly knew her—but it was a link.

Enzo asked Checco something which Ceccho didn't translate. "*Papà*, not here," he said.

"He wants Checco to look at a mole on his back," Chiara explained to Hildi.

"It's swollen," Enzo said, starting to take off his shirt.

"Look," Chiara said; "you make Hildi blush." She looked at Hildi. "It's nothing. Just Italian men."

It was raining harder, and according to the weather radio there was no letting up in sight.

Checco checked the mole. "*Papà*," he said, "it's no different from the last time I looked."

"Should I have a biopsy?"

"Is it sore?"

"No, but I think it's inflamed."

"I'm telling you—" Checco switched from English to Italian.

"I'm going to put this on film," Chiara said, but by the time she got her camera, Enzo was already buttoning his shirt.

"My son, the doctor," he said, "won't order a biopsy."

Checco tried to explain. He wasn't that kind of doctor. He did scientific research . . . But his father just shook his head and put his arm around Hildi.

"Not that kind of doctor," he said. "*Mamma mia.*"

It was the first time Hildi had heard anyone in Italy say "*Mamma mia.*"

Hildi almost stumbled on the steps outside Checco's apartment. She waited for him to unlock the door—a single-key lock for the front door, three locks for the apartment itself. One long key and two short ones. She had a similar long key and a similar key holder.

"Can I get you something?" he asked when they were inside. "An espresso? Chocolate? Campari?"

She picked up a peach from the bowl of fruit on the table, and he washed it for her. He brought her a plate, and she ate the peach, as she'd learned to do, with a knife and fork.

His apartment was not a rich man's apartment, but it made her think of the flight club, and of Oblonsky in *Anna Karenina*, who knew just what clothes to wear when he went hunting or fishing. Not the latest thing, but old clothes with some depth to them. She'd just read this passage to Nana.

"I've been waiting for something to happen," she said, "and I guess this is it."

"Accidenti!" Checco said.

Checco sat down next to her. He didn't push her at all, just the opposite, and Hildi understood that this too was a strategy. But she also understood that she was the one driving, the one flying the plane, the one deciding to bank left or bank right. Or just keep on going straight ahead. Which is what she'd wanted to do all along. From the beginning. The rest was all talk. It was time to shut up.

"Look me in the eye," she said.

He looked her in the eye, one eye at a time.

"What do you see?"

"I see myself swimming."

"Damn," she said, "that's just what Maddelena said you'd see. How did she know?" She didn't wait for an answer. She started undressing, sitting on the edge of the sofa and pulling her sandals off with her toes. She stood up and pointed at Checco, her wrist limp. "You. Checco," she said. "Follow me."

"*Subito,*" he said.

"I've been trying to live in the present moment," she said. "That's what you're supposed to do, right? But what is the present moment if it isn't a sackful of memories and thoughts about the future? If you had no memory—nothing but the present moment—you wouldn't understand anything that was going on."

"Maybe you don't want to narrow the present moment down quite that far. Maybe it just means not to worry too much about the past or about the future."

"Okay. I'm going to focus on what's happening right now. My whole body is focusing on that. But I'm still thinking about your father's mole and about going to Mexico with my ex-husband. Well, he wasn't 'ex' at the time. I feel like I'm inside a musical instrument—a big one—a piano or a cello like the one at Club Dante. It's so loud I can't hear the music. Or inside a painting, and it's so dark I can't see what the painter has painted." And then she shifted gears: "Is your father's mole okay?"

He laughed an easy child's laugh. "He's had it all his life."

"I'd like this to be some kind of ritual—what we're doing now—some kind of ceremony. So we don't have to reinvent the wheel each time."

"It *is* a ritual, probably older than marriage itself. The bottle of Campari, the bowl of fruit on the table, the peach, a man and a woman sitting next to each other."

"I'm trying to commit it to memory. Capture it. The bowl of fruit. The tablecloth. The pigeons on the balcony. It's like a painting by Chardin." She walked into the bedroom in her bare feet, holding her sandals by their straps.

It was like her first time and her last time. It was like climbing a very tall ladder. Climbing up to the top, she felt the strain in her thighs and her calves, ladder rungs under her arches, and then climbing higher and higher. She remembered a painter on a very tall ladder painting the belvedere on their house. Standing down below, in the drive . . . she'd been looking up at him. She'd just come home from school. She was not afraid of heights, but seeing him standing on the very top rung of the ladder had given her butterflies, the same butterflies she was feeling now, but she knew better than to say "I love you." Instead she said, "Not yet."

"Not yet," she said. "Not yet." Climbing higher and higher. "Not yet. Not yet." And then she was standing on the top rung, like the painter. "Okay," she whispered. "Now." And then she was falling over backward.

And she was thinking that now that that was out of the way, they could move onto something else. But what? What lay beyond *this*? Maybe *this* was as far as you could go. Two people who have made love for the first time and are looking forward to doing it again. And again. Maybe *this* was as far as she'd ever gotten.

CHAPTER III: CROSSING THE ALPS

By the end of their third week in Rome Louisa had to admit, at least to herself, that her spiritual quest had come to nothing. She'd dragged Hildi—always a good sport—to see most of the Caravaggios in Rome, but the Caravaggios hadn't spoken to her. Not even *La Vocazione di San Matteo* in the back of the French church. What had seemed perfectly clear at home in her kitchen when she'd looked at the reproductions in Helen Langdon's *Caravaggio*—which Elizabeth had given to her, and which she'd brought with her to Rome—now seemed confused and murky. Standing with a dozen other tourists in the darkness at the back of the French church and peering into the Contarelli Chapel, she wasn't even sure which of the men was Saint Matthew—the man with the beard or the man counting the money. She wasn't sure which man Christ was pointing at. Three people in the picture were pointing at other people: Christ was pointing, Saint Peter was pointing, and the man with the beard was pointing; but it wasn't clear whom any of them were pointing *at*. And Christ's limp wrist bothered her. She had to keep feeding the meter so the light would stay on.

It bothered Hildi too. "If you're going to point at someone and say 'Follow me,'" Hildi said, "you've got to do better than that." And she demonstrated, holding her arm out and pointing straight at her grandmother and saying in a loud voice that made the other tourists turn to look at her, "Nana, follow me."

She should have listened to Father Cochrane, who'd tried to tamp down her sudden enthusiasm for a spiritual adventure. She'd called him the night of Bart's death, feeling guilty about casting the first stone at her husband of over fifty years. Real remorse was something new for her. Down in the cooler with Bart stretched out between them, she'd laid out her spiritual agenda: fasting, prayer, a retreat at the Cistercian convent up in Dubuque, and the pilgrimage to Rome to see the Caravaggios. *The Calling of Saint Matthew.* Instead of applauding, Father Cochrane had counseled moderation, counseled her to go slow, but she'd ignored his advice and had spent a week in the convent preparing for the trip by fasting and praying, and had been so weak she'd lost control of her suitcase on one of the escalators at O'Hare. The suitcase had tumbled down the escalator, and she'd fallen down the moving steps on top of it. She was lucky not to have broken something, and when she thought about it now, she felt like a foolish old woman.

At the end of her junior year at Knox College in Galesburg, Illinois, Louisa had fallen in love with her Italian professor, Gianluigi Bevilacqua. Actually she'd been in love with him since the beginning of her freshman year, and had expressed her love by studying hard, spending hours in the language lab, and translating Leopardi. *"D'in su la vetta della torre antica,"* she said aloud, the first line of "Il passero solitario":

> *From high atop the ancient tower,*
> *Solitary thrush, you sing to the fields*
> *Until the day is done,*
> *And your melodies meander through this valley.*

What Louisa knew about passion she'd learned from Gianluigi one summer—the summer after her junior year—in Gianluigi's little apartment on Broad Street, just across the Santa Fe tracks. Passion had been a light that illuminated everything in her path, that lit up dark corners in the library and dark corners in her soul. She'd started smoking too, sitting next to Gianluigi on the edge of the bed after making love, enjoying one of his Italian cigarettes. And in the end it had been the cigarettes that gave them away, when Gianluigi's landlady had smelled smoke, burst into their room, and reported what she'd seen to the dean of women at the college. Gianluigi was dismissed and had to go back to Rome, and Louisa was forced to drop out. He'd promised to send for her, but by the time he wrote to her, it was too late. She'd been frightened; she'd had no money; her grandmother had washed her hands of her. She'd turned to Father Arnie, the young priest who ran the Newman Center at the college, and Father Arnie had found a job for her with the Oldfield family answering the telephone at the funeral home, which was where she'd met Bart. She never smoked another cigarette, but she missed them, and she would have smoked one now if she'd had a pack in her purse, though Hildi would have a fit when she came home.

So what? Louisa didn't care. She didn't like being left alone to fend for herself while Hildi went off with her doctor. The doctor who'd been stopping by to check on her *mal da gola*, Louisa realized, had really been stopping by to see Hildi, and really, she'd known it all along. This afternoon they'd gone flying—Hildi and the doctor. It was after eight o'clock, and they hadn't come back. Louisa tried to take some pleasure in Hildi's good fortune, if that's what it was, but she couldn't do it.

She decided to go out. She could at least walk down Via delle Mantellate, where Gianluigi had lived. She had it marked on her map. It was a short street next to Carcere Regina Coeli, Queen of Heaven Prison.

Walking down Via della Lungaretta she stopped to study the menus of the different restaurants. She hadn't eaten in any of them because her *mal da gola* had not only shaped their days, it had made everything, including the wine, taste *off*. By the time she crossed Viale di Trastevere it felt like rain. She was tempted to turn back, but instead she bought a small umbrella from a street vendor who was also selling suitcases, flashlights, and backpacks.

She passed the *farmacia* where she'd had her prescriptions filled. Signs outside the restaurants advertised strange drinks: caipirinha, mojito, sex on the beach. Sex on the beach cost four and a half euros. Five dollars.

Christmas lights were strung over the street, though it wasn't even Thanksgiving yet. Red stars at the apex of each string were flanked by icicle lights. She stopped outside Carlo Menta, where Hildi and the doctor often ate, and studied the menu. Hildi was right: the prices were very reasonable and the restaurant was full—people eating and drinking, talking and laughing. She looked through the mullioned window, searching for Hildi and Dottor Tonarelli, who had become "Francesco," and then "Checco."

In her navy cardigan and wool coat, Louisa felt invisible. Was she turning into one of those old people who complain about everything new—computers, smartphones, the Internet, MP3 players, e-readers (though she appreciated Hildi's Nook)? She kept her head down. In spite of the drizzle the street was full of young people. Piazza Santa Maria in Trastevere, where rival popes had battled it out long before the Great Schism, was crowded. The restaurants all looked inviting. The piazza itself looked inviting. More young people. Couples. Beggars. Buskers. Some of them a little scary looking. Rough. Loud voices. She was frightened. But energized too.

She sat for a while by the fountain to listen to a man playing a cello under a makeshift umbrella, opened the copy of Leopardi's *Canti* that had belonged to Gianluigi and read over some of the poems they'd studied in class, poems that she'd memorized as a student—"*Il primo amore,*" "*Il passero solitario,*" "*L'infinito*"—and then she read over Gianluigi's letter, folded in the book, begging her to follow him to Rome. It had been folded and unfolded so many times it was falling apart. She didn't need to open it to know what was in it. In it he wrote about the piazza, Piazza Santa Maria in Trastevere— the piazza she was sitting in now—how it could all be hers, not just the piazza, but Rome itself, the Eternal City.

Via della Scalla took her from the piazza to Via della Lungara, where there were no more lights, no more intimate restaurant spaces, separated from the sidewalks by rows of potted plants, where people ate outside even in November. The sidewalks on Via della Lungara were too narrow. She passed the Palazzo Corsini, where she and Hildi had seen another *John the Baptist*, and Hildi had asked her if Caravaggio was a homosexual. Actually John reminded Louisa of Gianluigi. Boylike. Fragile. It reminded her that she would never embrace a man again, much less a handsome young man like John the Baptist. It wasn't desire she felt, but the loss of desire, the longing that was left when desire was gone.

It was too dark to consult her map. She passed the prison Regina Coeli and almost missed Via delle Mantellate—Cloak Street, Robe Street. She would have liked an espresso, but the little bar on the corner across from the prison was closed. The traffic noise made her nervous. She turned down Via delle Mantellate. The huge blankness on her left was the wall of the prison. Past the prison the street opened up a little, but it was dark and empty except for people coming and going through the entrance of an art studio, which had a light over the door: Studio Stefania Miscetti. The rain had started up again, and the people were struggling with umbrellas. Louisa waited till she was past them before opening her own little umbrella. It was hard to see the numbers, and the numbering system was confusing. Red numbers for shops, blue numbers for apartments; they ran up one side of the street and then down the other. There were four or five names on the brass plates outside each door. When she finally found the name— Bevilacqua, bell three—she hardly knew what to do. What did she want to happen now? She couldn't conjure up any fantasies. Just a series of blank slates. What was she afraid of?

She worked up her courage and touched her finger to the tip of the brass button at first, feeling the cool metal, then pressed hard. She could still hear the traffic noise, but muted. She kept her finger on the bell. And waited. She pressed her ear to the little speaker, and waited for someone to say *Chi è?* There was no response. She took her finger off the button and then pressed it again. And waited. She couldn't be sure it was actually ringing.

Suddenly she was tired, as tired as she had ever been, on the verge of collapse. Rome had been too much for her. She hadn't been fasting, but she hadn't been eating well. Nothing tasted good. She was too tired to retrace her steps. Too tired to move, she started to cry, still holding her finger on the bell, still holding her umbrella against the thin rain.

She had no idea how long she stayed there, pressing the bell. She was still crying when a woman who'd been standing outside the art studio came up to her and asked her if she was all right.

"I've been in Rome for three weeks," Louisa said in Italian, "and I've been sick the whole time, and I fell in love with one man and then married someone else."

The woman ducked under Louisa's umbrella. "Did you ever know a woman who didn't do the same thing?" she said. "You never forget your first love. But it's good to hang on to that feeling when you want to have a good cry—to flush out your system."

"Is that what you do?"

"*Sì, sì.* Every now and then."

"I'm sorry," Louisa said.

"I always feel better afterward. And that young man. How old were you?"

"Twenty-one."

"When was the last time you saw him?"

"Over fifty years ago. Longer. Fifty-six years."

"And he hasn't changed a bit, has he? He's still lovely and kind and gentle, still has all his hair?"

Louisa nodded. "Something like that." She switched the umbrella from her left hand to her right.

"But you never had to live with him?"

"No."

"And the man you married? How long did you live with him?"

"Fifty-five years."

"So you got to know him very well?"

"When he died I was glad. For a while. I said terrible things, and so did everybody else."

"You know," the woman said, "it's like that for everybody. Well, not everybody. But for a lot of women."

"For you too?"

"Of course."

"But then that night I called the priest, and we went down to the basement, where my husband's body was still on a gurney in the refrigerator—my husband was a funeral director and so is my son. Father Cochrane blessed him, and he blessed me too, and I felt I'd stepped into the light."

"And so you came to Rome? A pilgrimage?"

"Sort of. I wanted to see the Caravaggios. I thought I did."

"There are no Caravaggios here." The woman laughed and removed her keys from her purse. "Not on Via delle Mantellate. Not one."

"Of course not."

"Let's get out of the rain." It took two keys to unlock the front door. "You'll see for yourself. Not one Caravaggio. But

I've just come from an exhibition by a woman from Bologna. She's made a map of Trastevere out of thread and hung it from the ceiling. It's astonishing, really." She looked at her watch. "Too late now."

"I'm sorry," Louisa said. "I was looking for my old Italian professor. I have a book of his that I want to return."

"Who would that be?"

"Gianluigi Bevilacqua."

"You won't find *him* here either."

"No, I didn't think so. But I saw the name . . ."

"You'd have to go to Campo di Verano. But not tonight. Too far, too dark. But there's no need, really. The dead are never far from us, don't you think?"

Louisa didn't know what to say. She followed the woman up a dark stone stairway. The dim lights on the landings went out before they got to the top of the stairs. Once in the apartment Louisa could see that the woman was about her age. Short. Thin. Gray hair. The apartment was simple and inviting. There was a bowl of fruit like a still life on the granite top of a handsome cabinet, and the bookshelves, full of books, had been built to measure.

"Tell me."

"It was a long time ago."

"You were one of his students?"

"For three years. He was the only Italian teacher. Most small schools in the United States offer French and German and Spanish but not Italian. We read Farina's *Fra le Corde d'un Contrabasso*, and then later we read Leopardi. That's the book I brought. Leopardi's *Canti*."

"Yes," she said. "Gianluigi read it every year. We read it together."

"'This lonely hill was always dear to me, and this hedgerow.'

59

Leopardi taught us about passion and about the beauty of nature."

"Gianluigi loved it in the United States, you know," the woman said, "but he was homesick. He wanted to come home. He missed Rome. Let me get you a glass of wine." The woman looked out a window recessed in the wall of books. "It's still raining, but you've had some nice weather. Not too cold. Not for November."

Louisa started to cough. "I've had this *mal da gola* ever since we got to Rome. It's done something to my taste buds. Wine tastes off. I haven't tried any for a while."

"Maybe a cup of tea." While the woman busied herself in the kitchen, Louisa looked at the books, many of which were in English.

"I'm Elena, by the way," the woman said, coming back with two cups of tea. "Elena Bevilacqua."

"Gianluigi's wife?"

"*Sì.*"

Of course, Louisa thought. *What was I thinking?* "I hope—" she said, but she wasn't sure what she was hoping.

"It's all right," Elena interrupted.

"I'm Louisa," Louisa said. "Louisa Oldfield."

"Here's what you're looking for," Elena said, pointing with her nose. "Next shelf up, a little to the left. Let me set this tea down." Elena set the tea down on the coffee table and went to get the sugar bowl.

Louisa wasn't actually sure what she was looking for. Elena came back with the sugar bowl and pulled a book off the shelf.

"He loved Wordsworth," Elena said. "Maybe even more than Leopardi. For Leopardi, nature was never our mother, always our stepmother."

Louisa opened the book and looked at the title page:

Il valore di ricordo: la poesie di William Wordsworth, un selezione, tradotto e curato da Gianluigi Bevilacqua.

"We went to England once," Elena said, "right after we were married. The Lake District. We didn't have any money. We stayed in youth hostels. Couldn't be together at night on our honeymoon! They were like dormitories, one part for men and another for women. We walked everywhere. And then one morning the woman who ran the hostel took me aside and told me it would be all right to go to my husband, and I couldn't understand what she was saying. She had to take me by the hand and practically pull me. Everyone was gone, you see. They were closing for the day. They close the hostels early. You have to be out by nine o'clock. I was already wearing my backpack. I don't wish to be young again, not really, but . . ."

"Was he your first love?"

She laughed. "My fourth or fifth," she said. "But that morning in the youth hostel, when everybody was gone . . . The earth moved."

"The earth moved?"

"*Sì*, the earth moved. I had to laugh when I read Hemingway—*The Sun Also Rises*—because I knew what the old woman was talking about. Pilar was her name, right?" Elena laughed at herself and poured more tea.

They'd been speaking in Italian, but now Louisa asked, "Do you speak English?"

"French. I used to teach French in the Liceo Scientifico Kennedy. Gianluigi taught English and did some translating too. I can *read* English, but I don't like to speak it. I read *The Sun Also Rises* in English, and Wordsworth's 'Tintern Abbey.' "That blessed mood," she said in English, "in which the burthen of the mystery . . .' I forget how it goes."

Her accent was terrible and Louisa wondered if this was

the way *she* sounded to Italians when she spoke Italian. There was no way to know. If you ask an Italian, he'll say, "You speak beautiful Italian." And you can't hear yourself in another language. But she was too tired to worry about her accent.

"How did you get here?"

"I walked. From Via della Luce, near the river."

"Let me walk you to the bus stop. The buses won't run much longer. Do you have a ticket?" Louisa didn't. Elena gave her one. "You don't want to get arrested."

The bus stop was in the piazza where the two streets on different levels came together. A list of stops was posted on the sign for the number twenty-three bus.

"Ponte Palatino's where you get off," Elena said.

They waited a long time chatting about this and that— about men and about love, about the Regina Coeli prison— and about the exhibit Elena had seen that night at Studio Stefania Miscetti. After about five minutes Elena lit a cigarette. She was still smoking it when the bus arrived. The smoke smelled good. Like an open fire. Like sitting next to someone you love on an unmade bed.

When Louisa caught a glimpse of Santa Maria in Cosmedin on the other side of the river, where she and Hildi had put their hands in the Bocca della Verità, she realized she'd missed her stop. At first she was alarmed. Hildi would be worried. Maybe that wasn't a bad thing. She'd spent enough time worrying about Hildi.

But she was frightened too. She should have gotten off at Ponte Palatino. Then she should have gotten off at the next stop. She thought of people hanging on to the ropes that hold down a balloon. If you don't let go right away, at the same time as everyone else, you're suddenly up in the air. If you let go within another two seconds, you're all right, but after that it's too late, you're too high up in the air. The bus crossed the river and she sat back. She would go to the end of the line and then ride the bus back. She was pretty sure it stopped on the other side of the Isola Tiberina.

They were on a big wide street. Was that the Pyramid of Cestius by the Protestant Cemetery? She'd like to be buried in the Protestant Cemetery. With Keats and Shelley. At least Shelley's heart, snatched from the flames.

It took half an hour to get to the end of the line. Out the window she could see big nondescript apartment buildings. Identical, with identical balconies.

She told the driver she was going to ride back into town, and he told her she'd have to wait fifteen minutes. The driver got off the bus, sat on a bench, and lit a cigarette. Louisa could smell the smoke through her open window. She got off the bus and sat down on the bench next to the driver.

"It smells so good," she said, holding back a cough. "I wanted to come closer."

He pulled a box of Marlboro Reds from the inside pocket of his bus driver's uniform, tapped out a cigarette, and offered it to her. "Good for a sore throat."

"I haven't had a cigarette in years," she said. "And I've had a *mal da gola* ever since I got to Rome."

"But tonight," he said, "something has happened?"

"I met the wife of a man I was in love with over fifty years ago. She lives on Via delle Mantellate. That's where I got on the bus."

"By the prison," he said. "This man you loved," he said, "he was in the prison?"

"No, no. This was back in the States. He was my professor. He's dead now."

"*Amore,*" he said, putting the cigarette to his lips and sucking in the smoke and then letting it out slowly. He held the cigarette out at arm's length and looked at it. "The world's best cigarette," he said. "Marlboro Red. When you're angry, they calm you down. When you're unhappy, they lift you up. Some people say they're too strong, but that's because they're too weak. The people who say that, I mean."

"Maybe I will have one," Louisa said. "If you don't mind."

"*Volentieri.* It will help your *mal da gola.*"

He lit a match and cupped his hands around it, and she leaned forward till the tip of her cigarette touched the tip of the flame. She sat back and relaxed, letting the smoke surround her.

"*Amore,*" he said again, looking at his watch. "Five minutes and we've got to go."

"I need to get off at Ponte Palatino," she said.

"On the way back," he said, "you'll be on the other side of the river. You want Monte Savello. I'll let you know when we get there."

Checco and Hildi were both at the door. Hildi was frantic and couldn't keep from scolding Louisa. "How could you do this to us, Nana? Do you have any idea how worried we were? If you'd just get a *telefonino*, this wouldn't have happened. You could have called me, or you could have called a taxi. You've been sick, and now— Where did you say you were? What did you think you were doing? Can you tell me that? What were you thinking? Were you thinking at all? And you've been smoking. Nana, what's got into you?"

Checco laughed, opened a bottle of Frascati, and poured three glasses. The wine was cold and slightly effervescent. Louisa couldn't believe how good it tasted.

* * *

It was not till two years later, after Hildi had been killed, that Louisa fully realized, as she relived it in her imagination, that the month in Rome had been one of the happiest times of her life, that like Wordsworth she had crossed the Alps into Italy without realizing it, that she'd been happy without realizing it—not just at the end, when she'd cooked a Thanksgiving turkey for Hildi's friends, and Maddelena had brought the dozen beautiful masks Checco had bought—but from the very beginning: from the waiting room at the *guardia medica* to the darkness at the back of San Luigi dei Francesi, waiting for a voice to say "Follow me"; even lying in bed with a slight fever, while Hildi read to her about Anna and Vronsky and about Kitty and Levin; even when Hildi, wearing a dress that barely covered her crotch, went out at night, leaving her all alone; even looking through the mullioned window of Carlo Menta at all the people laughing and talking, eating and drinking; even pushing Gianluigi's bell as hard as she could, standing in the rain with her ear pressed against the little speaker, waiting for someone to say, *"Chi è?"* Who is it? Even smoking a cigarette with the bus driver and then going back to a place that had begun to feel like home with the smell of tobacco on her breath and in her clothes; even being scolded by Hildi as if they'd traded places and Hildi was now the grandmother and she, Louisa, was a young woman again on the brink of a new life.

CHAPTER IV: PROFESSIONAL COURTESY

Simon and Gilbert were in Simon's office going over the details for the Connolly funeral when Marge, Simon's receptionist, said there was a phone call for Simon from Rome. Simon picked up a Bob Dylan CD from the desk and handed it to Gilbert. "You want to put this in the machine. Don't start it till about ten thirty." Mrs. Connolly had been one of Elizabeth's students at the college. Her husband was a musician and wanted *The Freewheelin' Bob Dylan* to be playing when people came in for the funeral. Gilbert wiped the CD case, which was smudged, on his pants: on the jacket Dylan and a girl were walking down a street in New York, Dylan in his thin jacket, the girl's head on his shoulder. 1963. Simon had been twelve years old, starting seventh grade at Churchill Junior High.

He picked up the phone, expecting it to be Hildi. It would be five o'clock in Rome according to the little alarm clock he kept on his desk set to Rome time. She'd completed a semester in the mortuary science program at the community college in Galesburg and then had gone back to Rome for the summer. But she hadn't come back from Rome in the fall.

He no longer worried about Hildi's brother, Jack, who was now running a very smart restaurant in New York—Bistrot Jacques. But he still worried about Hildi. An old habit. So far away. He'd been getting letters and calls, so he knew she was happy. He could feel it over the phone. He could feel the heat coming out of the receiver, as if it were a blow dryer burning his ear. He knew she had a job she loved, and he knew that she was in love herself. And he knew that she wasn't coming back, wasn't going to take over the business. And that was okay, even though he'd already changed the sign. He'd received an offer from one of the big chains—Service Corporation International. Elizabeth wanted him to take it. But he couldn't get himself to do it. Not yet.

It was nine o'clock in the morning in Galesburg, five

o'clock in the afternoon in Rome. Hildi had been killed in an auto accident at two o'clock that morning. Two o'clock in Rome. She'd been dead since eight o'clock last night, Galesburg time. Hit-and-run. Simon was prepared for almost anything from Hildi, but not this. The nervous young man on the telephone, who was probably Hildi's age, said she'd been hit by a car at the foot of Ponte Garibaldi, where Lungotevere Raffaello Sanzio turns into Lungotevere degli Anguillara— streets running along the Tiber—and had been taken immediately to a hospital on Isola Tiberina. She'd just crossed the Ponte Garibaldi. Lots of things would have to be done. He interspersed the list with condolences. How sorry he was. The papers, forms, arrangements. Simon would have to contact an Italian funeral director. The consulate had a list of funeral directors who spoke English. He could fax or e-mail the information.

Simon sat in the office for a while, but he couldn't get comfortable in his oak chair, one that tilted. One arm kept coming loose. He adjusted the chair in his mind and tried to adjust his mind too—or rather to let his mind adjust itself— to settle down. It was like waiting for the waves to stop up at the cottage on Lake Michigan, where they vacationed every year. But of course the waves just keep on coming.

The last image he had of her was from the veranda at the back of the house: She's getting into her mother's little yellow Mazda. Wearing jeans and a silk blouse. She turns and waves, eager to move on to the next thing. Elizabeth will take her to the airport in Peoria. Simon is preparing for a funeral and can't go with them. He looks out the window now, but there's no one there. The little Mazda is out of the way, in the big garage. Gilbert is backing out the hearse.

Simon's training prevented him from bursting into tears.

He continued to stare out the window. November. They needed rain. There hadn't been enough snow cover the previous winter and the summer had been dry.

He climbed the stairs to the belvedere. He could hear Elizabeth in her study on the third floor. Bart's Smith & Wesson was in a desk drawer. He took it out and put it on the table. The center of the town was to the west. He could see the courthouse and the bell tower on the college's Old Main, and the top of Central Congo—the Congregational Church.

He sat in his lopsided armchair and looked at the pictures, Elizabeth's prints. A Rembrandt etching had been replaced by Braque's *Woman with a Guitar*, Picasso's *Aubade* by Raphael's portrait of Castiglione. All clearly labeled with dates. When he heard her footsteps on the stairs coming up after him, he put the gun back in the drawer, but then she turned and went back down the stairs. She was as mysterious as the pictures. She'd been ready to leave him at one point, and at that point, he wouldn't have minded. But that was long ago now. That was ancient history, but he could remember, and the memories were no longer painful. They had weathered this storm, and others too. That was part of the fabric now, like the pattern in the Oriental rug she'd put on the floor for him—a dark red ground covered with leaves and small flowers in different colors: blue, gold, navy, green, tan. His brother-in-law had brought it back from Oman. Simon could see into the past but not into the future, not even five minutes into the future. He was lost in a fog. He had no compass. It was chilly in the belvedere, but he didn't turn on the little space heater. He was accustomed to entering into the grief of others without breaking down. This life had been hard for Elizabeth too and was still hard. She wanted him to sell, but he couldn't do it.

He looked at the pictures. He liked them, most of them, but they didn't speak to him, didn't move him deeply. He couldn't see what she saw. She'd taught him to pay attention to surfaces and not search for deeper meanings, but he couldn't help himself. He tried to look through them to the life behind life, the death behind death. She kept changing them, two or three new ones every week. A Van Gogh self-portrait had replaced Georgia O'Keeffe's *Iris*. She'd taught him to say "Van GAWCHH" rather than "Van GO." Van Gawchh was clearly unhappy, about to dissolve into the whirling blue chaos behind him. No wonder he'd committed suicide. Next to Van Gawchh was Francis Bacon's portrait of his lover, George Dyer. Dyer had committed suicide too. The man in the painting was certainly a mess—composed of splashes of paint, with an accident report at his feet, his body crushed, his face cut in half in the mirror, the man thrown from his chair but still sitting on it.

Simon took the pistol out of the drawer. He put the tip of the barrel in his mouth and closed his lips around it. Relief was possible. Let things take their own course, shape themselves without him. Just a squeeze. He could taste the gun's metal—like the color gray—the bullet in the chamber like a vitamin. But before he pulled the hammer back, he remembered he needed to leave a note for Elizabeth. He knew the importance of notes. He'd handled too many suicides. He put the gun down and started to write with a fountain pen. He wanted Elizabeth to be happy, or be as happy as possible. She could sell out to Service Corporation. Gilbert could stay on as manager. Then he started to write down all the things that would have to be done. He went down to his office and checked the computer for the e-mail from the consulate in Rome. It hadn't arrived yet. He'd have to explain that too.

Elizabeth knew his password, could handle the transition. She was a good manager. And she spoke Italian. She could deal with the Italian undertaker. She knew the business. He could hear her in the kitchen. He left his note on his desk and went into the kitchen, where she was making tea.

"Want a cup?" she asked.

"Yes," he said, sitting down. He waited for her to pour the tea. Two white porcelain cups. From the college food service. They seemed to accumulate.

"Sit down," he said. "Some bad news."

"You've been crying," she said, looking at his face.

The cup rattled on the saucer when she put it down in front of him, and he knew that a new life was about to begin. Another new life. But not entirely new. He still had to take the Connolly funeral. Gilbert had put on the Bob Dylan album. He could hear, faintly, *The Freewheelin' Bob Dylan*. "Corrina, Corrina, where you been so long?" He could hear Gilbert downstairs with the family. The guest book. The supply of tissues. He needed to check the body one last time. Adjust the hands.

There were no direct flights from Chicago to Rome in November. They had to change planes in New York. On the flight Simon and Elizabeth were not always in sync. Normal mental function alternated with grief and tears. The flight attendants brought packets of Kleenex. They took turns crying, softly, discreetly. The plane climbed over a storm; Simon could see flashes of lightning below them, fierce and beautiful, and wouldn't have minded if the plane had gone down over the Atlantic, and he didn't like keeping his seat belt fastened.

This was grief from the inside. What defenses did Simon

have? He held Elizabeth's hand. Interrogated it. *What will become of us now?* he asked her hand. His own advice, the advice he gave to people in great distress—take it one day at a time; write down your feelings in a journal; take care of yourself physically; get plenty of sleep—was good advice, but he didn't think it applied in his case. He thought of a line from Thomas Malory's *Morte d'Arthur*, which he'd read in a "boy's" version. *The Boy's King Arthur.* He thought, at the time, that the "boys" were the Knights of the Round Table, and he imagined that he was one of them, but then at the end it all comes apart: "Comfort thyself," the king says to Sir Bedivere, "and do as well as thou mayest, for in me is no trust for to trust in."

Elizabeth was asleep.

At the hotel—Hotel Antico Borgo in Trastevere—Elizabeth lay down on the double bed. She was the one who knew Italian, but she was going to stay and make phone contact with Simon's mother and with Hildi's brother, who were coming the next day. Simon took a taxi to the American consulate on Via Vittorio Veneto. He had trouble getting past security and had to leave his cell phone in a locker, and then he had a lot of paperwork to deal with. He knew the drill, but in reverse. He spoke not with the person who had called him on the phone but with a young woman, not much older than Hildi. She could not recommend anyone in particular, she said, but she steered him to a funeral director in Trastevere, not too far from the hotel.

The undertaker—Simon preferred the old word, at least in the privacy of his own mind—picked him up at the consulate. He wore a dark suit; his shirt was open at the collar; he had a GPS in the car but didn't look at it; he drove sensibly and didn't try to get Simon to talk.

"This is it," he said. "It" was an office. The sign over the door said IMPRESA FUNEBRE. Inside, the office was furnished with catalogs from which you could chose a hearse, a casket, flowers, and wreaths. Whatever you wanted.

Simon sat at a desk across from the undertaker, whose name was Guido. Simon understood that the man had to maintain a certain tone. You don't want your undertaker breaking down in tears for the same reason you don't want a bomber pilot to burst into tears as he releases his load of bombs. Or maybe you do.

There were lots of decisions to be made: cremation or burial or shipping the body home? Burial in an Italian cemetery? Guido could arrange whatever Simon wanted.

Simon hadn't thought it through. He was nervous, upset, bewildered by the catalogs, too many choices. And at the same time he experienced what he thought of as a kind of priestly fellowship, or undertaker fellowship—two men who understood and appreciated each other's work.

The *impresario*—Guido Fioravanti—reached across his desk and touched him, surprising him. He spoke pretty good English.

"This is it?" Simon asked.

Guido explained. There were no funeral homes in Italy, as in the United States. Well, maybe four or five. Guido was interested in Simon's business. The problem in Italy was space. There was no room. No parking. Embalming was not done, though it could be, but probably only if the body was going to be shipped back to the United States. Then it would have to be specially embalmed.

Simon wanted to talk to Elizabeth but couldn't reach her on her cell phone. She was talking to Louisa or to Jack. Coordinating.

A requiem mass? Probably not.

Cremation? Probably. But some kind of service? It was hard to know what to do.

"My daughter was planning to go into business with me," Simon said. "But Rome was too much for her. Rome and an Italian boyfriend."

"Yes," Guido said. "He's a doctor. He's been calling the consulate. I have his number. You could call him now, but it's probably better to wait."

"Hildi was full of ideas," Simon said. "She wanted funerals that tell the truth. Not a bunch of fairy tales."

"I understand exactly what you mean. But what is this truth? If you throw out the fairy tales, what have you got?"

They put their heads together but couldn't come up with anything beyond the shared conviction that *something* mattered, and that it was hard to say good-bye, and that you shouldn't have to do it alone. Beyond that, they could not go.

There were two hospitals facing each other on the Isola Tiberina. A Jewish hospital (Ospedale Israelitico) next to a large church in a piazza on the east side of the island, which was at a much lower level than the street they were standing on, and Ospedale Fatebenefratelli, which means "Do-Good Brothers Hospital," to the west. Hildi's body was in the morgue in the basement of the latter. Guido knocked on an unmarked door at the edge of the piazza, and they were admitted.

The body was in a walk-in cooler on a gurney. Simon was hoping for a mistake. But it was Hildi. A policeman was present for the official identification.

"Mi dispiace per la vostra perdita," he said, and Guido translated: "He's sorry for your loss."

Had the man been watching *Law & Order?* Better than "God called her home," or "She's in a better place" or "She's gone to glory."

"Your wife is here?" the policeman asked.

"At the hotel."

"Other children?"

"My son and my mother are coming tomorrow. They'll be coming on the same flight. Chicago to Frankfurt, and then to Rome."

"And your daughter? She was studying here?"

"Working for a consortium of American colleges and universities in Rome. She was helping edit their newsletter. She had an Italian boyfriend. A doctor."

"Yes. Francesco Tonarelli."

They wheeled the gurney out of the cooler. The body was covered with a sheet. They weren't the only ones in the morgue, the *obitorio.* Simon could hear sounds of weeping coming from behind the kind of curtains that are used to separate patients in a hospital room. And he could smell citrus: someone was eating a clementine.

They backed the gurney up to a sink. Guido filled the sink with warm water and added a few drops of lavender oil. Guido had brought a linen sheet and some light cosmetics. Simon had brought the dress that Elizabeth, just as they were leaving for the airport, had stuffed in a plastic grocery bag.

Simon remembered his first corpse. His first cadaver. Remembered helping his father. He was twelve years old. And he remembered his first cadaver in the morgue in Da Nang, and later at the Wisconsin Institute of Mortuary Science up in Milwaukee, where, because of his previous experience, he'd gotten his embalmer's license in only one year.

Simon held Hildi's hand while Guido kept a gentle pressure

on the eyes till they stayed closed, and then he sutured the mouth shut. Rigor had passed and the body was limp. There was a kind of truth in this. She was not a sleeping princess. She was already starting to dissolve.

"No fairy tales for us," Guido said, as if reading Simon's thoughts. Simon helped him turn the body and replace the bottom sheet, but he looked away as Guido closed the orifices with cotton balls.

"I've always been a Roman Catholic," Simon said. "I'm still a BCL. A Big Catholic Layman. I give a lot of money to the church. I always used to think that one day I'd sit down with all the great books—you know what I mean: the Bible, Plato, Aristotle, all the great books I'd never read—and sort everything out. I thought my wife could help me, and I thought that if I could just find the right metaphor—the journey, the awakening, the peaceful sleep . . ."

Guido shook his head. "Death breaks the back of metaphor. When my wife died, I didn't want a metaphor. I didn't want people to say 'She's in a better place' or 'She's at peace' or 'She lived a good life.' I just wanted to make the pain go away. Her *salma*, her corpse. It was an inconvenience. Everything. No fairy tales for me, I told myself. I went to see a psychiatrist. This isn't done in Italy. I mean, there's a stigma. He gave me some pills. As if I was sick. The pills helped, but I stopped taking them. I woke up. It wasn't right. Treating this pain, this grief, like a sickness, something to be cured. That's what's happening now. I don't mean here, with you and me right now, but today. Grief is becoming an illness, a medical condition, something to be cured. Maybe that's the new paradigm. Maybe we don't need grief anymore."

"But you don't believe that?"

"Grief is a signal. You've lost something vital; you've been pushed out of your ordinary life. Everything is called into question. You have to rethink everything, reaffirm your humanity, reaffirm everything that animated your life, and it's hard. Do you want to turn this into a medical problem? If I could give you a pill that would make your grief go away, would you take it? But that's what we're doing, as a society. 'Your wife died and you're feeling grief? Take a pill.' 'Your daughter died and you're feeling grief? Take a pill.' Maybe it's okay. Maybe in the future we can wipe out grief like smallpox or polio."

Simon let go of one hand so Guido could wash it with soap and water. He held the other hand and noticed that Guido wasn't wearing disposable gloves.

The injury was on the back of her head. He didn't see it until he helped Guido turn her over. She'd been thrown against a lamppost. Someone at the morgue had cleaned off most of the blood. Simon held her hand tightly as he had held her hand when she was a little girl. He gave her limp hand a squeeze, but she didn't squeeze back. That was the truth of the body, even if it was imperfectly understood.

Simon brought out the clothes that Elizabeth had put in the plastic shopping bag, a brightly colored patchwork dress, yellow and green. Guido looked at Simon. Simon nodded. They lifted her up and slid the dress over her head and adjusted the straps. Guido called the morgue attendant, and they wheeled her back into the cooler.

Afterward, standing at the foot of Ponte Palatino, Simon noticed helicopters.

"Keeping an eye on the river," Guido said. "Worried about flooding." Simon knew about the floods in Florence, but he didn't know that the Tiber flooded too.

"Oh my, yes," Guido said.

About thirty feet below them, in front of San Bartolomeo, a TV crew was covering a funeral. Simon and Guido watched the TV crew from the bridge. A big Mercedes hearse was parked in front of the church. An enormous wreath was carried into the church. "Four hundred euros," Guido said.

Simon nodded.

"The well of Aesculapius is in the crypt of the church," Guido said without offering any more information.

They stood and watched for a long time. A canteen had been set up for the TV crew. Simon couldn't see how the hearse got into the piazza in front of the church. You could walk down a set of stairs, but there was no visible road.

What were they waiting for? Simon was waiting for the end, for them to bring the coffin out of the church, for the people to spill out into the piazza.

But then the hearse drove off, along the broad sidewalk that ran along the river, and the TV crew began to dismantle the camera and another crew started loading equipment over the side of the embankment. A hoist of some kind was attached to a very tall ladder that went all the way down to the sidewalk along the river, where still more crew members loaded the camera equipment onto four-wheeled dollies, which they pushed down to the tip of the island. Huh?

Simon touched Guido's arm. "What's going on?" he asked.

Guido spoke to a man at the base of the TV crane and came back. "It's a *funerale finta*," he said. "A fake funeral. They're making a film. I guess it's a different kind of truth."

Simon laughed and shook his head, and then he started to cry. He pulled a tissue out of his pocket and a comb fell out onto the small square paving stones. Some of the stones had been dislodged, and Simon could see that they were pointed on the bottom.

He'd have to give her up. Might as well do it now. But no. Not yet, but . . . soon.

When Simon got back to the hotel Elizabeth was lying on the bed. She hadn't changed her clothes. Her eyes were closed, but she wasn't sleeping. Her cell phone was next to her.

"You get everything taken care of?"

Simon sat on the edge of the bed and put his hand on the top of her head. He spread his fingers out.

"It's all taken care of," he said.

"Now what?"

"People will come to a place at the hospital. They call it a *camera ardente.*"

"You have to pay?"

"Of course. There aren't any funeral homes in Italy. I didn't know that. Maybe six or seven. Guido is interested. Not easy to find space. Parking. He invited us to supper."

"Are you crazy? Italians don't invite you to their homes."

"It's a professional courtesy."

"It's very unprofessional, if you ask me."

"He's called an *impresario.*"

"I thought an impresario was someone who manages an opera company or who organizes concerts or magic shows. Like Andrew Lloyd Webber or Billy Rose."

"I guess they organize funerals too."

"You can go. I'll stay here."

"Lizzy—" She said nothing. "I'll call him."

Simon used Elizabeth's cell phone to call. He explained. Guido wanted to speak to Elizabeth. She shook her head, but Simon handed her the phone and she started speaking in

Italian. Explaining. But then he could see she was changing her mind. *"Va bene, va bene."*

"He's very persuasive," she said.

Via Santini, on the other side of Mercato Cosimato, was empty at night. It was a playground area. They stopped to buy some flowers on the way. Elizabeth insisted. It was just something you had to do in Italy. Guido lived above a shop that sold fresh pasta. Tortellini, tortelloni, ravioli. It was still open.

"Bell one," Elizabeth said. "Second floor, above the shop. Look for the name. Fioravanti."

A disembodied voice asked who it was and then buzzed them in. The door on the landing was open. Guido appeared briefly, a cell phone at his ear, and then retreated. As soon as they entered the apartment Elizabeth said, "He's lonely. That's why he invited us."

Simon shushed her. "He speaks English."

"Yes," Guido said, coming back into the room. "And your wife is right. I am lonely."

Elizabeth apologized. In Italian. They spoke in Italian, which Simon couldn't follow.

They ate a Roman dish that had been one of Guido's wife's specialties. *Cacio e pepe.*

"Parmigiano-Reggiano?" Elizabeth asked as Guido served the spaghetti.

Guido shook his head. Pecorino Romano. Parmesan didn't have enough bite. He asked about the funeral-home business in the United States, and they shared undertaker stories: bodies purging, falling out of caskets, misidentified bodies, bodies buried with valuable jewelry.

Simon told the story of the removal he'd gone on with

Hildi. How they'd played pinochle with Mrs. Johansen while they were waiting for the coroner to come to sign the death certificate, and how he and Hildi had sung "You Are My Sunshine" on the way home, and then they'd stopped for a beer, and how Hildi had wanted funerals that told the truth about death, which he'd already told Guido.

"You never told me that story," Elizabeth said, and she started to cry.

"I never told anyone," Simon said.

"So, she was going to partner with you, take over the business?"

"That was before she came to Rome. She loved it here. And she was in love. I'm glad she had this time, glad she had an Italian lover. Every woman deserves at least one Italian lover. My mother had one." And he knew that Elizabeth had had one too, and in retrospect he was glad. Why not? He reached for her hand.

"You'll do fine," she said.

The family kept Guido busy. Hildi's brother, Jack, wanted justice or vengeance. He wanted the driver of the hit-and-run car hunted down and crucified, but it wasn't going to happen. They stood at the scene of the accident, at the end of Ponte Garibaldi, with a policeman and with Checco. They looked up and down the one-way street along the Trastevere side of the river. Witnesses? Jack had read too many detective novels and thought there had to be someone who'd noticed. They could do a door-to-door. But all the old women who sat by their windows all day twitching their curtains would have been in bed at two o'clock in the morning.

Louisa wanted to have Hildi buried in the Protestant Cemetery with Keats and Shelley and Joseph Severn and

John Addington Symonds, but this would be difficult if not impossible. "It's not really the 'Protestant' cemetery," Guido explained. "It's really the 'non-Catholic' cemetery, for non-Catholics only, and (a) Hildi was nominally a Roman Catholic, and (b) she did not have an Italian identity card." Elizabeth wanted cremation, but this too presented difficulties. They would have to prove that cremation was in fact what Hildi herself had wanted. It could be done, of course. Guido could manage the paperwork, the affidavits, which would have to be notarized or authenticated. Simon and Elizabeth would have to testify under oath that their daughter had expressed a strong desire to be cremated.

About twenty people gathered in the *camera ardente* at Ospedale Fatebenefratelli, where Hildi's body was on display in the fiberglass casket that she would be cremated in. Guido had put up notices at the consortium office where Hildi had worked, outside her old address on Via della Luce, and outside her most recent address, where she'd been living with Checco in Piazza de' Renzi. It was awkward at first. People didn't know whether to speak Italian or English. Simon and Jack were the only ones who didn't know Italian. Checco's sister, Marina, was the only one who didn't know English.

Checco sat by himself with his head in his hands. His sister released her Seeing Eye dog, Bruno, who went around the room sniffing everyone, introducing them to one another. And then he went to Checco and sat with him. The body had not been embalmed, but it had been refrigerated and was still presentable.

Checco had moved to the casket and, in spite of Bruno's ministrations, was struggling to hold himself together. Simon recognized the signs and went to him, put his hand on his

shoulder. Touched him. The two of them stood by the cremation casket, as if they were guarding it. Simon, in undertaker
mode, adjusted Hildi's hands. Checco moved as if to stop him
but then put his hands over his face again.

Simon was glad to get a glimpse into Hildi's life in Rome.
Glad that there were people here, so far from home, who had
loved her. Not just Checco and his sister, but friends from
work, from the consortium, from her old neighborhood on
Via della Luce, who spoke to Louisa in Italian. A Dutch opera
singer, Italian neighbors, the woman from the mask store,
Maddelena. Hildi was leaving a trail of friends behind her.

There was nothing to eat or drink, nor was there any
service, but friends got up and spoke, mostly in Italian, which
Simon was able to understand—the feelings if not the words.
Louisa and Jack sat together. Simon and Elizabeth sat with
Checco, who had assumed the role of chief mourner. Simon
comforted him but did not give way himself till later. He
touched Checco's arm, and Elizabeth held his hand and spoke
quietly to him in Italian.

Simon and Elizabeth stayed in Rome to wait for Hildi's ashes.
They went to San Luigi to see *The Calling of Saint Matthew*.
Simon fed the light meter till he ran out of coins, and then
they walked back to the hotel over the Isola Tiberina, past
San Bartolomeo, where Simon and Guido had watched the
funerale finta.

They spent time with Checco and his family; they ate at
Carlo Menta; they went to hear Checco's sister sing at Club
Dante. She and Bruno came to their table and sat with them
during her breaks, and Elizabeth rested her hand on Bruno's
head. They went to the mask store and saw Hildi's face in the
window in different guises—masks made from the original

mold—and Simon bought a lot of masks: a clown, a plague doctor, the Caravaggio Medusa for Louisa, suns and moons and elves and Renaissance ladies, a Bacchus and a satyr, two long-beaked birds. Maddelena tried to restrain him, but he knew what he wanted, and she gave him a substantial discount.

The consulate said it would take seven or eight weeks to get the ashes, but Guido had them in three days, another professional courtesy. Checco wanted some of the ashes, and Simon asked Guido to open the urn. Still another professional courtesy.

Checco was almost apologetic for "stealing" their daughter, for living together without her parents' permission (or even their knowledge). Checco had been worried about this. He didn't know how Americans would react. He'd worried about preventing her from going into business with her father. She had assured him that her parents wouldn't mind their living together, but she hadn't wanted to disappoint her father. They both had worried about it. They had been planning to get married. They had considered various scenarios: spending half the year in Rome and half in Galesburg. Maybe Checco could practice medicine in the United States. Maybe Hildi could become an *impresario funebre* in Rome. Checco spoke about these ideas seriously, as if they were problems that still needed to be resolved.

CHAPTER V: THE TRUTH ABOUT DEATH

Hello, everybody. I'm Elizabeth. Simon's wife. I want to tell you about the last years of Simon's life. He was a good man, and I loved him with all my heart (at least most of the time). And I want to tell you about Olive (our black lab) and a little bit about myself too. And I want to tell you the truth about death.

PART I: SIMON

After Hildi's death a chilly wind blew through our lives, blew right through the double-glazed windows and the storm doors, whistled through the fireplace chimneys, hummed under the wide eaves. You don't get used to something like that, but you learn to work around it. And work was what we did.

I taught my classes and resumed work on a long-term project about the puzzling figures that decorate the margins of medieval books of hours and books of prayers—ass-kissing priests, sciapods, grylli, drunken apes, potbellied heads, putrifying corpses—which I planned to call *Marginalia*. (Sciapods, in case you're wondering, are humanlike creatures with one gigantic foot, big enough so that they can lie on their back and hold their foot up as an umbrella to shade them from the sun. Grylli usually have two legs, a head, and a tail, but no body or arms. They're often wimpled like nuns or have manes like lions.)

Simon instituted most of the changes Hildi had wanted. He encouraged people to have funerals at home. And he encouraged the bereaved to help him wash the body—or at least hold the dead person's hand, as he had held Hildi's hand in the *obitorio* in Rome—while he did the prep. Not during embalming, of course, but he made it clear that embalming was not necessary, that you could keep the body in relatively good shape for quite a while in the refrigerator or for several days at home by placing chunks of dry ice under it at strategic points. He encouraged cremation as an inexpensive alternative to a traditional burial. He hung paintings by local artists and people bought some of them. But the most important thing of all was the dog.

It had begun with a letter on a website. It was the end of August. We hadn't gone to the lake that summer and were restless. Simon had read the letter aloud to me as I had been watering the plants in the front windows.

"'Hi, everybody! I'm Olive! I'm three years old. I'm a big strong girl, but not *too* big, about sixty pounds with lots of love to give! I had a family a long time ago, but they weren't very nice to me. The Guardian Angels came to my rescue and have been very kind to me, but I've been living here at the shelter for almost a year, and I'm starting to get sad. Just look at my picture, and you'll see! Every time a car drives up I think maybe it's someone who will take me to my forever home. Maybe you'll be that person. If you think you might be that person, please call the shelter and leave a message for me. Okay?—Olive.'"

"Simon," I'd said. "You sound as if you think the dog wrote that letter."

Simon had taken off his glasses and was reading from the computer screen. "Well," he said. "It's a good letter. You want to hear another one?"

"No," I'd said. "It's shameless."

"That's all right," Simon had said. "Olive's is the best. Come and look at her picture. She's beautiful."

"I do not want a dog."

Olive—sixty pounds, a black lab mix, glossy black—was wearing a blue-and-yellow bandanna.

"If she's been at the shelter for a year," I'd said, standing behind Simon and looking at the picture on the computer screen, "there must be something wrong with her or someone would have taken her to her 'forever home.'"

"I suppose that means till she dies."

"What else *could* it mean?"

Well, I thought later, *maybe a dog would be good for Simon.* We picked up Olive for a trial run. She'd already had a litter, but the puppies had been adopted early on. "Sometimes a dog gets picked up and then has to come back," the woman at the Guardian Angels shelter said. "I guess it's just the way things are. People don't think it through. One lady brought her dog back because it barked at the neighbor's dog. What was she thinking when she got a dog? It's a terrible moment when the dog realizes it's going to be abandoned a second time." I took this as a warning.

The first night at the funeral home Olive checked everything out, but she wouldn't get into the crate we'd bought at the pet store. The crate was in the laundry room.

Olive barked and barked and kept on barking till Simon let her out of the laundry room, and then she slept on a quilt on the floor at the foot of our bed.

She didn't poop for a couple of days. But she peed a lot and ran around the enclosed parking lot. Simon got several books on dog training—books by monks and dog whisperers, books that recommended using treats as rewards for good behavior, books that recommended clicks, and books that said your dog wouldn't be happy until you completely dominated it. Simon spent some time working on the basic commands—though Olive already knew what she needed to know about "Sit," "Stay," "Stand," "Down," "Come," and so on—but he didn't bother with therapy-dog certification. He wasn't worried about her knocking people over or banging into their walkers, and after a couple of months she started working at the funeral home. She enjoyed her "work" and wore a smart forest green uniform with a yellow bandanna around her neck. Gilbert fretted about insurance—What if she bit someone? What if she jumped up on the casket?—but Olive always paid attention and took care of the people who were grieving hardest, and after a while he stopped fretting, because even Gilbert could see that the love Olive was offering was simple and profound, kind and compassionate.

Olive liked to empty every wastebasket in the house at least once a day. She liked to turn up dead pigeons by the railroad tracks or dead squirrels from Hope Cemetery and bring them to one of us. She liked it when I started yelling at Simon to take away the dead bird or the dead squirrel or whatever it was. I'd wave my arms as if I were trying to signal someone who was a long way away, and Simon would try to tug it out of her mouth till finally she'd drop it at his feet. She liked to pick up toads in the pachysandra patch around the oak tree at the back of the fenced-in area and carry them around in her mouth. She liked getting me up in the morning—Simon would already be downstairs in the kitchen and would have closed the bedroom door behind him—and in the evening she liked to drag the Scottish plaid wool blanket off the couch and make it into a bed on the floor. Sometimes she folded it over carefully, and sometimes she just wadded it up. She liked to stretch out on the couch (when I wasn't there), or at least pull a cushion off the couch and use it as a pillow.

She liked to chase live squirrels in the little park by the depot. She liked to lie on the living room floor with Simon. She liked to smell us, and she liked it when we smelled her back, pushing our noses into her neck fur. She liked to bump my arm when I was reading. She liked to patrol the whole house—including Nana's apartment and the bedrooms on the third floor—just before bedtime. She liked to "vacuum" the kitchen floor for things that I had dropped or spilled. Crumbs, cereal, sometimes an olive. She'd hold the olive in her mouth for a while and then spit out the pit. She liked to do this when there were guests. She liked running in the park at night, walking too, smelling all the messages left by other dogs, putting together a kind of olfactory map of the park. She liked running through the snow with her nose down. She liked wearing her uniform where there were a lot of people in the house, either in the children's room upstairs or in the visitation room downstairs. There was always one person who needed her most, and she liked to stand by that person.

She liked to bark when no one was around; she liked to lift her leg to pee instead of squatting; she liked to poop right in the middle of the little Girl Scout garden on Mulberry Street, at the edge of the park. She liked greeting people at the door. She liked chasing the Frisbee in the park. She liked putting on her uniform and going out with Simon in the middle of the night. Just the two of them. She liked to sit in the front seat of the van. She liked going duck hunting with Simon. Just the two of them. Simon was not a very good shot, but he usually got a couple of ducks. Olive liked to dive off the little boat into the water or burst out of the duck blind. Simon said it was something she'd always known how to do.

She liked to tease me by bringing me things and provoke me by peeing on my tomato plants. She liked to snooze in the sun on the Oriental rug up in Simon's tower. She liked the baby carrots that I tossed up in the air for her to catch, and she liked to break all of my rules about not getting up on the couch or bed. She liked sitting quietly with Nana up in Nana's apartment. She liked to put her nose in Simon's crotch when he was sitting on the edge of the bed trying to tie his shoes. She liked having her teeth brushed, which Simon did every morning. She liked sitting by my chair when I was reading. She liked Simon telling me not to baby her. She liked putting her head against Simon's leg when he was shaving. She liked to lie down and cradle her head on her paws till someone came to talk to her.

Olive didn't like my shooing her off the couch or off the bed or out of the kitchen. She didn't like walking on the leash when she could be running free. She didn't like not barking sometimes or not jumping up on me. She didn't like being left alone with Megan Thomas, who came to babysit the phone when everyone else was gone. She didn't like not being allowed to go into the prep room with Simon. She didn't like taking a shower with us and getting soap in her eyes. She didn't like it when I wiped her paws with a towel when she came in from the rain or the snow. She didn't like it when Simon and I packed our suitcases.

Olive was a natural comforter. Her stores of friendliness and attentiveness, open affection, and loving-kindness were inexhaustible. She put people at ease—extending the paw of affection, placing her head on a lap or a leg. Word got around and more and more people requested Olive. For the children. For the elderly bereaved. For everyone. It was fun for her. It was work too, and after a visitation or a funeral she would lie down on her bed in Simon's office or else on the quilt that she'd dragged into the back of our bedroom closet.

She comforted us too. Sometimes at a visitation she'd go to Simon as if he were the one grieving hardest. And Simon would have to shoo her away.

Simon was working too hard. "You take all the difficult cases," I told him one evening after a difficult funeral, "the suicides, the organ donors ... You're everyone's friend and comforter. But let's face facts: you're getting older; you worry about money all the time; you're drinking too much; you have to get up three or four times in the night to pee. And you're angry all the time. You're turning into your father."

I think this last remark hit home.

I was sitting at the little library table in the tower. Simon was in his big chair-and-a-half. The deceased—a chemistry professor at the college—had wanted to donate his organs. All the paperwork had been in place for weeks. At the last minute, just as the doctors were about to take him off the ventilator, his wife changed her mind, brought her lawyer to the hospital; she wanted Simon to pick up the body at the hospital before the surgeons had a chance to harvest the organs.

The organs were harvested nonetheless. First Person Consent makes your decision to be an organ/tissue donor legally binding—family consent is not necessary—but it was an ugly scene, and later the widow was unhappy with the way the body looked. There's only so much you can do with a dead body when the corneas and the organs have been harvested— tissue too, including some major bones, which had been replaced with plastic tubes.

Louisa had died in June and we'd canceled our plans to take Olive up to the lake. I had changed some of the prints around. Simon was seriously depressed. Hard work wasn't helping, and there was only so much Olive and I could do. I wanted something to keep his spirits up, but nothing too obvious. I didn't want the tower to look like a dentist's office with uplifting posters on the ceiling, but I did put up lots of Impressionists—Monet's gardens, Renoir's cafés, Matisse's dancing boys and girls—along with Giovanni di Paolo's *Five Angels Dancing Before the Sun* (from the Musée Condé in Chantilly); a picture of a Korean bowl that charmed with its imperfections, reminding us that we don't have to get everything perfect; and De Kooning's *Villa Borghese* and *Woman on the Beach*, which hang side by side in the Guggenheim.

Simon poured himself a second drink from a bottle of Bushmills that was standing on a little table next to his chair-and-a-half. He put his feet up on the ottoman. I was working at my laptop at the small library table.

"Let's go up to the cottage," I said, "for a dirty weekend. It's been a long time."

"It's October."

"It's still warm," I said. "Maybe warm days will never cease. We can take Olive. She'd love the lake."

He looked at me as if I were crazy. "I'm sorry," he said. "I didn't think you were interested."

I was indignant. It wasn't my fault that we hadn't made love since Hildi's death. It had been over a year now. "Not interested?" I said. "Simon, do you really believe what you just said?"

He shook his head. "Lizzy, Lizzy, Lizzy," he said. "What's going to become of us?"

"I like it when you call me Lizzy," I said. "I want you to keep doing it. I want to drive up to the cottage for our dirty weekend and I want you to call me Lizzy the whole time. I want you to call me Lizzy in bed, Simon. It's been over a year. Remember how horny you used to get after a funeral or a removal, and I did too? I could feel the heat coming off your body, both of us ready for a good no-holds-barred, sheet-ripping fuck. And then spooning afterward. We'll take Sally's mindful meditation DVD and watch it together. I've got the

Zafu meditation cushions she gave us for Christmas. There's even a meditation on Tantric sex. It's a dance. There's no beginning, no end, no goal. Just slowing everything down."

"You've been working too hard too," he said.

I'd finished a draft of *Marginalia* and had sent off a proposal to Douglas Richardson at Princeton University Press. I was ready for a break. "By the way, there's an e-mail from Checco. We could see if he'd like to come. We could pick him up at O'Hare. And we could scatter Hildi's ashes in the dunes. We could do a jigsaw puzzle together," I said. "You could throw the Frisbee out into the lake for Olive. You could read the first two chapters of *Marginalia*."

Hearing her name, Olive, who was lying on the Omani rug, stirred and looked up at Simon as if to endorse the idea. As if she needed a break too.

"We could build a fire in the fireplace."

I could see that Simon was on the edge of tears. I'd gotten through to him. "I'll call Mrs. Burian," I said, "so she can get things ready. I'll make all the arrangements. You can just lie back and enjoy it. I'll e-mail Checco too."

The vacation, however, was not a success. Checco could not get away; the jigsaw puzzle—*The Vocation of Saint Matthew*—reminded Simon of his mother. "I'm no good at this," he said. "I like the idea, but I don't think I've ever, in all the years we've been coming up here, been able to fit a single piece in. Not once." Simon was too restless to read my first two chapters, and Sally's mindful meditation DVD made him even more nervous. The goal was to slow the mind down by focusing on your breathing, but Simon couldn't sit still. "The minute I try to sit still," he complained, "my body starts to talk to me: to itch, to cramp, to tingle, to twitch, to ache."

"Try to interrogate the itch," I said, trying to guess what Sally (who taught yoga) would say. "Follow its progress, the way you might follow an insect crawling through a patch of tall grass."

"What about the tingling? What about the cramps?"

"Interrogate everything," I said.

"What am I, a goddamn prosecuting attorney?"

Sally could sit through the half-hour lectures without moving. I could manage about ten minutes. Simon couldn't last even thirty seconds. "Try to put your expectations aside," I said. "Wanting things to be other than they are is the problem. Attachment."

"I don't *want* anything," Simon insisted. "*Wanting* is not the problem. The problem is *not* wanting. I don't *want* anything."

He was on the phone a lot with Gilbert. The chemistry professor's wife had refused to pay her bill and was threatening to sue the funeral home. Simon wanted to go home that afternoon. I persuaded him to stay till the next morning.

"We still have to scatter Hildi's ashes," I said.

"We can do it this afternoon and then take off."

"You can leave if you want to, but I'm staying here till tomorrow." I wanted to spend one more night in the cottage, though I'd pretty much given up on a no-holds-barred fuck.

If it hadn't been for Olive, who was always in good spirits, I'm not sure what we would have done. It was her first time at the lake, and she loved it. Like all labs, she had webbed feet and was a strong swimmer, and she never seemed to tire of swimming out into the lake after the Frisbee.

On the last morning the lake was very calm, flat as a pancake. It was foggy. Simon threw the Frisbee farther and farther, as if he were trying to set some Olympic Frisbee record. I begged him not to throw it so far, but he wouldn't listen. You couldn't see farther than fifty feet.

"Not so far, Simon. Please."

"She loves it. You can't throw it too far for her."

"I don't want to watch."

"Go up and check the cottage to make sure we haven't left anything. I'll be up in a few minutes." But I didn't go, and after an especially long throw we watched Olive swim right past the Frisbee, saw her heading out into open water. Into the fog. We could see her, and then we couldn't see her. I was furious. "What the hell's the matter with you? Why did you throw it so goddamn far? What the hell were you thinking? What's the matter with you anyway? You're determined to spoil every fucking thing. You can't even take a fucking vacation."

"Everything is already spoiled," he shouted, kicking off his sandals and running toward the water. He wasn't a strong swimmer, but he was going to swim out after her. I ran after him and tried to hold him back, but he was in panic mode and fought me, as if he were drowning and I was trying to rescue him. There was no sign of Olive.

Simon suddenly collapsed at the edge of the water. There were not many people on the beach, but those who were there had cell phones and called 911.

By the time the ambulance arrived, Simon was unconscious. By the time Olive dragged herself up out of the water with the Frisbee, the ambulance crew had arrived, coming down the big wooden stairs at the public beach and running along the hard sand at the edge of the water.

Olive licked Simon's face, and Simon woke up and struggled with the paramedics, who strapped him onto a stretcher and carried him across the beach to the waiting ambulance.

* * *

They kept Simon for two days in the small hospital in Coloma, and then we drove home in our Mazda. Olive sat in the front with me and Simon lay down in the backseat.

Simon was out of danger, but I worried about a second heart attack, a sudden hammer blow striking from behind, a dark horseman galloping toward us across a fertile valley, swinging an ax or a mace. Simon refused to have bypass surgery, refused to do anything his doctors had suggested. He refused to cut back on salt and saturated fats, refused to cut back on his drinking, refused to take his ACE inhibitors, refused to keep his angina diary.

And so on.

He kept a copy of his living will on the table next to the bed: *No heroic measures. Do not resuscitate.* He mailed fresh copies to Dr. Currie and to both of the local hospitals, and he made me promise not to call 911 till it was too late. I had mixed feelings about this.

By the time we celebrated Simon's fifty-ninth birthday, I had signed a contract with Princeton for *Marginalia*; we had hired another embalmer, installed a new computer system, and hired a young woman to create a presence on the Internet. The website she created featured Olive in her uniform, photos of the family and staff and the home itself, and the opportunity to subscribe at no cost to a daily e-mail to help you through the grieving process. Gilbert composed the e-mails himself, and the first ones were very good—thoughtful and thought provoking—but after a while you got to number twenty and then number thirty. What more was there to say? And he started a blog. Simon wasn't happy about the blog, though he wasn't sure just what it was, and he was too tired to do anything about it.

Simon's health had not improved. When he read in the paper about new drugs that would enable people to live into their hundreds he became agitated. He wasn't interested in living that long. He didn't seem to be very interested in living at all. He was short of breath and couldn't handle the stairs up to the tower. I thought of moving Rembrandt and Caravaggio and the Impressionists and the Korean bowl and De Kooning down to our bedroom on the second floor. But I no longer maintained my unquestioning faith in the healing power of great art. Maybe Hegel had been right: Art has lost its genuine truth and life, and has been reduced to a mode of recreation or entertainment, decorative rather than necessary and essential. Or maybe I just had to accept the fact that Simon was never going to see what I saw.

It just wasn't going to happen. And then something else happened.

Instead of looking at great art, we started looking at *New Yorker* cartoons while Olive snoozed on the Omani rug, which we'd brought down from the tower to our bedroom. We'd always looked at *New Yorker* cartoons, of course, and the attic was full of old *New Yorker*s, stacked in no particular order in bankers boxes, many of them folded open in the middle of an article or story that one of us hadn't quite finished, or a cartoon that we'd wanted to look at one more time. You could fit over a hundred *New Yorker*s into a Fellowes Bankers Box if you made one flat pile and then filled the remaining space by standing another forty copies or so up on edge. We went through hundreds of old *New Yorker*s, cutting out one or two cartoons, sometimes more, from each issue and taping them up on the walls, not caring if the tape would pull the paint off later. We weren't thinking about "later." We were thinking about "now." About Charles Addams and George Booth and Roz Chast and Sam Gross (*My son stepped on a crack and broke my back*) and Charles Barsotti (*Fusilli, you crazy bastard! How are you?*). And the younger generation too—Marisa Acocella's sexy fashionistas, Drew Dernavich's woodcuts, C. Covert Darbyshire's stressed-out children, Eric Lewis's absurd captions, Matt Diffee's hapless losers.

When we ran out of wall space, we made space by taking down the old cartoons and pasting them in scrapbooks, till we ran out of old *New Yorker*s. When a new one came in the mail, usually on Tuesday, we'd go through it quickly, looking at the cartoons; then we'd read some of the articles, and then a few days later we'd go through it again, cutting out the cartoons we liked. Maybe it wasn't the happiest time of our life together, but it was the funniest.

For years we'd been unable to keep up with *The New Yorker*, but now *The New Yorker* couldn't keep up with us, and Simon begged me to draw our own *New Yorker* cartoons. He was enthusiastic, full of ideas. "How about this?" he said one afternoon, lying in bed with his laptop propped up on a pillow. (I'd just come back from lecturing on Rembrandt's self-portraits.) "Two explorers wearing those jungle helmets—pith helmets, I think they're called—come to a clearing in the jungle. What do they see? The lost—"

"The lost graveyard of the elephants," I said. "Like the explorers in those old Tarzan movies."

"No, no. Not the lost *graveyard* of the elephants, the lost *funeral home*. Not the graveyard but the funeral home. Get it? Why not the lost funeral home? Picture a funeral home in the jungle. You could draw some elephant pallbearers loading a casket into a hearse. The driver of the hearse is an elephant, of course, wearing a sharp uniform. What do you think? A sign in front that says JUMBO AND SONS, FUNERAL DIRECTORS."

"I like it," I said. "But I haven't done any drawing for years."

"It'll be a good exercise." Simon was so enthusiastic I thought I'd better seize the moment.

I hadn't done any serious drawing since the early days of our marriage when I'd thought I might switch horses and become an artist instead of an art historian. That night Gilbert helped me bring my old four-post drawing table down from the attic. We carried the storage drawers down separately, then the frame, then the top. I set it up next to the bed and pulled up a chair. Olive parked herself on the Omani rug and Simon sat on the edge of the bed and rubbed her with his feet.

I went out to Dick Blick on Saturday morning and came back with pencils, erasers, rulers, stumps, torchons, a pencil box, small sketch pads, large drawing pads, a pencil sharpener, a sandpaper pad, a glue stick, masking tape, a light box, a fixative spray, double-ended Prismacolor markers in every shade of gray, which I distributed among the six storage drawers. And half a dozen books on cartooning. Mort Gerberg, Bob Mankoff, Polly Keener, Steve Whitaker, and others.

By the time I got back Simon had located images on the Internet—images for me to imitate—drawing prompts, suggestions, jungle cartoons, trees, explorers with pith helmets, photos of funeral homes. I printed them out in Simon's office.

How hard could it be to draw cartoons? I thought.

Harder than I thought. I started with some warm-up exercises—scribbles and gesture drawings. In two minutes I could turn out a gesture sketch of a young girl reading or an old woman leaning on a cane or an old man trying to tie his shoe. But "the lost funeral home of the elephants"?

"By crikey, Wilson, it's the lost funeral home of the elephants." That was Simon's caption.

It took me two days just to get the perspective right. I went through dozens of sheets of paper and used up two of the Prismacolor markers shading in the jungle trees. I went across the street and studied our own Italianate funeral home with its five square bays, its wide overhanging eaves, its octagonal belvedere (from which, once upon a time, the farmer had been able to observe his workers in the fields), its open verandas and the guest rooms over the elaborate porte cochere on the west side. But it was too complicated, and in the end I decided on a more urban model, like the old Foley Mortuary over on Broad Street, which had been turned into apartments. We both liked the idea of an urban street running through the middle of the jungle.

I drew sketch after sketch till I got something workable. After a while it became easier, though never easy.

Simon liked heroes. "How about Beowulf picking up his steel grip," he said, "at an airport carousel?"

I had a lot of trouble getting the carousel right and finally worked from an image Simon had downloaded from the web.

"How about the *wind*shield of Achilles?"

I drew Achilles getting the windshield of a little sports car repaired at the Hephaestus Glass Company. We didn't caption either of these cartoons, but we added banners: BEOWULF'S GRIP OF STEEL and THE WINDSHIELD OF ACHILLES.

"How about hell freezing over?"

I drew Satan out ice fishing with one of his devils. Ice shacks all over with more devils. The devil fishing with Satan

said, "Well, I suppose it was bound to happen sooner or later."
A lot of people didn't get this one; Gilbert didn't get it; neither
did Marge, but I guess that's the way it goes with *New Yorker*
cartoons.

"How about an old-fashioned carnival midway? But instead
of the world's fattest woman and a two-headed baby and the
incredible five-legged calf, the barkers tout 'Plato's Cave'
('Experience the thrill of a lifetime'); 'The *Ding an Sich*' ('See
things as they really are'); and 'The Veil of Maya' ('See Swami
Krishna lift the Veil of Maya'). A little boy standing with his
father says, 'Daddy, You promised we could see the *Ding
an sich*.'"

I thought I did a pretty good job with that one.

Simon liked elephants. "How about an elephant artist at an
exhibit of his works. Draw a couple of women drinking white
wine. One of the women says, 'They say he studied with De
Kooning.'"

I liked the idea but never got the drawing right.

Simon didn't have many friends in the ordinary sense, except
Paul Childs, our lawyer, who'd gone to school with him. "Keep
your chin up," Paul would say. "You'll beat this thing." And he
was full of stories about people who'd made miraculous recov-
eries, had "beaten" angina, survived double and triple bypasses.
No comfort there. But comfort came from an unexpected
place: families Simon had helped, families whose kith and kin
he'd buried. They read about Simon on Gilbert's blog—which
had become locally famous (or infamous)—and sent cards,
notes, e-mails. Some of them even stopped by to thank Simon
and to see how he was doing. Simon pretended not to be
affected, but in fact he could remember all the details of every
funeral, all the particulars, and he was deeply moved. And he

was looking better. He was in good spirits and had dropped his opposition to bypass surgery. At the same time, we grew closer, more trusting; we opened our hearts to each other, and our arms too, as if we were young lovers. We paid attention to each other the way some artists pay attention to the leaves on a tree, noting their individual characteristics. And Simon started to take more of an interest in my work. He asked me to bring down a Rembrandt self-portrait from the tower—Rembrandt as a young man, from Schloss Wilhelmshöhe in Kassel, which I've never seen—and he read the first two chapters of *Marginalia* and offered some sensible suggestions. And one night he told me—it was a kind of confession, really—that actually he'd been happy in Vietnam in the morgue at Da Nang, though he hadn't realized it at the time. Not exactly "happy," but happy that he'd confronted his worst fears and had mastered them, that he'd made the mythical journey to the underworld and made it back safely.

"And I thought I knew everything there was to know about you," I said.

Sally sent Simon one of those drinking birds that you used to find in gas stations. The bird dips its beak in a glass of water and then swings upright. The water evaporates from the felt on the head, which lowers the temperature of the head . . . We never did figure out how it worked, but we enjoyed watching the bird dipping and bobbing on the top of Simon's dresser, and Simon asked me to get more. I found them in a catalog and ordered a case, a dozen, and we set six of them up on the dresser. He had another idea for a cartoon, and I was sketching it, following his directions. Birds in a long row, stretching all the way to the horizon, were hooked up to electric power lines—the great towers that carry electricity around

101

the country. The whole area is surrounded by a tall chain-link fence. A pickup truck has pulled up to the gate. The driver and a man in a guard's uniform stand facing each other. The driver of the pickup is asking the guard, "What happened to all the wind turbines?"

Simon had been pushing me to submit some of our best efforts to *The New Yorker*, but I didn't have a very clear idea of how you submitted cartoons to *The New Yorker*, didn't have any idea, in fact (though I'd looked through all my cartoon books and searched the Internet), so I put it off. Until it was too late.

He was lying on the bed, looking through some of my sketches, sorting them into yes, no, maybe. I was working on the last idea he'd come up with—"The Truth About Death." I was sketching rapidly, trying not to overthink the conceit. I nailed God's face with a few strokes of my pencil, and then with a few more strokes a dog emerged out of nothing. I'd been looking at Harry Bliss's dogs, and Matt Diffee's too, but this dog was my own. But when I stood up to show it to Simon, the room was quiet. Simon's breathing had stopped. The little tremor of excitement I'd felt when the dog's face appeared out of nowhere was Simon's heart giving out. A last flutter. I didn't realize it till I'd finished the drawing. It was over; he was dead. He was still sitting up in the bed, not even slumped over, my sketches scattered around him like autumnal leaves on the comforter. It wasn't what I'd expected. Maybe it never is.

I didn't dial 911, but I called the hospital, whose number was on the table next to the bed on top of a copy of Simon's living will. Simon was an organ donor. You can't donate your organs if you die at home—organs need a continuous blood supply—but you can donate corneas and tissue (including veins and bones) within twenty-four hours of death. The hospital would notify the eye bank and MTF (the Musculoskeletal Transplant Foundation). I told them I'd have Gilbert bring the body, and then I sat down for a few minutes on the edge of the bed and massaged Simon's feet. Olive paced up and down the Omani rug. I called Gilbert and asked him to take the body to the hospital. In a few minutes I heard him coming up the stairs with the Med Sled. When I tried to stand up, I almost fell over. I had to push my feet down hard against the floor to hold steady.

I helped Gilbert wrap up the body. Then I lay down on the bed, and Olive jumped up and lay down next to me. After a while I called Jack and Sally in New York. They said they'd be here the next afternoon at the latest.

Gilbert brought what was left of Simon back from the hospital the next morning, which was sunny and cold. I told him I wanted to be there when he prepped the body. I wanted to get it done before Jack and Sally arrived. Gilbert had always been opposed to organ and/or tissue donation. They're messy and make the undertaker's job a lot harder. "His body's been terrorized," he said. "You know what they do . . . The organs are in a separate bag . . ."

"Is this why you let Simon do the tough jobs, even when you could see he was worn-out?"

"You really don't want to see this." We were standing outside the door of the prep room.

"Gilbert," I said. "I'm the boss here. If you don't want me here, I'll find somebody else to do the prep."

"I'm just saying. It won't be pretty. The body's a mess, like a gunnysack full of packing peanuts and plastic tubes, the eyes . . ."

"Gilbert," I said. "You're not a very kind person, and right now I need kindness, not your bad temper. I'm just going to hold his hand while you do what you need to do. You're getting an extra hundred and fifty dollars from MTF for your trouble."

"You're right," he said. "I'm sorry. I wasn't thinking. I loved him too."

What was left of the body had already been washed in the hospital, but I held Simon's hand while Gilbert washed it again and did what needed to be done.

Jack and Sally arrived that afternoon, and the next day we pushed the coffin to the cremation chamber, located in what had once been the paddock for Grandpa Bart's horses, Stormy and Salty. Sally read a poem by Emily Dickinson:

> *Tell all the truth but tell it slant—*
> *Success in Circuit lies*
> *Too bright for our infirm Delight*
> *The Truth's superb surprise*
> *As lightning to the Children eased*
> *With explanation kind*
> *The Truth must dazzle gradually*
> *Or every man be blind—*

I pushed a button and the cardboard coffin rolled into the fifteen-hundred-degree Matthews oven.

Two nights later—a week before Thanksgiving—we had a small reception at the funeral home. Simon's cremains were in an urn that rested on the mantel over the fireplace, where a pyramid of oak logs was crackling. The small reception turned into a big reception. Families Simon had helped through difficult times came to pay their respects and to see Olive too. Olive in her uniform greeted everyone, but she was bewildered. She kept looking around for Simon. And then she came to me and extended the paw of affection.

The visitation room was full of bright colors—our new gallery of local artists—and Sally read another poem. I could hear the first line—"How hard to take the trail as it comes"—and then everything shut down.

That night Olive spent more time than usual patrolling the house, like an old-fashioned cop on an old-fashioned beat, a cop who sensed that something was not quite right but couldn't figure out what it was.

Dr. Johnson (Sam Johnson, that is) was right when he said that attempts to divert grief when it is fresh only irritate, and yet the conventional wisdom—most of the things we say to people because we don't know what else to say—is in fact wise: time is a great healer, take it one day at a time, write in your journal, acknowledge your feelings, don't pretend you're just fine, eat well, get plenty of exercise, get plenty of sleep, and be kind to yourself. This is good advice. I hadn't taken it after Hildi's death, and I didn't take it after Simon's. No one does. I didn't want people asking me *how I was doing* in the special voice that is usually used when addressing the newly bereaved—"How *are* you?"—or asking if there was anything they could do. I didn't want any more casseroles, didn't want any more lasagna or trays of peeled pink shrimp. I admired my good friend and colleague in the art department Alice Duncan, who had proclaimed her own grief from the rooftops and forced everyone to acknowledge that no one's grief had ever been as profound as her grief, who went over and over the details of her husband's death—where she'd been sitting when she got the phone call from the hospital, how many minutes it had taken her to get to the hospital, the delay at the tracks on Seminary Street, where she had waited for an endless train to pass—as if she'd have been able to prevent the death if only she'd made it to the hospital five minutes sooner. I admired Alice, but I soon found her tiresome. I did things in my own way, defended myself in my own way. I sat up in Simon's tower, looking at the pictures that covered the walls— Monet and Matisse and De Kooning and the rest—or looking out the windows, watching the shapes made by the clouds, watching the sun coming up in the southeast in winter, the northeast in summer. Through the sixteen windows in the octagonal belvedere I could watch it rise and set without moving my chair. Simon's chair. I sometimes imagined it was just the two of us, and . . . and what?

We had few regrets. We had not embarked on great adventures. We'd had some romantic entanglements that at the time had threatened our marriage, but that was long ago, and those entanglements had become part of the fabric, part of the warp and woof of our lives, rather than stains on the carpet. We'd lived the lives we'd wanted to live, done most of the things we'd wanted to do, though I never got Simon to go to Italy with me except after Hildi's death.

About a week after the funeral I started to think about that trip as I was sitting quietly at the library table up in the belvedere. I closed my Clairefontaine notebook and went down to the office to get a note card with a picture of the funeral home on the front. I refilled Simon's pen and went back up to the tower and started to write a note to the *impresario* in Rome to thank him for his kindness, and for the *cacio e pepe* he fixed for us our first night in Rome. "Caro Guido . . ." I wrote. But then I put down the pen and just sat, listening to the familiar sounds of our old house as it settled into a November evening, no longer thinking of myself as the protagonist of my own story but as an extra in a larger story, a part of a pattern. But what is the pattern? Could I see it myself? I thought maybe so, out of the corner of my eye. But it was only Olive flicking her tail.

PART II: OLIVE

I didn't draw any more cartoons after Simon's death. November tenth. Most of the leaves had already fallen and would have to be raked—by someone else. If I worked hard at other things, it was because I didn't know what else to do. I proposed a new course (Varieties of Visual Experience) at the college; I agreed to chair a session at the International Congress on Medieval Studies in Kalamazoo.

Olive and I stayed put in our apartment—the two upper floors on the west side of the house—and Gilbert and his family moved into the apartment on the east, which had originally been Bart and Louisa's. Jack and Sally wanted me to move to New York, but I didn't want to give up my teaching. Not yet. Besides, I'd always thought of the funeral home as home. I didn't want to live anywhere else. There was plenty of room, and it was convenient for everyone. I didn't mind baby-sitting the phone for Gilbert every now and then or helping with a funeral.

I kept busy—teaching, securing permissions for the thousand and one images I wanted to include in *Marginalia*—and Olive kept busy too, looking after me, keeping me company, patrolling the house at bedtime, "working" visitations for Gilbert and even going along on removals. I walked her three times a day, letting her loose in the park by the train station. I never got the hang of throwing the Frisbee, but Dr. King, our vet, said that jumping up in the air to catch the Frisbee was not good for her back. She was satisfied with a ball, which I threw underhand. We went everywhere together. To my office in the Fine Arts Center, to the grocery store, to the library, to Cornucopia, to Innkeeper's for coffee—Guatemala Antigua coffee at the drive-up window, where there was always a treat for her. And when I walked her past Hawk's Tattoos on Simmons Street, there was always a baby carrot for her on the window ledge.

Olive and I had a year together—not quite a year, actually—before she started to leak. I noticed damp spots on the Omani rug in the bedroom. She never squatted down to pee in the house, she just leaked a little when she was snoozing on the rug in the afternoon or sleeping in her bed at night. I didn't notice it at first. It didn't really smell. Dr. King said that this was because she wasn't concentrating her urine. I started giving her Proin and bought a spray to clean the rug. The Proin worked for a while. Several months. But then the leaking started again. Dr. King examined her. She was eight years old, the healthiest dog he'd ever seen. Apart from the leaking.

But sometimes she missed her footing on the stairs. It was hardly noticeable, but I noticed, and at the end of September I took her to a specialist in Peoria. It was a beautiful day for a drive, the trees starting to turn. It took an hour to get there, then half an hour for the paperwork. The lovely doctor reminded me of Checco, Hildi's friend and Nana's doctor in Rome. Open, warm, friendly. Olive took to her right away. A good sign. She said the same thing as Dr. King in Galesburg.

Olive looked like the healthiest dog she'd ever seen. "She must have some English stock in her," she said, "because you can see waves in her fur."

But half an hour later she returned, and she didn't bring good news. She couldn't do the ultrasound, she said, because there was a tumor in the way. It was probably spleen cancer. Probably not life threatening. "I take out a dozen spleens a month," she said. Did I want to go ahead with a biopsy, which would confirm the diagnosis? Of course I did.

In another half an hour she came back with more bad news. Liver cancer. Nothing to be done.

I wanted to call Simon. I didn't want to face this alone. I called Jack in New York. He wasn't home of course, but I talked to Sally, and she stayed on the phone with me and asked a lot of questions: Can they do X? Can they do Y? I let her talk to the doctor. They couldn't do X or Y. The doctor held me while I cried. Olive had about three months to live.

That evening on the way back from our walk, Olive stumbled again on the stairs. Just a little stumble, as if she'd misjudged a step. It was hard to be sure, but I was sure, and it broke my heart. That night I talked to her, and we made a list of all the things we were going to do in the next couple of months. I hadn't been planning on going to Lake Michigan again, but I changed my mind. I looked into her eyes, and she looked into mine. I thought she was trying to explain to me why things were the way they were, how they were all tied together.

I put my face in her thick ruff and then kept my hand on her head while I made arrangements with Mrs. Burian about a four-day weekend at the cottage. There was electric baseboard heating, and a fireplace too, which we'd never used. I didn't think Olive would be able to walk down the sixty narrow steps to the beach, but there was another easier way down to the beach from the state park—the one the paramedics had used after Simon's heart attack.

That was on a Monday. On Thursday, coming back from the park by the depot, she stumbled badly, but made it up the stairs. She ate her supper. Half an hour later she threw it up. I cleaned it up and sat with her in the living room.

At about nine o'clock she got up to go to bed. Walking down the hall, she had a seizure. Frothing. Flailing around. Banging into the walls, then falling down. I called Dr. King at home. He said to meet him at the clinic right away. Olive was able to walk. I took her down in the elevator. Gilbert went with me. But then she had another seizure in the garage. When it was over we managed to get her up into the back of my Mazda hatchback.

Dr. King and his assistant were waiting for us at the animal hospital on Fremont Street. He said that the medication to control the seizures would feed right into the tumor and kill her. We decided to put her down. I kept my hands on her head while Doctor King injected a tranquilizer into her shoulder, and then—after few minutes—three cc of ketamine. She kept her eyes open for a bit, but she didn't look at me. She was looking past me. Then the eyes closed. The life flowed out of her, into my hands and into my body and then into the air. Olive was dead. And that was about as close to the truth about death as I ever got. Not something you can *tell* anyone. You have to experience it.

This is what Olive was trying to tell me. Maybe. None of the "meanings" we assign to Death—like the meanings we assign to life, to poetry, to great art, to music—can define the experience itself.

As I said before, I've never rejected the conventional

wisdom about grief, but Olive's death pushed me to the limit, brought me to my knees, not to pray, but because I couldn't stand up. Maybe it's that we can't explain death to a dog. Not that we can ever "explain" death. Not any more than we can explain beauty or love or sorrow. But at least we can talk it over, the way Simon and I did. You can— I don't know what you can do.

I didn't call anyone that night. I knew I wouldn't be able to talk. But I sat in the tower. I was lonely, homesick. I was waiting for something to happen. I didn't know what it was. I was still waiting when I drifted off to sleep in Simon's big chair-and-a-half. When I woke up in the middle of the night, I reached down for Olive, but she wasn't there.

The Omani rug in our bedroom started to smell. It had taken a while for the ammonia in Olive's diluted urine to activate the odor-causing bacteria in the rug itself. I took the rug to have it professionally cleaned. A big job. Gilbert helped me carry it down the stairs. Afterward it still smelled. I took it back and had it professionally cleaned a second time. This time the carpet-cleaning company added a special formula. It was okay for a few days, but then the smell came back. I complained and got a refund of twenty-five dollars in the mail and a note saying not to bring the rug in again. Then one day on Simmons Street I passed a parked truck with a sign that said PROFESSIONAL RUG CLEANING and a Chicago address—more promises. It was parked in front of the radio station. Someone in the station said the rug guy was across the street in the Weinberg Arcade. I found him there. He turned out to be a former student. His business was in Chicago, but he did a lot of work in Galesburg. He thought he might be able to help, but I'd have to bring the rug to the

Weinberg Arcade. I got Gilbert to help me again. We got the rug into the removal van. The rug guy cleaned it on the floor in the hallway. He gave it a special treatment with an impressive machine like a steam roller. We took it home and left it in the garage over an old bedstead. It was a lot better. But it still smelled, and I didn't want it in the bedroom. I liked it where it was, in fact. Every time I go out I take a sniff. I can still smell Olive, and her smell still makes me tear up a little. I have to be careful, but I'm glad for this remembrance.

What I understand now is that Olive gave a shape to all our days. First thing in the morning—walking her to the park, throwing the ball to her, fixing her breakfast, brushing her teeth, and so on, all through the day. What a good dog she was. The hardest thing was that I couldn't talk things over with her, and she couldn't talk things over with me. I tried to imagine what she'd say if she could write us a letter, and she did write a letter. I could read it as clearly as if it had come in the mail:

Elizabeth, you and Simon were so good to me. You loved me from the beginning, after I'd spent a whole year at the shelter. You gave me a good home. Always kept my water bowl filled. I could have eaten more food, but I suppose you didn't want me to get fat. I loved going to the park three times a day and chasing the Frisbee. I always stayed put for you till you said "Okay" because I knew you meant it when you said "Stay." I tried to be a good hostess when you had dinner parties or when people gathered downstairs. I barked at the first guests, because I thought that was my job, but after more people started coming I just walked around to greet them. I liked wearing my uniform during the visitations. I liked circulating and making everyone feel at home. But the best thing of all was the time we went up to the lake, just the three of us. I loved playing with the other dogs, and I loved the lake. I loved swimming out after the Frisbee. I'm just sorry we never got to go back.

Remember when Simon threw the Frisbee way, way out in the water and I swam right past it, and you started screaming and yelling at him because you were afraid I'd keep on going? But I knew I had to get the Frisbee. After a while my back legs started to cramp. And then the fog cleared a little bit; a bit of sun came through, and I could tell I was going in the wrong direction, heading out farther and farther into deep water. But then I could hear voices calling my name. "Olive. Olive. Olive." I could hear a siren too. My legs were on fire. My back was hurting. My bottom half was sinking. I had to work harder with my front legs. I didn't know how long I'd been in the water. But I wasn't afraid. I was pretty sure I could turn around and get the Frisbee and swim back to shore. And I did. But this time I won't be turning back. I'm not afraid, and I don't want you to be afraid. This is just the way things are, and it's okay.

PART III: ME (ELIZABETH)

Marginalia, which was published six months after Olive's death, was an unexpected success, relatively speaking, of course, and within a year I was enjoying the kind of success every academic hopes for at the end of a long career. The book—350 pages of text and over a thousand images—had generated strong reviews in all the major art-history journals, including the *Oxford Art Journal*, *The Burlington Magazine*, and *Studies in Iconography*; it had stirred up a lot of controversy by placing the sciapods and the grylli and the potbellied heads and all their exuberant obscenities—pissing, shitting, farting, puking, coupling—at the center of the great medieval project rather than at the periphery. It had put me on the map: I'd been invited to chair a session at the CAA Conference in Chicago and to give a talk at the Morgan Library on medieval marginalia as the first cartoons and to discuss with Cyrus Walker, one of the curators of medieval and Renaissance manuscripts, the possibility of curating an exhibit. And, unfortunately, I'd been named chair of the art department because (a) it was my turn and (b) no one else wanted to do it.

So by the time Checco and Enzo came from Rome for the Stearman Fly-In, in September, I had a lot on my plate. I wanted to see Checco again, of course, but Checco had married the woman who ran the mask shop, Maddelena, and they had a son, Giorgio, who was three years old now. I was unnerved by the prospect of embracing someone who, in an alternate universe, might have been my son-in-law and whose son might have been my grandson. If only Hildi had crossed the Tiber on Ponte Palatino instead of Ponte Garibaldi . . .

We embraced nonetheless by the Lincoln statue in front of the train station. They'd flown to O'Hare, spent the night at the Congress, near Union Station, and taken the Carl Sandburg to Galesburg. The Fly-In didn't officially begin till the next day, but the sky was already full of blue and yellow biplanes, and we watched a four-ship squadron flying in formation—the planes peeling off one at a time, breaking and rejoining—before loading the suitcases into the back of the little yellow Mazda, which I was still driving.

Enzo rented a car at the station and he and Checco spent

most of their time out at the airport. They hitched airplane rides to Kewanee—Hog Capital of the World—for the annual Fly-In Breakfast; they flew back and admired the planes (over a hundred of them) in the little airport in Galesburg; they drank coffee and swapped stories in the pilots' tent; they partied at night.

I joined them at the airport on the second afternoon, and Checco persuaded a local Stearman owner—George Young, who serviced the funeral home vehicles, including the Mazda—to let Checco take me up for a quick flight. I wasn't keen to go, but Checco was very persuasive and I couldn't figure out how to say no. Fifteen minutes after I said yes I was strapped into the rear cockpit of a Boeing Stearman E75—powder blue with bright yellow wings—and then we were describing a big sky circle around Galesburg: the Sandburg Mall, St. Mary's Hospital, the old Maytag plant, Oldfield and Daughter, Seminary Street, Knox College, Hope Cemetery. Checco talked to me through the headsets, which were incorporated into our leather helmets, explaining everything he was doing—leveling the wings, throttling down to minimum speed, putting the plane in a sideslip by putting the control stick to one side and kicking the opposite rudder, adding power when we were too low. (There were no loops or rolls, thank goodness.) When we flew over the cemetery where Hildi's ashes were buried next to Simon's, he told me that on their first flight together he and Hildi had flown over the ancient Necropoli di Porto on the Isola Sacra near the airport in Rome, an artificial island created by Emperor Trajan—a cemetery I had once visited with a group of students, a cemetery where you can trace the shift from pagan cremation to Christian burial, just as you can now trace a shift in the opposite direction in the cemetery below us.

* * *

We would have to talk about Hildi—I saw that—and that afternoon after the Accuracy Landing Contest and the Four-Ship Formation Competition, Checco and I drove back into town and walked around the Knox campus. We took a peek at my office in the Fine Arts Center, stopped at Cottage Hospital so Checco could see an American hospital, went back home, and took a bottle of wine up to Simon's tower. Checco had brought another mask of Hildi, made from the original mold. When he took the protective Bubble Wrap off, Hildi's face emerged from a red-gold autumn leaf on a long stem. "You don't wear it," Checco explained. "The stem is a handle. You hold the mask in front of your face." He held it in front of his face, and there was Hildi looking back at me.

"I'm going to put it up right away," I said. I took down Matisse's *Danse (II)* and put up the leaf—which had a hook on the back—on the west wall, below a still life by Chardin and Giovanni di Paolo's *Five Angels Dancing Before the Sun*. It was almost six o'clock. The sun itself, which had moved to the south, was pouring in the windows, and I had to shade my eyes to look closely at the leaf. I couldn't tell if it was an oak or a maple. The lower lobes dropped down over the stem like a maple, but the top was pointed like the leaves on the red oak in our front yard, though it had too many lobes for a red oak.

"Non è una vera e propria foglia," Checco said. *It's not a real leaf.* *"Maddalena crea le foglie d'autunno nella sua immaginazione."*

Checco and I had been speaking in English ever since he arrived, but up in the tower we started speaking Italian. Were there things we wanted to say in Italian that we couldn't say in English? I remembered Checco weeping in the *camera ardente* in Rome, standing next to Simon in front of Hildi's cardboard cremation coffin, his face in his hands; I remembered his sister's Seeing Eye dog trying to comfort him. And I think Checco was a little embarrassed to reveal that now, in spite of his grief, he was happy—that he and Maddelena had been living together for three years and had finally gotten married and that their son, Giorgio, had already been up in the plane with him three times despite Maddelena's objections. And maybe I was a little embarrassed to admit that I was happy too. Not as happy as I'd been when I first married Simon; not as happy as I'd been when Jack and Hildi were young and our family was all together and I hadn't even been aware that I was happy; not as happy as I'd been when Jack and Sally got married or when Hildi and Nana came back from Rome the first time; not as happy as I'd been when I signed the contract for *Marginalia*. But happy enough. And maybe it was easier for both of us to share our thoughts about happiness in Italian.

"Enzo said he won't be home till late," I said. "We could go out, or I could fix some pasta here."

"Let's stay here," he said. "But why don't you fix an American dinner?"

"All right," I said. "We'll go to Hy-Vee. I think they still have some local sweet corn."

"Corn?" he said. "*Mais? Granturco?* You mean like we feed to pigs in Italy?"

"That's more or less what I mean," I said. "We'll open a bottle of California wine and cook some big hamburgers on the grill and have some *granturco* on the cob."

"And maybe an *insalata* too," he said. "With tomatoes from your garden."

And that's what we did, and then we looked through *Marginalia* and talked about the past and about the future while we waited for Enzo to come home.

*   *   *

Museum time moves slowly. I pitched the exhibit at the December meeting of the director and the curatorial staff at the Morgan Library and spent Christmas with Jack and Sally. The exhibit—"Medieval Marginalia"—was green-lighted by the planning committee the following June, and I flew to New York in July to meet with the new director and with Cyrus Walker, who would be overseeing the exhibit, and to help Jack and Sally celebrate their fourteenth wedding anniversary. I couldn't have been more excited about what was the culmination of my life's work as an academic, but I had another agenda too, which I kept to myself: I wanted to show some of my cartoons to Bob Mankoff at *The New Yorker*. I told myself I would be carrying out Simon's dying wish. And I would be.

I'd called Mankoff as soon as I'd known I was coming to New York. I hadn't been able to find his number—or any number—on the *New Yorker* website, but I was able to get it from my editor at Princeton. I talked to Mankoff's assistant, Colin, and told him I was going to be curating an exhibit at the Morgan Library and wanted to talk to Bob Mankoff about medieval marginalia as the first cartoons. He said he'd tell Mankoff. Five minutes later I got a call: I outlined my plan for the exhibit at the Morgan, and I offered to send him a copy of the talk I'd given there in October, and he was interested. We set up an appointment.

I could have taken the cartoons to the "open call" on Tuesday, when anyone can bring in his or her cartoons, but I thought I'd have a better chance if I had a private audience, like a private audience with the pope. I wasn't sure how I'd introduce the subject of *my* cartoons. I'd just have to see how it played out. Maybe I could just say, "By the way, take a look at these." I was confident that he'd take one look at my batch of cartoons and bless them on the spot.

I arrived in New York on Monday night, spent Tuesday and Wednesday with Cyrus at the Morgan, laying out a four-year timeline for mounting the exhibit and going over what we'd need to borrow, if anything, from the Met—limiting ourselves to items that Morgan himself had donated to the Met. At breakfast on Thursday Jack and Sally were annoyed at a cartoon in the latest *New Yorker*: a couple lying in bed on their backs, staring up at the ceiling. "Hey," the woman says. "You're the one who wanted a three-way."

Jack and Sally couldn't get it. They passed the magazine back and forth.

"What's that thing on her glasses?" Jack asked. "Take a look." He passed the open magazine back to Sally.

"Maybe she's wearing Google Glasses," Sally said. She handed it to me.

"I'm not sure what Google Glasses are," I said.

"It's like a little computer screen attached to your glasses."

"I've got to run," I said. "Let me take it with me so I'll have something to read on the train."

"It just got here," Sally said.

"I'll bring it back—don't worry." I told Jack and Sally I was going back to the Morgan, but I took the C train downtown toward Forty-Second Street.

Some of my confidence evaporated on the subway, as if I really *were* going to a private audience with the pope and the pope knew what I was up to. I was thinking that if Simon were with me, or Hildi or even Olive, I'd be able to explain myself better, at least not make a fool of myself. I seemed to see them out of the corner of my eye. But the young woman getting off at Seventy-Second Street wasn't

Hildi. Later, the Seeing Eye dog on the platform at Columbus Circle wasn't Olive. The man in a dark blue suit, rep tie, and crisp white shirt, as if he were heading for a funeral, wasn't Simon.

I held my MetroCard in my fist, afraid I'd lose it if I put it in my large briefcase, which was very full: a tin of homemade shortbread for Mankoff; a small collapsible umbrella; a copy of *Marginalia*; a draft of an article about the Egerton MS 1894, from the British Library, which was—I was planning to argue—the very first comic strip, though it wasn't something we'd be able to borrow for the exhibit; Mankoff's *How About Never—Is Never Good for You?*, which was very large and heavier than *The Naked Cartoonist*, which I'd shoved into the side pocket of the briefcase.

Sally's *New Yorker* was on my lap. I looked again at the offending cartoon. It didn't make sense even if the woman *was* wearing Google Glasses, whatever they were. I showed it to the man on my right, and then to the woman on my left. They both shook their heads. I could always ask Bob Mankoff to explain it. Would that be a good icebreaker or would it just reveal my ignorance?

In the station at Forty-Second Street my cell phone started to vibrate. Subway stations, Jack had warned me, now had Wi-Fi, but my phone was a cheap flip-top and I couldn't hear anything. All I could do was shout into the phone and hope that Jack or Sally or whoever had called could hear me. "I'm in the subway station," I shouted. "I'm in the subway station. I can't hear you." Jack had offered to buy me an iPhone, but I wasn't sure I wanted one.

I don't know what happened, but suddenly I was very disoriented. I suppose, in retrospect, that I'd taken a wrong exit and was heading north on Seventh Avenue instead of east on Forty-Second Street. Everything had turned around.

I asked several people where the *New Yorker* was. No one had heard of the *New Yorker*. "How about the Condé Nast Building?" No one had any idea, and I wondered again if I'd gotten off at the wrong stop. I couldn't tell east from west by looking at the gray sky.

Finally I asked a Bible salesman—a large African-American man standing in front of a little booth set up on the sidewalk. There were several people at the booth selling Bibles and handing out pamphlets and tracts. The man I spoke to had no idea either, but he pulled out his iPhone and tapped it several times. "It's right there," he said. "You see that Walgreens? It's just before Walgreens."

I turned around and saw the Walgreens, and all of a sudden the world did a 180-degree turn and I was facing the right direction. I knew where I was. I pulled the tin of shortbread out of my briefcase, struggled to get it open, and gave each of the Bible people a piece.

"God bless you and keep you," the leader said, "and may His face shine upon you," and all of a sudden I had a vision of myself as a New Yorker. I was tempted to explore this fantasy, but my briefcase was very heavy and I was a little bit dizzy, and I thought I'd better sit down first.

There was no place to sit down in the lobby of the Condé Nast Building. Not a chair, not a bench, not a ledge, so I plunked myself down on a long step that ran across the entire lobby in front of the desk, which was staffed by a dozen men in uniforms. I guess I didn't look like I belonged—in jeans and flats and a man's white shirt—because after about sixty seconds one of these uniforms came over and told me I couldn't sit on the step. Maybe I should have worn the outfit I'd worn at the

Morgan: a two-piece dark suit, patterned blouse, and closed-toe pumps. I stood up and walked over to the desk.

I got out my tin of shortbread and offered him a piece.

"Look, lady," he said.

"Try it," I said. "It's really good."

"You got business here?" he asked.

"I'm here to see Bob Mankoff," I said. "I'm a little early."

"Nobody's supposed to sit on the step," he said. "Look," he said again. "I got a little stool you can sit on for a few minutes, okay?" He brought a little three-legged stool for me, and I offered him another piece of shortbread.

"Okay," I said, holding up five fingers. "I'm a little early. Just give me five minutes."

"Who'd you say?"

"Bob Mankoff."

"He work here?"

"I hope so."

"This is good," he said, biting off a piece of shortbread. "Five, ten minutes." He looked at his watch. "Then you got to check in at the desk. They'll page this Mankoff guy and tell you where to find him and check if it's okay to go on up. I'll let you know."

"Thanks," I said. I tried to imagine what it would *feel* like to be a New Yorker. Maybe I *could* move to New York. Jack and Sally wanted me to move to the city. They'd even picked out a condo for me to look at on Eighty-First Street. I could sell the funeral home. From Eighty-First Street, I could walk to the Met and the Guggenheim and the Frick. It would be an easy commute to the Morgan, where I'd be spending a lot of time during the next four years. I could see my grandchildren every day. Become a new person. Start a new life.

I opened the tin again and ate one of the pieces of short-bread. It was raining outside. I was glad I had a small umbrella in my briefcase.

I'd seen pictures of Mankoff and was prepared for the unruly hair, the beard, the heavy black glasses, and the big smile. He looked from a distance almost like a cartoon drawing of himself, one of his own drawings. I was looking across a warren of cubicles. He was standing in an open office doorway, just as he was in the photo on the jacket of *How About Never—Is Never Good for You?* In that photo there's a banana peel on the welcome mat. A warning?

At first I thought there was something wrong with his eye, and then I realized he had something stuck to his glasses like the woman in the cartoon. He was wearing Google Glasses. The cartoon still didn't make sense to me. I held it in my hand as if it were a ticket or a bus pass or a passport that would admit me to Mankoff's world.

"Do I know you?" he asked, studying my face.

"Hey," I blurted out without thinking, holding out the magazine, "you're the one who wanted a three-way."

He looked at the cartoon and laughed.

"You didn't used to be able to get away with that," I said, recovering.

"That was before Tina Brown. All edge. You disapprove?"

"Not exactly. Just never appealed to me. I suppose that corresponds to some defect in my character. Reluctance to take risks, for example."

He laughed. "You came to see me," he said.

"She's wearing Google Glasses, isn't she? Just like you. That's the little white thing on her glasses, isn't it? But I still don't get it. Where's the 'three-way'?"

123

"She's been streaming everything to a third party, and it's singular, by the way: 'Google Glass.'"

"That's what Google Glass does? Takes pictures of what you're doing in bed and sends them to someone else?"

"Well, that's only one thing. What it does is take pictures of what you're looking at and streams them to your followers on the web."

"I see."

"Come in," he said backing into an office that was the opposite of Cyrus Walker's office in the Morgan. No Persian rugs made you want to take off your shoes. No chandeliers sparkled like stars in the vault of heaven. No inlaid walnut bookcases displayed precious volumes. No inlaid walnut library table held a vase of fresh flowers. No Renaissance paintings graced the walls. The walls, like Mankoff's desk, were covered with cartoons.

And Mankoff himself was the opposite of Cyrus Walker. Cyrus could have passed for an undertaker, like the man I saw in the subway—dark blue linen suit, probably Italian, with a crisp white shirt and rep tie. Mankoff was wearing khakis and a loose short-sleeved turquoise-and-yellow shirt that wasn't exactly Hawaiian, but that made you think "Hawaiian."

I suppose we were both dressing too young. "You know what I think?" he said, reading my thoughts. "Don't pay any attention to what other people think about you, because it doesn't matter."

"Am I in the right place?" I said.

"If you're looking for Bob Mankoff," he said.

"I meant New York," I said. "Everyone's so nice—one of the uniforms in the lobby even brought me a stool to sit on. I thought I must be somewhere else."

"That's because everyone here is from the Midwest."

"On the subway," I said, "I suddenly had a vision of myself as a New Yorker. My son and daughter-in-law want me to move to New York. They even want me to look at a condo."

"You're from the Midwest," he said again. "You'd fit right in."

"*You're* not from the Midwest," I said.

"That's why I *don't* fit in," he said.

We sat down with the desk between us. I had a good view of the city through the window behind Mankoff, but I didn't recognize anything and wasn't even sure what direction I was facing.

I put a copy of *Marginalia* down on his desk on top of a pile of cartoons, and we leafed through it.

"These images," I said, "function like *New Yorker* cartoons. There they are around the edges. Nothing to do with the main story, but they affect the way you read the main story. Like the 'three-way' cartoon right in the middle of a long article on the Federal Reserve or nuns and the penis tree in the *Roman de la Rose*." I had the page marked and opened the book to it. In one image a black-robed nun is plucking penises from a tree and putting them in a basket. In a second image two nuns are gathering penises and sticking them in their robes. "Or this snakeman playing the bagpipes through his anus." I had this page marked too. A crowned head is attached to a long snakelike neck. At the other end of the neck the man is farting into the chanter of a bagpipe. "These would be good for the caption contest," I said.

He laughed. "Never get away with it."

"All these images are in the Morgan," I said. "They're images of dissent, transgression. They liven things up. They remind us of our bodily reality. Most scholars dismiss them as graffiti, scribes bored out of their minds, but I think they belong at the center like the cartoons in the *New Yorker*.

I can't remember a single article or story from the *New Yorker*, but I can remember hundreds of cartoons."

He laughed. "Got a theory?"

"Not exactly, but let me tell you about my husband. He worked in Graves Registration in Vietnam before he became an undertaker. He faced death every day, but he never got over our daughter's death. I never got over it either, but I've tried not to let it poison my life. And then after he had a heart attack, he was even more depressed. Refused a stent; refused bypass surgery. Wouldn't do anything his doctors wanted him to do. And then about two months before he died, we started looking at *New Yorker* cartoons. We had hundreds of old *New Yorker*s in the attic. It gave him a new lease on life. He even started talking about bypass surgery, which is what his doctors had wanted from the beginning. When we ran out of cartoons he wanted me to draw more—our own cartoons. He was full of ideas. I couldn't keep up with him. I had to stop working on my book—this copy's for you, by the way."

"Well," he said. "Death can be pretty funny. Like sex."

"If you'd ever been to the National Funeral Directors conference in Atlanta and heard the jokes, you wouldn't say that."

"Give me an example."

"A man says to an undertaker, 'Your wife has really nice tits. Mind if I cop a feel?' 'Go right ahead,' the undertaker says. So the man fondles the wife's breasts. 'Thanks,' he says. 'They're really nice.' 'Before you go,' the undertaker says, 'would you help me close the coffin lid?'"

"You're right," he said. "That's not funny. That's disgusting." But he laughed.

"'We made good time,'" I said. "'We're already in the valley of the shadow of death.' Now *that's* funny."

"Sam Gross," he said. "A woman talking to her husband as they drive past a road sign reading FEAR NO EVIL.'"

I started tossing out captions, and he caught every one.

ME: "'Death takes a personal day.'"

MANKOFF: "Arnie Levin. Death lying in bed watching TV and drinking tea."

ME: "'The Founding Fathers were clear. You must win by two.'"

MANKOFF: "Two people playing Ping-Pong in front of the Supreme Court. That was a caption contest—last April. I don't remember who did it."

ME: "'Oh darn, and just as I was starting to take charge of my life.'"

MANKOFF: "That's one of mine. A man opens his apartment door and Death is standing there."

"I'll stop there," I said.

"So," he said. "What's to laugh about?"

"'Sudden glory'?" I said, shaking my head. "No. 'The presence of inflexibility and rigidness in life'?" I shook my head again. "No."

"That takes care of Hobbes and Bergson," he said.

"I mention them only to show them the door. How about 'Release of tension'?"

"Getting warm, warmer," he said.

"'Incongruity,'" I said. "That's where *you* come down."

He nodded. "Mashing two or three frames together."

"But the problem with incongruity," I said, "is that it's a necessary cause but not a sufficient cause. It always seemed to me that Simon's laughter came welling up out of something deeper. The cartoons were just triggers, vehicles, like the little cars that bring up coal from the depths of a mine. He was an undertaker, but he loved to laugh. Until Hildi—that's our daughter—was killed. But then at the end he started laughing again, as if he'd discovered something funny at the bottom of things."

"Here's what I think," Mankoff said. "Grim Reaper cartoons are a coping mechanism, but they're something more than that. Laughter is holier than prayer. I'm not a guy who talks a lot about holiness. Or prayer. But I think a lot about laughter. When you laugh, your ego disappears. Like dancing. Your whole body becomes part of the dance, part of the laughter. Lao Tzu, the Chinese philosopher, used to say that without laughter, there is no Tao. He used to ride a buffalo backward. I mean, he'd sit backward on the buffalo. A water buffalo, not a bison."

"So the buffalo's going one way and Lao Tzu's looking the other way. He must have gotten a lot of laughs."

"So life's a comedy, not a tragedy."

"Do you think that's what Simon was doing at the end? Riding backward on a buffalo."

"You could do worse."

"Do you think that's what *you're* doing?"

"Maybe that's it," he said. "But I'm still waiting for my ego to disappear." He looked at his watch. "Listen," he said, "I've got to go to a meeting. I've got to take these cartoons to David Remnick. I'll take in fifty roughs—rough drawings. He'll pick seventeen or eighteen." He moved the copy of *Marginalia* to one side and scooped up a pile of cartoons from his desk.

I was disappointed. I was afraid I wouldn't get to show him *my* cartoons. But he said he'd be back in fifteen minutes. I conjured up a picture of Simon riding backward on a buffalo, looking back at me as the big animal plods along, swishing its tail back and forth, its great thick horns curving backward, white socks on its feet.

When Mankoff came back I said, "Let me show you some of Simon's cartoons before I go. They're not all about death, but they all came to him while he was dying. He always wanted me to send them to you, so let's pretend." Of course, I wasn't pretending. I was imagining how astonished everyone would be—Jack and Sally, my colleagues at Knox, Cyrus at the Morgan—when I told them I'd sold a batch of cartoons to the *New Yorker.*

I laid out the seven cartoons I'd brought. They were on sheets of good quality eight-and-a-half-by-eleven paper, smaller than the large sheets that Mankoff had taken to show David Remnick. Even so, I was expecting Mankoff to jump at the chance to publish them, but that's not what happened.

"This is my favorite," I said—"'The lost funeral home of the elephants'"—expecting Mankoff to chuckle at the mashed-up frames of reference.

"The reader," he said, "has to be familiar with the trope of the lost graveyard of the elephants."

"That's a problem for *New Yorker* readers?"

He shook his head. "The real problem is that the caption doesn't complete the drawing. The drawing says it all. The clearing in the jungle. The white hunters. The reader can see that it's a funeral home. There's even a sign: JUMBO AND SONS, FUNERAL DIRECTORS. The caption is redundant."

I knew right away that my fantasy was just that. A fantasy. I forgot about death for a minute.

"And these trees," he said. "They look like giant rocks."

I knew better than to argue or to point out that this was the

THE TRUTH ABOUT DEATH

way a lot of cartoonists shaded their trees, to say that these drawings were just roughs.

He looked over the rest of the cartoons.

"There's no consistent style," he said. "No signature. They're all different. As if you're imitating different cartoonists. This one is totally different from the funeral home in the jungle. You'd never know it was by the same cartoonist—and by the way, why are they ice fishing?"

"That's Satan, you see. Hell has frozen over, and the other devil says, 'It was bound to happen sooner or later.' Hell freezing over." I could feel the blood rising to my face.

He put it at the back of the stack, which he held in his hand. He was looking right at me with the stupid Google Glass. What did he see?

"Are you streaming this now?" I asked. "Right now?" I didn't want him broadcasting my red face out to the World Wide Web.

He shook his head and put his hand on *Marginalia*. "This is an astonishing book," he said, and we took another look at some of the images and talked about the exhibit at the Morgan and about my prospects as a cartoonist, which were not good. He explained the facts of life, cartoon life.

"You can't just walk in off the street and expect to sell a cartoon to the *New Yorker*. It'd be like me going to the Morgan Library and asking them to let me curate an exhibit."

"I didn't realize that," I said. "I'm sorry I took up your time."

"You're not really risk averse, are you?" He laughed again. "Don't answer that. I'm glad you came," he said. "You don't need to apologize. But I want you to forget about drawing cartoons. Stick with your marginalia." He paused. "I *am* going to hang onto this last one, though," he said. "'The Truth

About Death.' Pretty funny. You did a nice job on God's face. Uncanny. The dog too. I think you found your line here, your style. The others are too labored. This one does what a good cartoon should do: it simplifies everything."

"My husband was dying—I mean really dying—while I was drawing this," I said. "I labored over the other ones, but this one just happened."

He wanted me to change the drawing a little. "Give God a cell phone instead of a landline. But don't touch the dog. The dog is fine as is."

"I can do that," I said.

"You don't need to do it now," he said.

"Can you see things on your Google Glass? I mean the whole world?"

"As long as it's on the Internet."

"Could you see my home in Galesburg?"

"The funeral home?"

"Yes."

"I'd like you to see it," I said.

"Galesburg, right? What state?"

"Galesburg, Illinois."

"Okay, Glass," he said. "Funeral homes in Galesburg, Illinois." He looked through the glass and then at me. "There are three, right? Oldfield, that's you, and Lake Mortuary, and Peterson-Ward?"

"Do you see any photos?"

He tilted his head, ran his finger along the temple, and tapped, once, twice. "Oldfield and Daughter, Funeral Directors," he said.

"It used to be *Oldfield and Son*. Simon's grandfather started the business."

He tapped again.

"That must be your husband and your daughter standing by that sign, and that's your dog. In a green uniform."

"That's Olive. Next to Simon."

"Do you want to look?"

"No," I said. "I don't need Google Glass to see them."

"Your daughter was going to take over the business?"

I nodded. "She was, but then she went to Rome and fell in love, and then she was killed in a hit-and-run. Olive is dead too. Liver cancer." I could feel the tears welling up in my eyes.

Mankoff didn't say he was sorry for my loss. He didn't say anything for a while, and then he said, "So now you're trying to figure out the truth about death?"

"I am," I said. "I was hoping we could put our heads together."

"You don't need any advice from me."

"I do," I said. "At least I did. I needed to come here. I needed to show you some of our cartoons."

"Are you going to write something about this?" he asked.

"I am now," I said.

"Good," he said. "Just remember all the things I've told you, and pump up my part, okay?"

We exchanged books. I signed *Marginalia* with "Warmest wishes" and drew a little gryllus wearing a Google Glass. Mankoff gave me a copy of *How About Never*. He signed it and drew a self-portrait under his name on the title page. I already had a copy in my briefcase. Now I had two. I asked him to sign the second one for Jack and Sally.

I gave him the tin of shortbread and he pried off the lid and took out a piece.

"I gave away a few pieces on my way here," I explained. "That's why the tin isn't full. But you can make more." I handed him the recipe, which I'd typed out. "Give this to your wife. Put it in the tin."

"This is delicious," he said, taking his first bite. He put the recipe in the tin, and we said good-bye, and Colin, Mankoff's assistant, led me through a maze of cubicles to the elevator. I gave him my card. "Give this to Mr. Mankoff," I said.

I walked through Central Park on my way back to Jack and Sally's. Four miles, but I was in no hurry. I sat on a bench by the reservoir and fed two packages of crackers to the pigeons.

By the time the boys—Jack Junior and Adam—came into my room to wake me up from my nap, the anniversary dinner had begun. I fluffed up my hair with a brush and slipped on the red dress I'd bought for the occasion. The guests had arrived and were eating slices of pâté on crusty bread, drinking champagne and a French rosé, and were inhaling the aroma of a bouillabaisse that had just been delivered from Bistrot Jacques in a big tin stockpot. We watched Jack assemble a *salade de gésiers de canard* on a beautiful white oval platter: mesclun, tomato wedges, green beans, hard-boiled eggs, boiled new potatoes, sliced cucumber, and the *gésiers*—sautéed duck gizzards.

"You can't really do the *gésiers* at home," Jack explained as he cut them into thin slices. "They've got to be cooked over low heat for a long time. In France you can just buy them already cooked in the grocery store. They come in little plastic pouches. The boys love them," and to demonstrate he picked up a couple of slices with his fingers and placed them in his sons' open mouths.

I'd never shown my cartoons to anyone except Simon, and now Bob Mankoff, and suddenly I was hungry for a wider audience. I didn't want to make a faux pas by interrupting the drama of the duck gizzards, but I thought of Mankoff's advice—"Don't pay any attention to what other people think about you, because it doesn't matter"—and fetched my portfolio—a manila folder—from the guest bedroom. I laid six cartoons out in a row on the sideboard.

I soon had everyone's attention. Who can turn away from a cartoon? No one. Everyone, the boys included, admired them and even laughed out loud at some of them. "The lost funeral home of the elephants" was the favorite. Everyone insisted that I should send all six of them to the *New Yorker*, and I realized that I hadn't mentioned my trip there to anyone, not even to Jack and Sally, and I didn't mention it now, didn't mention "The Truth About Death," which I'd kept to myself; didn't mention the fact that Mankoff had wanted to "hang on" to it.

I put the cartoons away and had a glass of the rosé—Côtes de Provence—which was from a vineyard in Provence co-owned by Brad Pitt and Angelina Jolie. "It's very hard to come by in the United States," Sally told me. "No one can get more than six bottles." She leaned toward me and whispered in my ear: "Jack says it's not just another crappy celebrity wine. He says it's really good." And she started to laugh.

"It *is* really good," I said. And it was, and the *salade de gésiers de canard* was really good too, though most of us were a little apprehensive about the gizzards. At least at first. And the bouillabaisse was heavenly, the *tarte aux abricots* divine. The coffee was robust, the pear cognac sweet and tart at the same time.

We toasted Jack and Sally and wished them many happy returns of the day, and Jack promised another dinner as soon as "Medieval Marginalia" opened at the Morgan.

* * *

I'll be staying in New York for a few days while Jack and Sally fly up to Quebec for a little vacation and to check out some French-Canadian restaurants. I've got three long meetings scheduled with Cyrus at the Morgan. Even though it's summer vacation, the boys will be at the Calhoun School from eight thirty to three thirty every day, working on a full-scale production of *Romeo and Juliet*. I should still have time to take in the Unicorn exhibit at the Cloisters, the Parmigianinos at the Frick, and the Jeff Koons retrospective at the Whitney, but I'll probably have to skip the Italian Futurist exhibit at the Guggenheim. After lunch I'll stop by the school's performing arts center on Eighty-First Street to watch the boys working on the set or rehearsing their lines or figuring out their blocking. Jack is Mercutio on stage and a carpenter when he's working on the set; Adam is a torchbearer in the first act, Mercutio's page later on, and a scene painter when he's not on stage. We may grab some sandwiches at Zabar's around the corner and take them home for supper, or we may wait till later, take a cab to Bistrot Jacques, and eat bouillabaisse or pasta with grilled artichokes, or we may pick up something at the little grocery store on Eighty-First Street near the condo that Jack and Sally wanted me to look at. Or we may order pizzas, or maybe we'll just break out the peanut butter and jelly. We'll figure out something.

Jack and Sally will be back in time for the performances of *Romeo and Juliet*. And then, unlike Olive, I'll be turning back, back to Galesburg, where I'll live the life I've been given. Bart is dead. Louisa is dead. Hildi is dead. Simon is dead. Olive is dead. Everything that I know about them happened in the past. That's just the way things are, just the way Olive explained them to me. I'll sit at the library table in Simon's tower, surrounded by great works of art, though I'll probably change things around as soon as I get home. I'll have to give it some thought. I'm aware, of course, of the limits of great art. Even of the greatest art. You can't eat it or drink it. You can't curl up on it and go to sleep. It won't keep you dry if it's raining or warm if it's snowing. It won't keep you afloat if you're drowning. It won't cure a cold or replace a broken hip. Well, you can't explain it, but then you can't explain any of the great mysteries, can you? A sword blade in an old painting flickering with the light of burning towers; a dog extending the paw of affection; the tip of a lover's finger tracing your name on the inside of your thigh; Renaissance angels balancing effortlessly on stepping-stone clouds; your first oyster.

I'll look through our scrapbooks of cartoons too, and I may even sit down at my drawing table and sketch some of Simon's ideas—I have a long list. But later. I already have too much on my plate—classes to prepare, a session to chair for the CAA Conference in Chicago, a plenary lecture to write for the International Congress on Medieval Studies in Kalamazoo, and an exhibit to curate for the Morgan Library.

Just one more thing, though, before I go. I'm going to leave my cartoons with you. Six of them. So you can judge for yourself. But the last one—"The Truth About Death"—I'm going to keep to myself till I hear from Bob Mankoff at the *New Yorker*. It shouldn't be long now. He's got Jack and Sally's landline number here in New York, he's got the number of the new iPhone that Jack gave me, and the number of my landline in Galesburg, and he's got my street address and my e-mail address. I expect to hear from him any day.

"By crikey, Wilson, it's the lost funeral home of the elephants."

"*Well, I suppose it was bound to happen sooner or later.*"

"What happened to all the wind turbines?"

"'To be or not to be, that is the question.' Good, now we're getting somewhere."

"Daddy, you promised we could see the Ding an sich.*"*

"I can have her for you by tomorrow noon."

A CHRISTMAS LETTER

I WAS IN FLORENCE, Italy, when my father died. It was Easter Sunday and I was staying with old friends, the Marchettis, in their apartment near Piazza delle Cure, a quiet neighborhood on the north edge of town that you entered from Via Faentina. We hadn't gone into the center for the big Easter celebration, but we'd watched the dove and the exploding cart on television.

We were just sitting down to our first course—a rich broth thickened with egg yolks—when we got a telephone call from my sister. Signora Marchetti answered the phone. My sister didn't speak Italian, but she managed to make herself understood, and Signora Marchetti waved me to the phone in the small entrance hallway.

"Are you ready for this?" my sister said.

"I'm ready."

"Dad's dead," she said. "Out at the club, he fell down in the locker room. Drunk. They couldn't rouse him. He was dead by the time they got him to the hospital."

"I thought they kicked him out of the club?"

"He got reinstated. He got a lawyer and threatened to sue them."

My father had taken up golf late in life. He was a natural athlete and soon competed with the club champion. After my mother's death he'd bought a small Airstream trailer and rented space on a lot across the road from the club entrance so he wouldn't have had to drive home at night if he stayed late at the bar, which he often had.

"Where are you now?" I asked.

"I went out to the trailer earlier just to have a look, but I'm at the house now. Dad's house."

"It must be pretty early."

"Seven o'clock," she said.

I pictured my sister, Gracie, in the breakfast nook of the kitchen we'd grown up in, a lovely Dutch Colonial house about a mile north of town—a house that my father had built himself with help from *his* father. I pictured her sitting on the built-in blue bench at the built-in blue table, the cord from the phone on the wall stretched over her shoulder.

"What are you doing?" I asked.

"Just sitting here."

"How are you?"

"I'm fine, in fact. How about you?"

"I'm fine too."

"Have you met up with your friend yet?"

I'd come to Florence ostensibly to borrow one of Galileo's telescopes for the Galileo exhibit at the Museum of Science and Industry in Chicago, where I was employed as an exhibit developer. But really I'd come to see a woman with whom I was madly in love, a Scottish-Italian fresco restorer, Rosella Douglas, who was working on the frescoes in the apse of Santa Croce.

I looked up at the Marchettis eating their soup at the long table in what was a combined kitchen–living room–dining room. Was someone listening to me? Luca was the only one who understood English, but he was seated at the far end of the table next to his grandmother.

"She's skiing in the Dolomites," I said. "She'll be back tomorrow night. I'm going to meet her at the station. Have you called people yet?"

"I'm going to do that today."

"Do you want me to come home?"

She laughed.

"What about the funeral?"

"His body went to the junior college. They did the removal last night. They've started a mortuary science program. They'll cremate what's left—send us the ashes."

"Dad was full of surprises, wasn't he?"

"We'll have to have some kind of memorial service when you get back. Maybe out at the cemetery."

My sister and I had been looking forward to this moment, but we hadn't really planned ahead. "Whatever you want to do will be fine," I said. "You're the one who's had to put up with him."

"Sometimes I think I should have moved away like you did." But then she met Pete, and that was that. No way Pete was going to leave Green Arbor. Though they were divorced now, and Pete had in fact left Green Arbor. Probably to get away from my father, who had treated him like an errand boy.

There were sixteen of us at the long table. Signora Marchetti (Claudia) had kept a bowl of soup warm for me. Chiara, who was my age, forty, put it on the table in front of me and stood for a moment with her hand on my shoulder. I'd spent a year at the Marchettis' as an exchange student when

I was in high school, and then again when I came back to Florence on a study-abroad program, and then at various other times over the years. Chiara was like a second sister, and Luca like a younger brother. I got on well with all of them and with their cousins and aunts and uncles and with the grandmother, Nonna Agostina, who was seated in the place of honor at the head of the table.

Faces turned toward me as I took my place at the opposite end of the table from Nonna Agostina.

"My sister," I said. "Calling to wish me a happy Easter."

I had to make a conscious effort to suppress my relief, my sudden joy, though in fact it was more complicated than that. I was glad that my father was dead, but I wasn't glad that I was glad. I would have preferred to be grief-stricken. And I was saddened by the sharp contrast between my own little family—Gracie, Dad, and me—and the extended family— four generations—passing their empty plates to Chiara and Luca, who were helping their mother and father clear the table. But the soup was delicious, and so was the roast baby lamb. Sensation is sensation.

When I first heard of the Oedipus complex at the University of Michigan—we were reading *Oedipus* in a "Great Books" course—I knew exactly what Freud was talking about. Dad had become more and more abusive toward my mother, who suffered from tic douloureux. She was a lovely woman, small in stature, but bighearted, generous-spirited, deeply religious. She played the organ and directed the choir at Methodist church. *You just married me for the money,* he'd say to her. Drunk. *For a free ride.* It would have been a blessing if he'd died first. She could have lived out her last years in peace instead of in a nightmare.

And where was I? I'd run away. To Ann Arbor. And then Chicago. It was my sister who bore the brunt of my father's anger during the last years of my mother's life, and beyond. I was afraid of my father—most people were—and my only attempt to intervene was a disaster: It's Christmas Eve. I'm a wise fool, just home from Ann Arbor for Christmas vacation. My sister has taken Mom out on a last-minute shopping trip. They're not home by five o'clock and Dad is working himself up into a rage. Every fifteen minutes or so he goes out to his gun room at the back of the garage for a nip of Jack Daniel's, which he has to do because drinking is not allowed in our house. "I try to be a good husband . . ." he says, over and over. "I do everything I can . . . And now look at this . . ." He shrugs helplessly. "She'll be overtired." He's indulging in his favorite fantasy, which is that everything he does is for my mother's sake. He calls me in Ann Arbor, for example, on Sunday mornings. If I'm at home, in my dorm room in Adams House in the West Quad, which I usually am, he'll want to know why I'm not in church. "Your mother wants you to go to church— And you'll go. Next Sunday you'll attend the Methodist Church or I'll come up there and find out the reason why."

It's late when my mother and sister get home—after six o'clock. They've had a wonderful time, but Dad blows a gasket, is in a towering rage. I can hear him chewing out my mother in the bedroom. "You know better than to get overtired. I try to be a good husband; I try to do the best I can, and now look at you. You've been gone for four hours . . . You've tired yourself out. You know better . . ." And so on.

The bedroom door is not locked. Mom is sitting on the bed. Dad is shouting at her, repeating himself. "What were you thinking? ... How could you? ... I do everything I can ... I try to be a good husband, but ..."

"Leave her alone," I say. "She had a good time. Why do you have to ruin it?"

Dad gives me a look of contempt. "Get out."

"Leave her alone," I say. "You're too drunk to know what you're doing."

This is the Oedipal moment. I would kill him if I dared, if I could.

He's a big man. Drunk. "Like a raging bull elephant in musth," as my sister and I sometimes say to each other.

He slaps me so hard I fall down.

My mother is crying

I get up and he slaps me again, backhanded, on the other side of my face.

I run out of the room.

And that's a story I've never told to anyone before, but I've had to live with it for years. I've never been able to forget, or to forgive. But there's more.

Later on—Dad asleep in his chair—we do the usual. My sister and her husband, Pete, and their daughter, Megan, are there. Mom reads the Christmas story from the Gospel of Luke. We've decorated the tree, and there's a fire in the fireplace. We don't talk about what happened. Maybe that silence is the greater act of cowardice.

Megan, age twelve, is the only one who stands up to my father. When she was little he would force her to eat sweet potatoes or candied carrots, which she couldn't stand, and he'd make a big battle out of it. She'd eat the sweet potatoes or candied carrots or whatever it was and then throw up on the table. Finally he gave up. But he respected her. At least he left her alone.

Later on, in the middle of the night, I can hear him typing. He's retired early—too early—in order to spend more time hunting and fishing. He's turned his wholesale lumber business, which specialized in choice hardwoods—cherry from western Pennsylvania and West Virginia, yellow poplar from Appalachia, yellow birch from Canada, black walnut from Indiana—over to some of his key employees, who have embezzled so much money that the company has fallen into the hands of the receivers, a phrase that my father repeats over and over: "fallen into the hands of the receivers." He wants to go back into business and repay the creditors, firms he'd done business with over the years. But the credit rating agency won't give him back his old credit rating, and without his credit rating, he can't, or won't, go back into business, and that's what the letter is about—addressed not to the men who defrauded him, but to the credit rating bureau. He's been working on it—sending it out, demanding meetings, switching lawyers—for six or seven years, working on it day and night, including Christmas Eve. On Christmas morning we go over the letter again. It's the same letter every year. It's a good thing he doesn't have a computer, because then he wouldn't have to retype it, and the typing is a kind of therapy for him. He types so hard he ruins two or three Underwood office typewriters a year.

In any case, we go over the letter as if nothing had happened the night before. I advise him to go easy on the capital letters, and he agrees. He retypes the letter, jabbing at the keys with two thick fingers, a job that takes him about twenty minutes. I look it over again. There are a couple of typos. He retypes it again, and then again. Pretty soon all the nouns and verbs are recapitalized. For emphasis. "Although I am neither RICH nor POWERFUL, nonetheless if you

THINK . . ." Then the adjectives and adverbs. And then every word: "ALTHOUGH I AM NEITHER RICH NOR POWERFUL, NONETHELESS, IF YOU THINK . . ."

On Easter evening at the Marchettis', after most of the relatives, including Nonna Agostina, had gone home, I played a beautiful mahogany guitar that Luca, a professional musician, had got in Paris the year before. I knew a handful of Italian songs and we sang "Bella Ciao" and "Il Cacciatore Gaetano." It was a twelve-fret classical guitar with a wide neck and short scale, very easy to play. I tuned it down to an open G and played a new version of "Corrina, Corrina"—by an Italian group, TamboGnola—that I'd found by accident on YouTube. The song articulated the kind of melancholy I often experience after a few glasses of wine, and I was moved to open my heart to the Marchettis. I did not, however, tell them that my father had died drunk in the locker room of the Green Arbor Country Club. I just said how moved I was to see four generations together with the grand-mother at the head of the table. Four generations.

And then the truth came out with a bang: No one could stand the grandmother, Signora Marchetti's mother. Signora Marchetti had one brother and two sisters, and they moved Nonna Agostina around from house to house. But she kept her old *casa* near Palazzo Strozzi, even though she went back to it only once a year. She was tight with money. She was always changing her will to punish her children, usually the son or daughter she was living with. Everyone hated her. Even the grandchildren.

I was floored. It was like discovering that there's no Santa Claus—or no Easter Bunny. It was worse than that. It was like discovering . . . I didn't know what it was like discovering. I still don't.

*   *   *

Rosella—the woman I was in love with—was going to take the bus from Cortina d'Ampezzo, where she'd been skiing with her *friend* and his children, to Venice and then an express train to Florence. I drank a coffee in the station bar, checked the schedule, and then waited for her on a bench at the end of track 6. We'd met at a party in Hyde Park (Chicago, not London) to which I'd been invited because I spoke Italian, which turned out not to be necessary. "We'll speak Italian when you come to Italy," she'd said. "But in the United States we'll speak English." Her mother was from the Orkney Islands and her father was Italian, and she spoke English fluently, but with a pronounced Scottish accent. She didn't say "wee" and "bonny," but she rolled her *r*'s and collapsed her words into as few syllables as possible, and the first time we made love she'd said, "Whun ye feel it coomin, luv, tock it oot," because she'd suddenly remembered that she'd forgotten to take her birth control pill. I took it out, spilled my seed on the bed, and she'd laughed and drawn me down to her. She'd tasted sweet and salty.

She'd come to Chicago for a conference on fresco restoration. I'd taken some time off and went to a couple of her lectures at the Art Institute, and one at the Newberry Library, and I showed her the main sights, including some of the exhibits I'd worked on at the Museum of Science and Industry: "The History of Computers," "Life Tech," "Blue Planet, Red Planet." She'd spent time in California and New York, but it was her first time in Chicago, and she expected to find an old bluesman on every street corner, but she had to settle for Roy Book Binder at the Old Town School, and Cephas & Wiggins at Buddy Guy's, and all the time I was thinking that what we were doing was having a little adventure, *una piccola avventura.* But by the time I dropped her off at O'Hare—she was on her way to New York—she had become the person in whose eyes I wanted to shine, and I gave her a Galilean-style telescope kit I'd created for the Galileo exhibit out of a cardboard mailing tube and a pair of lenses. It was two feet long, but we managed to squeeze it into her suitcase at the last minute.

She wasn't married, and neither was I, but she was somebody's mistress and lived in a house on this somebody's estate on the side of Mount Ceceri, above Fiesole. "It's one of those complicated European affairs," she said. "You Americans, you Middle-of-the-Westerners, wouldn't understand." She laughed. I was standing with her in the check-in line at the United terminal.

"I understand all right," I said. "You've got yourself a sugar daddy in Fiesole, and he cheats on his wife and now you're cheating on him."

"*Sugarrr daddy,*" she growled. "That's exactly what I told you: you don't understand a thing."

Sitting by the tracks in the station in Florence, I could close my eyes and still hear her laughter over the sound of the trains. Love made the world bigger, louder, more surprising, brought what was blurry into sharp focus. But what about my parents? What had happened? What had gone wrong? Would things have been better if my mother had allowed my father to drink in the house? That was one theory, Pete's theory. It made a certain amount of sense, but it was an interpretation I didn't want to pursue. Going back even further I could remember the first time I heard them quarreling. Adults didn't quarrel in Green Arbor, Michigan. Not when I was growing up, and that's why it made such an impression on me. I woke up in the night. My mother wasn't saying anything, but my father was shouting something about the new mantel over the fireplace in the living room. "Goddamn it," he shouted, "if you didn't want it that way you should have said so." I couldn't hear my mother, and I never figured out what the problem was with the mantel.

At the University of Michigan I majored in philosophy. I read Thomas Kuhn and Karl Popper and specialized in the philosophy of science, which is how I wound up in Chicago at the Museum of Science and Industry as an exhibit developer. On Tuesday I was going to ask the director of the Museo di Storia della Scienza in Florence if I could borrow Galileo's telescope for the Galileo exhibit at the MSI. It was out of the question, I'd told my boss. The famous telescope that Galileo used for his observations for *Sidereus Nuncius* was going to the Franklin Institute in Philadelphia. But there was a second telescope, a smaller prototype that we were aiming at. It had a magnification of 14x, as opposed to 20x, and a focal length of 1330 mm with a 26 mm aperture.

I was thinking about this second telescope—comparing it in my mind to the telescope kit I'd put together for the exhibit—when Rosella came up behind me and put her arms around me. "*Sorpreso?*"

"*Stupito,*" I said. *Stupified.* I really was amazed. Amazed to be taken by surprise like that and to hear Italian coming out of her mouth.

We backed up a little, looked each other up and down, and stepped into each other's embrace. The train, which had backed into the station, was already pulling out, on its way to Rome. We walked to the new parking lot and I hoisted her big suitcase into the trunk of her smallish Alfa Romeo.

"Is this a Spider?" I asked. It was the only kind of Alfa Romeo I could name.

"A Brera," she said. "It's small, but not too small. I couldn't fit this suitcase into a Spider. Would you like to drive it?"

I declined automatically. I'd never driven in Italy and had no desire to. But then all of a sudden it hit me: I could buy a car like this. I could buy two of them. I could buy anything I wanted. Now that my father was dead, I was rich.

"Momento," I said. "Maybe I will drive."

I hadn't been to bed with a woman since Rosella's two-week stay in Chicago the previous October, and I didn't want to disturb the prospect of bliss by telling her about my father's death. In my mind what had started as a *piccola avventura* with a predictable trajectory had turned into the real thing. Even before she left Chicago. But what was the "real thing"? And how would it turn out? On the one hand, I wanted to deromanticize it. We were both adults, after all. This wasn't a teenage infatuation. On the other hand . . . But you can't think about these things when you're driving in Italy. Rosella guided me through a complex maze of streets in which you have to go south in order to go north, east in order to go west, until we were finally on the familiar bus route up to Fiesole, then through the piazza in Fiesole and onward, up Mount Ceceri, and then down a narrow wooded lane that was like a tunnel, green as dark as midnight, till we came to a big wooden door in a stone wall. It was thrilling. Rosella got out, opened the door. I drove through, and she closed the door and got back into the car. It was like a fairy tale, and the house—her house, provided for her by her sugar daddy—was like a glass palace. Like the Philip Johnson glass house in New Canaan, Connecticut.

"I'm the one who suggested the glass," she said. "So now he

says I have to live here. I used to live closer to the villa." Farther along a road that disappeared into the darkness.

"Well, you're pretty isolated," I said.

"We can pull the drapes," she said. "If you're self-conscious."

Maybe I *was* self-conscious, but I didn't say so.

"Let's go to bed right away," she said, once we got into the house. "Then we can enjoy our dinner later. Besides, it's chilly in here. That will give it a chance to warm up." She adjusted the thermostat. "We can talk later. You can tell me all about Galileo. His tomb's in Santa Croce, you know."

"Yes," I said. "I'm going to see if we can borrow it for the MSI exhibit."

"The tomb?" She laughed. In the bedroom she unpinned her hair in front of a mirror and then combed it out. Hurry up and wait. But I didn't mind. I studied an etching on the wall signed *Rembrandt f. 1646*—a young couple making love.

"Is this real?" I asked. "I mean really a Rembrandt?"

"Yes, but it's not mine. It comes with the house."

"The woman has three hands."

"He forgot to erase one when he changed the position. But look at the smile on her face."

It was a lovely smile, a wonderful smile, like the smile on the face of a young woman I'd been watching over and over on the YouTube video—a slide-guitar version of "Corrina, Corrina."

I watched Rosella's shadow moving on the wall as she took her clothes off. When she turned toward me and smiled a smile that spread through her whole body, I could see tiny creases under her eyes. She was irresistible. But over her shoulder, in the mirror, I could see something moving outside the bedroom window, something at the edge of the darkness. The drapes had not been pulled. I turned to look. It was an enormous white pig coming closer, walking stiff-legged. The pig came right up to the glass wall and pressed its nose up against it. For a moment I thought I was coming unstrung, but Rosella put her hand on my back, as if to steady me.

"It's Elena," she said. "She's supposed to be penned in up at the villa, but sometimes she gets loose. She's attracted to the light. They have quite a few animals."

"*They?*"

"The family."

"She's huge."

"Over two hundred and fifty kilos. Do you want me to chase her away?"

"No, no," I said. "It's all right."

"She'll wander off when I turn out the light."

After we made love, Rosella cooked spaghetti with garlic and oil, the simplest meal in the world and one of the most satisfying. No salad—the shops had been closed on Easter Monday evening. There was nothing else to eat in the house except some crackers and a bowl of apples, big green apples past their prime. We each ate an apple using knives and forks.

After supper we went outside and looked at the night sky through the crude cardboard telescope I'd given Rosella. No sign of Elena. The moon was full, but because of the small field of vision inherent in the design, you could see only half of it at a time.

"Before Galileo," I said, "astronomers thought that the sky had been completely explored. Everything—all the planets, all the fixed stars—had been cataloged. There was nothing more to discover. Who would have thought that by sticking two eyeglass lenses into the ends of a tube . . ."

"They had eyeglasses?"

"Eyeglasses were invented in the late Middle Ages," I said. "That's what you've got in this tube, more or less.

Sixteen dollars for a pair of lenses, thirty-five dollars for the whole kit."

We looked at the North Star and at Vega, which was rising in the northeast, and at Jupiter, though the telescope wasn't powerful enough to pick out its moons, and then we went back inside and watched—on a computer—a slideshow of Rosella's restoration work between the Gothic ribs at the top of the apse of Santa Croce—the Cappella Maggiore. We looked at hands and feet and robes and faces that had been cleaned and the tips of an angel's wings, the feathers newly restored to their original luster.

"I love this job," she said. "You've got to be an artisan, working with your hands without leaving a mark. And you've got to be an artist, using your imagination, and you've got to be a scientist too, a chemist. And you've got to be an historian, hanging on to things that are passing away, to preserve the old visual culture. Now we're in a new visual culture. It's impoverished in some ways, but rich in others. The problem is that people don't know how to understand the symbols, how to read them critically. You'll have to come up on the scaffolding with me. Then you'll understand."

Scaffolding? The top of a Gothic cathedral? I was picturing Juliette Binoche in *The English Patient*, hoisted up to the top of a church so she can examine the frescoes. No, thanks. But I didn't want Rosella to know that I was afraid of heights. I wasn't cripplingly acrophobic, but I never stood close to the floor-to-ceiling windows in a high-rise, and I never took the glass elevators in Water Tower Place.

"You'll have to wear a hard hat," she said, too interested in the slideshow to notice my lack of enthusiasm, interested in the frescoes not so much as works of art but as things, physical objects, subject to decay in a way that a poem or a piece of music is not. "When they're covered on the outside," she said, "with an accumulation of dirt and grime and candle smoke, you can clean them. When they're threatened from the inside by corrosive salts erupting from within the very stones of the cathedral, you can dissolve the salts. But when they're gone, like half the Giotto frescos in the Peruzzi Chapel, they're gone forever."

When the slideshow was over, I sat down at the computer and went to the YouTube video, the one with the smiling woman. The men you see at the opening are Italian, and the man wearing headphones says something in Italian—too fast for me—and counts down in Italian. The voice of the singer sounds like an old black man from the Delta, but the video doesn't match the audio. The young man playing a guitar in the video is strumming away wildly with a flat pick, but what you hear on the audio track is someone fingerpicking a slow blues: *Corrina, Corrina, where you been so long?* And then, during the second and third verses, you see the young man and this lovely woman sitting together. Talking. She turns to him and smiles.

"Look at her smile," I said. "It's like the smile in the etching."

Rosella looked at me, astonished. "That's Joan Baez," she said. "And Bob Dylan."

"Really? It doesn't say that on the website."

"*Porcamadonna!* How could you not recognize Joan Baez and Bob Dylan? You're kidding me."

"No, I had no idea."

"Well," she said, "they're very young."

"That's not Bob Dylan singing, is it?"

"I'm not sure."

"He can do gravelly," I said. "And he's the one who made that song popular."

We went back to bed. Rosella left the light on. She couldn't stop smiling. "I can't believe you didn't recognize Joan Baez and Bob Dylan." And she—Rosella—seemed to have three hands like the woman in the etching, all pinching, tickling, massaging, scratching, poking.

Afterward she fell asleep, but I was wide-awake. I propped myself up on one elbow and watched her for a while, and then I got up and went outside. I slipped on my leather jacket, which I'd bought at a discount store in Chicago, and put an apple in one of the side pockets. I turned the porch light on. A bicycle was leaning against the side of the house, and I was tempted to go for a spin. The road, or lane, led back down to Fiesole or up to the villa. But it was too dark to see, and the house was too isolated. Low streaky clouds covered the moon, and there was almost no light except the light from the house itself—the porch light and a lamp on the table next to the bed that I'd left on. I could see into the bedroom. Rosella had covered herself with a sheet.

I walked out to the edge of the darkness, out of sight of the house. I could sense trees, but I couldn't tell what kind they were. Maybe olive trees. I felt a branch but couldn't find any olives. It was too early anyway. It wasn't cold, but it was chilly, and after a few minutes I was ready to go back inside. But I'd forgotten about Elena. Two hundred fifty kilos. A third of a ton. Pure white like the moon. She was standing under the light, between me and the door. I walked around the house. There was another door that opened into the kitchen, but it was locked. I knew enough about pigs not to challenge her. I'd helped my girlfriend's father rustle hogs a couple of times when I was in high school, and what I knew was that if a farmer had a heart attack in his field, the pigs would eat him.

I took the apple out of my jacket pocket and held it out to her. "Elena," I said. "How about a nice mushy apple?" She really was enormous.

"Elena, Elena, *vieni mi qua*, come and get this nice apple." I took a bite out of the apple. She moved her head, and I could see she was tempted. It took about five minutes to lure her away from the front door. She moved toward me in her stiff-legged gait. Closer and closer. She seemed interested, rather than hostile, as if she were interrogating me. I thought about throwing the apple down on the ground, but decided against it. I held it in the palm of my hand as she came closer. She knocked it off my hand with her snout, waited for my reaction, then picked it up with her mouth. I walked around her, slowly, on my way to the door, trailing my fingertips over her back, which looked furry but felt as scratchy as sandpaper.

She raised her head, looking for another apple. I went inside, brought out the bowl of apples, and fed them to her one at a time till they were all gone. And then I got back into bed with Rosella.

On Tuesday morning I met with the director of the Museo di Storia della Scienza, who was pleased that I spoke Italian. He didn't make any promises about the second telescope, but he sent me to the Fondazione Scienza e Tecnica on Via Guiseppe Giusti, near the Protestant Cemetery, where I spent a pleasant afternoon, though our own collection at the MSI already contained most of the sixteenth-century astronomical and mathematical instruments that we needed for the exhibit.

On my way to Piazza Santa Croce to meet Rosella I stopped and browsed the windows of several real estate agencies. I liked the looks of a two-bedroom apartment on Borgo

Pinti for six hundred thousand euros. It would be perfect. Rosella could walk to work. The words of the notice embedded themselves in my brain: *appartamento luminoso*. It was on the *piano nobile* of an old palazzo that had been recently restored. Large living room. Modern kitchen. Two bedrooms. Two baths. Rooftop terrace. I was feeling optimistic that evening as the waiter at the Osteria dei Pazzi, who knew Rosella by name, seated us at a table by the window. But Rosella was preoccupied, because out of the blue the Italian government had decided that it needed to exercise more control over restorers. The first step was a decree that all restorers would have to have a university degree.

"All of a sudden twenty thousand restorers aren't restorers," she kept saying. "This country is impossible. You can't live here." She tore off a chunk of *pane toscano* and put it in her mouth. "And this bread is ridiculous. Everywhere else in the whole world they know enough to put salt in their bread. The Florentines are the only people in the whole world who don't know this. What is the matter with these people? It's insane."

"That's because their food is so salty already."

"Instead of putting so much salt in the food they should put some of it in the bread. Twenty thousand restorers won't be restorers if the Italian government has its way." She shook her head.

She ordered the *antipastone* for both of us. I understood that *antipastone* meant "big antipasto," but I didn't understand that it meant that the waiters would keep bringing us food till we couldn't possibly eat any more, not even one more olive: salami, prosciutto, cheeses, octopus salad, anchovies, roast vegetables, roast beef, *lardo Colonnata*—thin white slices of lard that has been specially cured in marble basins at Colonnata, near Carrara. But lard nonetheless, a Tuscan delicacy.

It was while we were eating straight lard that I proposed to Rosella. I didn't know what I'd do if she laughed in my face. My clothes, my suitcase, were at her house, so I couldn't have just walked out of the restaurant. I was trying to stay focused in the present moment, to detach myself from the result, to identify with the watcher watching myself rather than with my ego.

She didn't laugh nor did she throw herself into my arms. She listened as if she were listening to a business proposition. The fact that we were in love was very important, but it was only one part of a larger picture.

She called to the headwaiter, a man who burst into song every so often, and asked for another *quarto* of wine. It wasn't a fancy place. Comfortable. Not too expensive.

I told her about my father's death, though I didn't mention that he'd died on Easter Sunday, only four days ago, and she became tender and understanding. But, she said, she had her own situation to consider, the situation that was too complicated for an American to understand, the situation that involved a rich older man who had a life of his own—a wife, several children, old money, old aristocracy, a big estate with several houses, animals … She was right. I didn't understand.

"How would we live?" she wanted to know. "Fresco restorers don't make a lot of money. How would you find a job in Italy?"

I had in fact given this question some thought, but I didn't want to play my trump card, didn't want to tell her that now that my father was dead, I was a rich man too. I wanted her to meet me halfway.

"Museum jobs," she said, "any state jobs, are impossible to get. You'd have to enter a *concorso*, a competitive examination, along with hundreds of other people. And even if you won, which you wouldn't because the exams are rigged—there's a lot of horse trading—you might be sent to Calabria."

"One of the American programs? There are forty-three of them in Florence."

"You wouldn't make enough money."

Our waiter had cleared the table and brought a bottle of vin santo and some biscotti di Prato. Rosella dipped a biscotto into her glass of wine.

"Rosella," I said. "I want this to matter. I want *us* to matter, you and me. I want us to be important. This isn't a little adventure."

"You never know what's important and what's not important till it's over, do you?"

On Wednesday and Thursday afternoons, around five o'clock, we met at the statue of Dante in Piazza Santa Croce and then took the number seven bus up to Fiesole, where she'd left her Alfa Romeo Brera parked near the Roman amphitheater. Sometimes she took the tunnel-like lane, sometimes a regular road that took us past the villa where her sugar daddy lived.

We made love first thing every evening, early, so we could enjoy our dinner later. Elena did not reappear, but on Thursday we went up to visit her in her pen behind the villa. The signora was in Rome; the signore and his older son were still in the Dolomites, where the slopes were covered with snow year-round.

"She's got a very low center of gravity," Rosella said as we admired the gigantic sow. "But she's very fast. If you want her to move forward, you have to enter her flight zone from behind the point of balance, which is right between her shoulders, and you have to remember her field of vision is almost three hundred sixty degrees, so the only time she can't see you is if you're right behind her. If you want her to back up, you have to enter the flight zone from in front of the point of balance."

"You know a lot about pigs," I said.

"I know a lot about Elena," she said.

She'd borrowed a guitar from a fellow restorer so I could play for her. I tuned it down to an open G and played "Corrina, Corrina" while she cooked. I used a table knife as a slide.

"You know," she said. "I don't like the second verse of that song. He doesn't have his girlfriend and now his life 'don't mean a thing'? I don't think you can look to another person for your salvation, to give meaning to your life."

"Then I won't sing it again," I said.

On Friday morning—we were going to have lunch later at the Osteria dei Pazzi—we met at Dante's cenotaph in the right aisle of the basilica. She wanted to take me up to the vault at the top of the apse, where she was working on the feet of Saint Francis himself. The vault at the top of the apse was about the last place I wanted to be. The scaffolding was massive, not at all like the sort of thing painters put up at the side of a house. It filled the entire apse of the Capella Maggiore. Even so, looking up into that airy dome—I counted nine levels or floors—made me a little bit seasick.

I had secured the second Galileo telescope as well as an unusual astrolabe, so I wouldn't be going home empty-handed. There were still contracts to negotiate regarding the insurance, method of transportation, dates, and so on. I wouldn't be carrying the telescope, which looked like a piece of broom handle, in my suitcase, of course, but I would finish up my part on Monday. The MSI lawyers would worry about the fine print. But I was not in a mood to congratulate myself because I didn't know if I'd see Rosella again after today, didn't know if she'd be back from organizing a demonstration in Rome, didn't know what she'd decided or what would be settled up in the apse, didn't know if whatever it was we were doing was important or if it would turn out to be just a *piccola avventura*; I wasn't going to tell her about the *luminoso* apartment. Not yet, anyway.

The elevator made me nervous—though it was huge—so we put on hard hats and took the stairs. Up nine stories, each floor supported by metal braces inserted into holes in the wall that had been made when the church was built in the thirteenth century.

Rosella stopped to chat with someone on each level and to introduce me and to explain what was going on. You could see the joins where one day's work, or *giornata,* had overlapped another. In places you could see traces of the preparatory drawing in *verdaccio,* a sort of second underdrawing that repeated and corrected the *sinopia* or first underdrawing. You could see places where the pigment layer was flaking and areas where the pigment itself had been weakened by the binding medium or by surface abrasion. She explained the properties of the different fixatives (organic and inorganic), emulsions, and solvents (volatile and polar) that were used to remedy these problems.

We stopped on the eighth level for a cup of coffee in a large office, the sort of office you might find in downtown Chicago—full of desks, wastebaskets, lamps, a copy machine, a fax machine, telephones, and an espresso maker.

The apse had been frescoed by Agnolo Gaddi, who had learned from his more famous teachers—his father, Taddio, and Giotto—but who had done something different, moving toward the International Gothic style. But the scaffolding made it impossible to take in the big picture, *Scenes from the Legend of the True Cross*.

Rosella was working on the frescoes between the ribs of a vaulted arch at the very top of the apse. We were face-to-face with Saint Francis, the four Evangelists, and the risen Christ, and we had to take off our hard hats so we wouldn't scrape the ceiling.

"Vaults need special treatment," she said, "because the undersurface is lath rather than stone."

"What about these big cracks?" I asked. "Are you going to seal them up?"

"No," she said. "If you fill them, that just redirects the stress. You smooth them out and seal the raw stone at the edges so it doesn't disintegrate any further."

I was so overwhelmed just by the idea of being up there that I forgot to be afraid. Overwhelmed and feeling very special, very much the insider. I even let Rosella walk me to the edge of the scaffolding so I could look down into the big barnlike nave. She put her hand on my back to steady me, as she had done when Elena first appeared at the glass wall of her bedroom.

Far below us groups of tourists followed guides holding bright umbrellas, stopping in front of the famous tombs: Dante's (empty), Machiavelli's, Michelangelo's, Galileo's, Rossini's. A service was being conducted in one of the smaller chapels directly below us. We couldn't see the priest, but we could see the people in an area that had been roped off. Everywhere you looked people were taking photos. Isolated worshippers were scattered here and there. In the right aisle a mother and father consulted a guidebook while two children ran up and down the aisle. They had to make way for a mother and teenage daughter pushing an infant in a stroller. Workmen rolled a cart of stuff to the elevator. Some women in blue aprons were polishing the altar railings. (The main altar had been relocated to make room for the scaffolding.) A priest hurried toward the sacristy—we couldn't see the entrance from the scaffolding. Two other priests, crossing paths in front of the pulpit, stopped to chat. A line snaked out in front of a confessional. Two young lovers held hands. Two middle-aged women held hands. A beggar sat on the pavement by the ticket booth. You couldn't just wander in anymore. You had to pay. A bridal party had gathered around the ticket booth and the bride was arguing with the woman who sold the tickets. Probably a wedding party on their way to the wedding hall in Palazzo Vecchio.

What had happened to the original Franciscan vows of poverty? Legend has it that one of the friars responsible for the construction of the elaborate basilica was now in Purgatory being struck on the head by two hammers continuously.

Rosella pointed out the line of the floodwater from the big flood of 1966. The basilica—the whole Santa Croce district— was in the flood plain. The water had burst the huge doors.

I thought this view of the nave was what Rosella had wanted to show me. But I was wrong. What she wanted to show me was in a corner, in a small space at the base of one of the ribs, where the *intonaco* had been completely worn away. She pointed to a small oval portrait. A man in a floppy medieval hat, bright red—a jester? A peasant? A noble? A holy fool? I didn't recognize him at first. I was reading it as a late-medieval portrait, and I was only semiliterate. It didn't make sense. I had to adjust my eyes. And then I recognized myself. It was me. This was her gift to me. At first I didn't understand, and then she put her hand on my back, and I did. I understood that she was saying good-bye, that it was too late now to play my trump card, my ace in the hole. Too late to say I was rich, too late to tell her about the *appartamento luminoso* on Borgo Pinti with the terrace on the roof.

"It's true *affresco*," she said. "The lath, then the arriccio, the sinopia, the intonaco, the paint applied to the wet plaster. Then a few details al secco. Certain pigments you can't use in true fresco. It will be there for centuries. You can see Saint Francis and the Evangelists."

"And they can see me," I said. "Can you do this?" I added. "I mean, can you get away with it?"

"I've already gotten away with it."

My sister and I spent the week before Christmas in the old family home surrounded by old familiar things—the bright blue table in the breakfast nook, the deep red davenport in the living room that was always threatening to collapse, my mother's walnut Steinway piano, the silverware and the plates we'd eaten off as children, the glasses we'd drunk out of, Dad's typewriter on the desk in the little office off the front hall, a copy of the letter still curled up in the rollers. Two of the keys—the *s* and the *t*—were completely broken, but he'd kept typing anyway: ALHOUGH I AM NEIHER RICH NOR POWERFUL, NONEHELE, IF YOU HINK . . .

I had never gotten around to playing my trump card in Florence, and it was just as well, because my father left his estate, valued at about eight million dollars, to the Methodist Church. Except for the house, which went to my sister, and the Airstream trailer, which went to me. The church already had a new roof and a new electronic organ. The brick walls had been tuck-pointed, and the pastor was living in a new parsonage. It wasn't Santa Croce, but it was something.

On Sunday, two days before Christmas, my sister and I went to the ceremony in which the new organ was dedicated to my mother. Afterward we went out to the cemetery, just the two of us, and buried the urn that held Dad's ashes. The ground was frozen, but the hole, which had been dug months earlier, had been filled with straw. All we had to do was stick the urn in the ground. Someone from the cemetery would cover it with dirt and sod. But later.

We could have contested the will, but we didn't, and we didn't experience the rancor we might have felt. Eight million dollars. I could have bought the *appartamento luminoso* in Borgo Pinti. Gracie could have quit her job at the library and moved to the Florida Keys with her new boyfriend. Liberation, not rancor, was what we experienced. We were finally out from under. The money would have weighed us down. We were better off as we were. The Galileo exhibit was on schedule. Gracie had become the head librarian in Green Arbor. The library was planning to expand. We were almost festive at the cemetery.

On Christmas Eve we panfried a couple of small steaks and cooked some mushrooms and made a salad and drank most of a bottle of Bordeaux, and then we sat on the davenport in front of the fire in the living room and enjoyed the Christmas tree we'd decorated earlier. In the morning Gracie's boyfriend and his two kids were coming. We were going to cook a turkey and everything that goes with a turkey. Gracie had already baked the pies.

I'd sold the Airstream, and Gracie had put the house up for sale. We opened another bottle of wine and fought off the ghosts of Christmases past, though many of them were happy ones, and I told her about Rosella, told her the story I've told you: Easter dinner at the Marchettis'; the Rembrandt etching of the woman with three hands; the huge sow pressing her

169

nose against the glass wall and then knocking the big green apple out of my hand with her snout; the YouTube video of Joan Baez and Bob Dylan; looking through the window at Rosella asleep; the *lardo Colonnata* in the Osteria dei Pazzi; the *luminoso* apartment; drinking coffee in an office on the eighth floor of the scaffolding; removing my hard hat so it wouldn't scrape the ceiling of Santa Croce; Jesus and the Evangelists; looking down at the nave, without fear, overwhelmed by beauty. And my picture. Painted in the true fresco manner. A gift from the heart.

"Did it matter?" I asked my sister. "Was it important? Did it matter? Does anything matter? You know what she said to me? Rosella?"

"What did she say?"

"She said, 'You never know if something matters till it's over.' And now it's over, and I still don't know. What's the measure of change? Shouldn't something be different now? If she'd said yes, then it would have 'mattered' because it would have been a turning point in my life. Everything would be different. I'd be in Italy right now. You could be in Italy too. Or Florida. Down in the Keys."

"But she didn't say yes. And you couldn't have bought the *luminoso* apartment anyway because you didn't inherit any money." Gracie leaned forward and poured the last of the wine into my glass. I thought the davenport was going to collapse under the weight of my questions: *Was it important? Is anything important? What does it all mean? What does anything mean? Does anything mean anything? Was it a* piccola avventura *that turned out to be a* grande passion *or a* grande passion *that turned out to be a* piccola avventura? "A story like mine," I said, "should end with a comes-to-realize moment. But I haven't realized anything."

170

"Or a fails-to-realize moment," she said.

"But if it's 'fails-to-realize,' that means there must have been something to realize, something I missed. Doesn't it?"

"Stay calm and carry on," she said.

"Sorry," I said. "I'll be all right."

"How about this, little brother: maybe it's like money in the bank, a savings account, or an IRA or a money-market fund at a brokerage house. When you need some emotional capital, you'll be able to draw on it." She stood up. "But I'm going to bed."

"Sleep tight," I said. "Don't let the bedbugs bite."

That night, lying in the bottom bunk of the old cedar bed that matched my old cedar desk, I read for a while—Thucydides's *History* in Rex Warner's translation. A book I'd read in my first year at Michigan. But I didn't get very far. I turned out the light. The silence was unnerving—an occasional car went by on Kruger Road, the lights swishing across the room. The old house creaked, my sister closed and opened the bathroom door. I listened harder, kept listening harder and harder till I could hear Rosella's voice in my ear: *"Whun ye feel it coomin, luv, tock it oot,"* till I could hear my mother playing *The Harmonious Blacksmith* on the piano downstairs, till I could hear Gracie sobbing at the kitchen table after Pete left her and moved up to Battle Creek, and someone who was not Bob Dylan singing "Corrina, Corrina" on YouTube, and the sharp whistle of the coal mine at the Museum of Science and Industry, and Elena grunting with pleasure as she chomps down the apples that I hand-feed her, and even the *clack-clack-clack*ing of my father's typewriter in his little office off the front hall, and I knew that I had nothing to lose, that nothing is ever lost.

FOR SALE

IN 1996, THANKSGIVING AT the Unterkircher house in Chicago was the same as always—turkey, mashed potatoes, sweet potatoes, cranberries, apple pie—except that Margot, Rudy's youngest daughter, was in Florence, Italy, where she'd gone to volunteer her services after the big flood; and Molly, his second daughter, had stayed in Ann Arbor, Michigan (where she was studying to get her real estate license) in order to be with her new boyfriend. Dan, Rudy's son-in-law, had taken the car down to get gassed up for the trip back to Milwaukee; Meg, the oldest of the three girls, had put the kids down for a nap and was helping Rudy with the dishes. Rudy was washing and she was drying bowls and plastic containers and wooden spoons—all the stuff that didn't go in the dishwasher—and spreading them out on towels on the kitchen table.

Meg and Dan had bought a house up in Milwaukee, and when she said, "Pop, uh, we've, uh, been kind of wondering," he thought she was going to ask him for some money, which he didn't have. But she said, "We've, uh, kind of been wondering about having Christmas in Milwaukee this year."

Rudy rinsed off his hands, dried them on a dish towel, and poured himself another cup of coffee from the pot on the stove. He wasn't sure who was included in the "we."

She started to talk a little faster. "Molly would probably be staying in Ann Arbor," she said; so Rudy knew that the two of them had already talked it over. "She was really working hard," Meg went on, "and the New York Central schedule was really impossible, and she'd sold her car . . ." But all Rudy and Margot'd have to do—if Margot got back from Italy—was hop on a train in Union Station and they'd be in Milwaukee in about ninety minutes if they didn't feel like driving or if the weather was bad.

Rudy's life—or maybe it was just *life*—had a way of sneaking up on him, catching him by surprise. He'd think a chapter was about to end, and then it would go on and on. Or he'd think he was in the middle of a chapter, and all of a sudden it would end. It wasn't so bad when you were young, because most of the chapters were ahead of you; but when you were Rudy's age, sixty-five, there weren't so many chapters left. You hated to see a good one come to an end, which was what was happening.

"Well," he said, swirling the coffee around in his cup, "suit yourself, if that's what you really want." This was a phrase he'd used a lot when the girls were in their teens. One of them would want to hitchhike out to California with her boyfriend, and he'd say, "Suit yourself, if that's what you really want."

And that's the way they left it, because just as Meg was about to say something that might have settled the matter one way or another, Dan came in the back door, kicking snow off his boots, saying that the weather looked bad, and they ought to get going before it got really dark.

After they'd gone Rudy sat at the table and started to work seriously on a jug of wine that he'd put away earlier, imagining what Christmas would be like with just him and Margot and the dogs—Heathcliff and Saskia, a German Shepherd and Husky—and by the time he got to the bottom of the jug he'd pretty well convinced himself that he ought to sell the house and go down to Texas and buy an avocado grove. Then they'd appreciate what it meant to come home for Christmas to the place you grew up in.

He went down to the basement and pulled out an old one-by-twelve board that had been lying on the floor behind the furnace ever since he'd taken down the bunk beds in Meg's old room—the board had been used to keep Meg from falling out of the top bunk—and cut off a two-foot length with his new saw. The saw—a present from the Central Texas Avocado Growers Association—was Japanese and cut on the upward pull rather than on the downward thrust, which confused him a little but didn't stop him.

He didn't bother to sand down the edges; he just opened a can of the paint he'd been meaning to use to paint the storm windows and painted

FOR SALE

in big black letters. Underneath FOR SALE he painted

by owner

When he was done he brought down an electric fan from the attic and turned it on and pointed it at the sign to make the paint dry quicker—he was in that much of a hurry—and then he went back upstairs and turned on the radio and lay down on the living room floor with the dogs.

Meg and Dan decided to come home for Christmas after all, and Molly was coming too, bringing her Indian boyfriend, whose name was Tejin or Tinder or Ginger—something like that. He taught mathematics at the University of Michigan. She'd met him, she told Rudy on the phone, at the family table at Metzger's German Restaurant. He'd really like to see an American Christmas.

Rudy was relieved like a man who'd come through a serious traffic accident without a scratch. He vacuumed up the dog hair and brought down the boxes of the old Christmas decorations: the crèche that his wife, Helen, who'd taught art history before she died, had brought back from a sabbatical year in Italy and the snowman candles, like skaters on a pond made out of a mirror. He bought a tree but he didn't put it up, because they never put the tree up till Christmas Eve. He got out the old ornaments that the kids had made out of baker's clay when they were little: salt and flour and water rolled into a paste, cut with cookie cutters, baked in the oven, and then painted. And on the day before Christmas he bought two fresh capons instead of a turkey. It wasn't till he carried the capons down to the basement in the big roaster—to keep them cool but not frozen—that he remembered the For Sale sign, which was propped up against the freezer. The electric fan was still blowing on it. His first impulse was to hide it, in case one of the girls came downstairs to get something out of the freezer; but then he decided it might be a good idea to put it up, just for one night, just to shake them up a little, make them think. Sometimes it takes a little jolt to make us appreciate what we've got, to keep us from taking it for granted. That's what Rudy had in mind—a little jolt.

The ground was frozen too hard to drive a stake into, so he nailed the sign to the porte cochere and turned the outside light on so you couldn't miss the sign as you drove up the driveway. Then he went inside and rolled out the dough for the sour cream apple pies, which he made in springform pans so that they stood straight-sided, about four inches high. He used eight big Granny Smith apples in each pie.

He hadn't heard from Margot since right after Thanksgiving, when he'd gotten a card saying she was staying in a convent. The card was up on the refrigerator, held by a magnet shaped like a ladybug. It was a picture of the Virgin Mary and an angel with great, big gold wings. He figured he'd come home from work one day and she'd be there—Margot, not the Virgin Mary—but she wasn't. Icelandic Airlines had flights to New York on Tuesdays and Thursdays, but it was Friday, and she hadn't come home. He called Alitalia and TWA, which had direct flights from Rome to Chicago, but they wouldn't release the passenger lists, so he had no way of finding out if she was booked on any of the flights. By Christmas Eve he had just about given up hope. "How sharper than a serpent's tooth," Helen used to say, "it is to have a thankless child." She was joking, but there was some truth to it too. How much trouble was it to write a postcard? Or to pick up the telephone? What was she doing for money? Was she going to become a nun? Nothing would surprise him.

Christmas was a time to make allowances. Take Molly's boyfriend, for example, whose name turned out to be Tejinder, which means "the embodiment of power" in Punjabi. He was a Sikh and wore a cream-colored turban made out of some kind of soft material that reminded Rudy of some fancy underthings he'd bought for Helen once. Concealed on his person, Molly had told him, were several items—five, to be precise—of great importance: a comb to comb out his long hair, a knife to defend himself against his enemies, a ring, a bracelet, and some special underwear called *kaccha*.

Rudy had given considerable thought to where Tejinder ought to sleep and had finally decided on the floor of the study. He lugged one of the extra mattresses down from the attic and made it up nicely with matching sheets and pillowcases and a Pendleton blanket. He's probably used to sleeping on a mat on the floor anyway, Rudy told himself. But Molly carried Tejinder's suitcase right up to her own small room with its single bed. Rudy followed her.

"I've got a bed made up for him in the study," he said.

Molly plopped the suitcase down on the floor, sat down on it, and looked around at the empty aquarium, the books, the portable Smith Corona on the desk, and the beanbag chair.

"Wouldn't he be more comfortable in the study?" Rudy asked.

"He might be more comfortable," she said, "but he wouldn't have as much fun."

"Well," he said, "suit yourself, if that's what you really want."

Or take the portable television set that Meg and Dan brought, with a bright red ribbon tied around the handle. "Merry Christmas," they said. It took him a while to realize that it was his Christmas present.

Rudy and Helen had never had a TV. With Helen it had been a matter of principle—on account of the kids. Rudy'd never cared much one way or the other, but he'd gotten used to not having one, and he got a kick out of telling people that he didn't have one. *"WHAAAAT?"* they'd say. "You don't have a TV?" No one could believe him. He might as well have told them that they didn't have indoor plumbing. Babysitters had looked around the living room in disbelief and then desperation. Guests at Thanksgiving couldn't believe they were going to miss the football games.

"We just never got around to getting one," he'd say, or, depending on his audience, would add, "On account of the kids, you know. We'd rather they read books or played the piano."

And now Dan was hooking the thing up in the living room. He'd brought along the sort of antenna you set on top of the TV, with two spikes sticking up, and was turning it this way and that. The TV was making a loud static sound. Daniel, five, and Philip, seven, were waiting impatiently.

"C'mon out here, you guys," Rudy shouted from the kitchen. "I've got some baker's clay here; you can make Christmas tree ornaments like your Mama used to. We'll bake them and then you can paint them."

But either the boys couldn't hear him or they preferred to watch the snowy screen.

One Christmas was much like the next at the Unterkircher house, just like in the Dylan Thomas story, *A Child's Christmas in Wales*, and one of the things that was always the same was that somebody would give Rudy a copy of *A Child's Christmas in Wales*—a record in a red-and-white jacket with the text printed in a little booklet. There were half a dozen of them in the record cabinet. On the other side of the record was a poem called "Do Not Go Gentle into that Good Night," and sometimes Rudy wondered if maybe *that* was the real message they were sending him. He liked to think so.

For supper Rudy, Molly, Tejinder, Meg, Dan, and the children ate spaghetti with clams, which is what they'd eaten every Christmas Eve after Helen's sabbatical, because that's what they'd eaten on Christmas Eve in Florence, and Helen had liked traditions, especially Italian ones.

After supper they put the lights on the tree and decorated it with strings of cranberries and popcorn and the baker's clay ornaments. Rudy must have had three or four hundred of them, enough for several trees. Daniel and Philip had not forgotten about the TV, which could not be coaxed into working, much to Rudy's satisfaction, but Tejinder entertained them with a trick involving two hats and two or three little wads of paper, which he passed back and forth through the solid surface of the dining room table, and by demonstrating several yoga positions which the boys were eager to imitate: the Lotus, the Fish, the Crow, and finally the Dead Man's Pose, which, he said, was the most difficult of all. The boys lay quietly on their backs.

"Not even your toe must twitch," Tejinder warned. "Not even the tip of your finger must move."

Rudy put a little applejack in their cider and helped them write a note to Santa, which they left in front of the fireplace, along with a glass of milk and a plate of cookies.

Nobody said anything about the sign till it was almost bedtime and they were finishing off the last of the applejack in front of the fire. The dogs were on the side porch, banging to get in. Tejinder and Dan had gone upstairs, one to meditate, the other to settle the boys down.

MEG: "I see you've got the house up for sale."
RUDY: "Oh, that."

Molly got up to let the dogs in. Rudy suddenly realized that she'd quit smoking.

MEG: "Molly and I've been talking; we think it's a great idea. This place is too big for you. You must rattle around here all by yourself. You'd be better off in an apartment or one of those retirement condos. Dan and I heard talk about one on the radio on the way down—Fairview Estates, something like that. You'd have everything you need right there. A pool, a sauna. You'd have your own kitchen if you want to cook, but there's a dining room too. The best of both worlds."
RUDY: *A pool? A sauna? What do I need with a pool and a sauna?* "What about Margot?"
MOLLY: "She's twenty-nine years old; it's about time she got a place of her own. You're too protective. She's got to get out in the world."
RUDY: "Where do you think she is? She sure as hell isn't upstairs in her room. And what about Heathcliff and Saskia?"
MOLLY: "They're getting old, Papa. How much longer do you think they've got?"
RUDY: "Well, I dunno. They don't look so old to me."
MEG: "We could take them, Pop. We've got plenty of room now. We were thinking of getting a dog anyway. It would be good for the kids."
MOLLY: "This neighborhood's going to hell, Papa; I can tell just by looking down the street. It's going to go

down, down, down. These old houses used to be trendy, but now they're a drug on the market. Sell now while you've got the chance. Give me three months. I'll have my license. I'll take care of everything for you, the listing, showing, financing, closing, the works."

RUDY: "You going to have a license to practice in Illinois?"

MOLLY: "I'm planning to take the test for Michigan, Indiana, Illinois, Wisconsin, New York, and California. But listen to this. I've already got a listing figured out. It's right here in my purse."

She fiddled with her purse and pulled out piece of paper, which she handed to Rudy:

Victorian fantasy. Shingle-style. 5 BRs. Study. 2 bath. Parquet floors. Baccarat crystal chandelier. Leaded glass. Butler's pantry. Beautiful millwork. 2 fplcs. Mod. kitchen, Lndry rm. Full bsmt. Excellent condition. Lower 80's.

"How does that sound? Not bad, eh? You'll get eighty thousand for this place; I promise you."

Rudy didn't know what to say. He was dumbfounded. "You might as well get on the phone and call the undertaker right now," he said. "Tell him to bring the hearse around to the back door. Or call the knacker, for cryin' out loud. I've lived in this house for over thirty years. You don't think I'm going to pack up and move out just like that, do you? After thirty years? Your mother and I paid seven thousand dollars for this house. Why, you couldn't build a house like this today for a quarter of a million dollars."

"Papa, that's not what we meant and you know it." Meg unfastened her hair, tipped her head back, and shook her head. "What we meant is that we want you to do whatever you want to do, and that if you want to sell the house, it's okay with us. You don't have to worry about us. We'll go along with anything. *You're* the one who put it up for sale without saying anything to anybody."

The sign. The sign'd been a bad idea from the beginning.

"Suit yourself," Molly said, "if that's what you really want to do."

Rudy had to laugh. He didn't know how to tell them how much he loved them, and how much it meant to him to have them come home at Christmas, but he thought they knew anyway.

About an hour later the phone rang. He was sitting at the kitchen table filling stockings and he grabbed it on the first ring. There was a click and the phone went dead, and Rudy froze. The phone always clicked like that and then went dead on overseas calls. And then it would ring again in a little over a minute and the overseas operator would be on the line. It was a special kind of click; he always recognized it. He knew that the click was the same for good news as it was for bad news, but he associated it with bad news, because it had always been bad news.

Spread out on the table before him were six large gray wool hunting socks with red tops and six piles of additional stuff: oranges, apples, dried apricots and raisins (wrapped in Saran wrap), chocolate kisses in foil, salted peanuts, ballpoint pens, mechanical pencils, little bars of scented soap for the girls, penknives for Dan and Tejinder—*He could keep it in his turban!*—crayons and protractors for Daniel and Philip. He'd always filled stockings, and he didn't see any point in stopping now. He opened one of the penknives and tested the blade; he started to clean his fingernails. His pulse was speeding up, and he was experiencing a choking sensation. He was afraid that if anything was wrong he'd start to cry and wouldn't be able to talk. He'd have to get a hold of himself. The house was strangely silent except for the occasional clink of a metal dog collar and a strange pounding that might have been his heart. It was strong enough to rattle the copper saucepans that dangled from a rack over the table.

It was Margot, all right. At first he didn't pay any attention to what she was saying. He was listening for something else, like a mechanic listening to an engine idling.

"Is it really you, Papa? I had trouble getting through. Say something."

"How are you?"

"Oh, Papa, I'm so happy. I'm in love, really in love. Head over heels. Can you hear me all right? I don't want to say it too loud."

"Where are you?"

"At the post office."

"In the middle of the night?"

"It's nine in the morning here. Why? What time is it there?"

"It's two o'clock in the morning."

"Oh, Papa, I thought it would be afternoon. Is it Christmas yet?"

"It's still Christmas Eve. I'm filling the stockings. I gave yours to Molly's boyfriend. His name's Tejinder and he's from Punjab. He's a Sikh and he wears a turban."

When he knew she was all right he was tempted to scold her: *Why didn't you write? Why didn't you call? Why didn't you come home? You promised . . .* But he was too overwhelmed, too happy.

"Well," he said. "That's wonderful. Who's the lucky guy?"

"He's an Italian."

"Married?"

"No, Papa. Well, yes, but he's getting a divorce. He's from the Abruzzi. He's the head restorer for the whole region of Tuscany. He's working on the frescoes in the Pandolfini Chapel in the Badia Fiorentina. You remember the Badia? The monastery where they had the foosball game in the cloister? It's still there."

The foosball game he remembered, after all these years. But that was all.

"It doesn't matter. And the Simone Martini *Annunciation*. I sent you a postcard of it. Didn't you get it?"

"I got it; it's up on the refrigerator."

He tried to picture her in the post office. He couldn't remember anything about Florence—he and Helen had gone there to bring Margot back home after her nervous breakdown, and then he'd gone again when Helen was having that affair—but he imagined Margot in a red phone booth, with her friend—her lover—standing outside, waiting, impatient, eager.

"What are your plans? I mean, are you coming home, or what?"

"We're going to the Abruzzi sometime in January to see Sandro's parents, and then to Rome."

"Have you written to your boss at the Newberry? He called here the other day. To tell you the truth, I don't think you've got a job anymore."

But she didn't hear him, and he didn't repeat himself. *It might just be possible,* he thought to himself. *A mature man with a good job, a responsible position. But married?*

Rudy suddenly realized what the pounding was that was shaking the saucepans. It was the bed upstairs in Molly's room. The Indian was humping his daughter. They were shaking the whole house with their lust. It gave him a hard-on, just the cruel fact of it. It made him ache for his wife.

"I didn't know you could get a divorce in Italy," he said.

"It's an annulment; it's the same thing. You'll see. Don't worry, Papa. I'm all right. I'm fine. I'm not cracking up again. I'll write to you, Papa. I really will. I have to go now."

"Take care of yourself."

"You take care of yourself too, Papa. I love you. Tell everyone I love them."

That was all she said. But it was enough.

Rudy finished filling the stockings and carried them into the living room, where he spread them out on the coffee table in front of the fireplace. He moved the TV into a dark corner in the dining room, ate the cookies the boys had left for Santa, and wrote an answer to the note they'd left:

Thanks for the milk and cookies. Be good.

—Santa

He filled the humidifier, turned down the thermostat, let the dogs out to go the bathroom, turned off the tape deck, which had been left on, let the dogs back in, put the garbage container up on the kitchen table so the dogs wouldn't empty it, got a hammer out of his toolbox, pulled on his jacket, and went outside to take down the For Sale sign.

He still had a hard-on, a great lump of sensation swelling against his trousers. He'd almost forgotten how good it felt, and even though he didn't know what he could do about it, he was grateful. It was good to be alive. He felt like a young man, young and strong, the way he'd felt when he and Helen had moved into the house, which looked just the same now as it had then. They'd kept the red trim. Chinese red. He thought of the first Christmas they'd spent in this house, after his father's death; of Mr. Hamilton, the previous owner, whose paving-brick business had fallen into the hands of the receivers, and who had driven off to California with his whole family in a broken-down Pierce Arrow; of the French doll-house that the Hamiltons had left in the attic; of the steamer trunks; and of the letter that Hamilton had sent him about a year later, telling him about the house, how Harald Kreutzberg, the famous German dancer, had been entertained there and Cornelia Otis Skinner and Matthew Arnold and Aleka Rostislav, who was Princess Galitzine and whose husband's mother was the older sister of the last Czar, and many other famous people. He kept the letter in the safe-deposit box at the bank.

The sign had worked its way loose—he hadn't hammered the nails all the way in when he put it up—and he could have pulled it off with his hands. He didn't need the hammer. But instead of pulling it off, he walked down the driveway to the street to pick up the empty garbage cans that had been sitting there for two days and to have a look.

It was windy and the snow blew upward in spiraling flurries; the ornamental streetlights glowed like beacons marking a broad channel. Most of the big old houses on the street had long ago been broken up into five or six apartments—sometimes even more. Most of the owners didn't live there anymore, and the lawns didn't get cut as often as they should have, and the houses got painted every ten or twelve years instead of every six or seven. Helen used to say that when she looked down the street at night through the leaded glass of the mullioned windows in the master bedroom at the front of the house, she could imagine—if she squinted a little—that she was living in a suburb of Paris—Saint-Germain or Saint-Denis. To Rudy, who'd lived in Chicago longer than he'd ever lived anywhere else, it just looked like home.

The living room window, which was curved, was divided into three panels, like a triptych. The window was filled with little white lights that were doubled by the beveled edges of the glass; in the large center panel stood the Christmas tree, full of light and promise. The light under the porte cochere was on too and the For Sale sign was clearly visible from the street. Rudy loved this house. "Come on in this old house," he used to sing to Helen. "Nobody here but me." But now it was time to move on, time to let go. He didn't know how he knew this, but he knew it. He knew it as surely as migratory birds know when it's time to leave everything behind them and head out who knows where, and no one has ever figured out how they find their way, but they do. It was as if he were sprouting wings, big golden wings, like those on the angel on Margot's postcard, wings that would carry him out of the past and into the future, wherever he needed to go.

THE SECOND COMING

RUDY LET THE DOGS in, filled their water dish, and spread out the mail on the kitchen table. There was nothing from his daughter Margot, who was in Italy, but there was a letter from the University of Chicago, where Helen had gone back to school, asking for money, which he tossed in the garbage—Helen had been dead for almost ten years—and there was a large formidable envelope bearing a stern warning:

This Cash Winner Notification may not be delivered by anyone except U.S. Government employees.

A partial list of sweepstakes winners was enclosed. Rudy could see his own name displayed through a little window, but he tossed the envelope, unopened, into the garbage with the letter from the University of Chicago. There was also a trial issue of a senior citizens' magazine called the *Golden Age Digest*, and finally, there was a letter from his nephew in East Africa.

He set the letter aside and glanced through the *Golden Age Digest* to see what his age-mates were doing. They were mostly playing golf. Happy foursomes in fruity two-toned shoes with fringe on the tongues, like the hair that hangs down over a sheepdog's face, waved from pea green links. The men wore cardigans and blue or white Oxford shirts; the women wore bright-colored skirts and pale blouses with wide collars. The same folks were buying condominiums with little work islands in the kitchens, which were tiled for easy maintenance. The idea was that old age wasn't just a downhill slide but the culmination of life, the peak.

Rudy tossed the magazine into the garbage, poured himself a cup of coffee, and then retrieved the sweepstakes envelope. He was, he learned, a "verified sweepstakes winner." But it wasn't clear just what he had won. He read through a lot of fine print. There were prizes in his category that ranged from two hundred fifty thousand dollars to one thousand dollars "to many thousands of substantially lesser cash prizes (as stated in the official sweepstakes rules)." He started to toss it again, but then his eye was caught by another stern notice:

Failure to claim prize will result in loss of your cash award. Company is not responsible for unclaimed cash awards. There is no entry fee or purchase necessary to claim your award.

But in fact they wanted him to buy some perfume, real perfume, not cologne or toilet water. Perfume that cost two hundred dollars an ounce in fine stores in New York and Paris, but which he could buy for only five dollars an ounce: Chanel No. 5, Opium, Melograno, Joy, Aramis. They came in different-shaped bottles, but it was hard to tell how big they were. Zen was shaped like a bowling ball. Aramis looked like a pint of whiskey. *Aramis,* Rudy thought. *He was one of the three musketeers, wasn't he?*

You didn't have to order any perfume to enter the sweepstakes, or claim your prize, but they made it very difficult for you if you didn't. You had to cut out your computer-printed number from one place and paste it on a three-by-five card, and then you had to cut out other bits of information from other parts of the official form and paste them on different parts of the card. And you had to cut out the "NO" paragraph from the lower left-hand corner of the Grand Prize Claim Document and affix it to the card too. There wasn't enough room; and if you didn't have them arranged in a certain way, you would be disqualified. You were also disqualified if you used staples or cellophane tape. In the end Rudy decided to order some perfume: presents for his daughters, Meg and Molly and Margot; and one for Mrs. Johnson, the cleaning lady; one for Mrs. Lake and another for Miss Heckathorne, the secretaries at the Agostino Co. Anyone else? That was six bottles, all different: Joy, Opium, Seduction, Chanel No. 5, Aramis, Diva. He wrote out a check for thirty dollars and then had to tear it up because he hadn't allowed for postage and handling, another $3.95, per bottle! What the hell!

Two hundred and fifty thousand dollars. A quarter of a million dollars. What would he do? He wasn't sure. He closed his eyes, tried to imagine. He could get to the feeling he'd have right after he'd opened the letter telling him he'd won, how he'd hold himself together, not tell anyone but the dogs for a few days, just riding high, till he'd gotten used to the idea. And then he'd tell Gus Agostino: "Gus," he'd say, "looks like I'm going to be leaving."

THE TRUTH ABOUT DEATH

"Rudy, what's the matter?" Gus would ask, concealing the extent of his interest behind a cloud of cigar smoke. "Where you going to go?"

"I was thinking about Florida, Gus, or Southern California, or maybe Texas; get myself a little spread of my own, maybe a hunderd acres, hunderd an' fifty. Run things my way."

"Rudy, that's great. You won't forget us, will you?"

"Of course not, Gus."

Why should he forget Gus? Gus had given him a job when he'd needed one.

When he was a boy he used to have daydreams like this—waking fantasies—about women, about success, about how everyone would be forced to acknowledge how extraordinary he was. But he'd thought that when you got older, when you grew up, you wouldn't do that anymore. Now here he was, no better than a kid. It wouldn't have occurred to him in a million years that his dad or his mom might have had thoughts like that. He could see his dad, standing in the door of the empty packing shed, looking out at the empty trees. Three years in a row they lost the entire peach crop during the Depression. What was his dad thinking to himself?

"Well," he'd say, "looks like you and me can eat the whole crop again." And they'd wander up and down the rows, looking, and find maybe three or four peaches. But what had he been thinking, imagining, dreaming?

And his mom, her hands up to the elbows in soapy water, looking out the kitchen window. What had she been looking at? The pump? The packing shed? Or something beyond? What had been *her* heart's desire?

The letter from his nephew in Africa was a birthday card. "Dear Uncle Rudy," it said,

I meant to get this off in time for your birthday but didn't get around to it. Everything is chaotic, and in fact I've been down with a parasite found in the water here called Giardia, so now I drink bottled water only, which is a nuisance.

Deedee and I sold the house and moved to Switzerland for a year to learn French, and then to East Africa and who knows how long we'll be here. Switzerland is beautiful, the natives are friendly, but it's very expensive. One of the most expensive places to live in the whole world.

The way things are going it seems to me the Lord Jesus Christ is coming very soon, any minute. I fervently hope so. This is a very wicked world these days and I wonder at God's patience with humanity.

I hope you had a nice birthday and will have a good year.

Lovingly,

Gary and Deedee

There was some literature from Gary and Deedee's employer, the Christian Bible Institute, an international organization dedicated to the task of translating the Bible into every single language in the world, including Kikuyu, and a request for support. Rudy crumpled it up and tossed it in the garbage, stepping down so hard on the pedal that the lid flew up into the air. There was a lifetime guarantee on the container, and this was the fourth one Rudy had gone through in two years, though the last time they just sent the little catch that's supposed to keep the lid from flying into the air.

What kind of a birthday message was that? *The Lord Jesus Christ is coming soon, any minute*? What got into people?

Rudy didn't give another thought to Gary's letter till two weeks later when he woke up at three o'clock in the morning in a motel room just outside of Mission, Texas. He had a hangover and couldn't get back to sleep. He'd drunk too much Lone Star Beer and eaten too much chili at the diner across the highway from the motel. His head and his stomach were churning, like electric motors running at different speeds, pulling against each other, and there was a neon sign that made a loud buzzing noise like a giant wasp as it blinked on and off, on and off, outside his window. It made you realize why a lot of people preferred Howard Johnsons and Holiday Inns, where there were no surprises, no crumbling tiles in the bathroom, no smell of roach powder in the closets. He lay there in the dark thinking, *What am I doing here? What on earth am I doing here?*

He'd flown down to look at some property, an avocado grove. That's what he was doing there. It had seemed like a good idea back in Chicago, but it didn't seem so hot right now. A man his age ought to be thinking about retiring, not raising avocados.

He reached over and turned on the clock radio on the stand next to the bed. He turned the dial but didn't get anything except a lot of static. There was lots of space between stations down here. He finally picked up a talk show way down at the other end of the dial, on the right. He started back toward the left and then reversed. There was an urgency in the slow Texas voice he'd heard that spoke to his condition. Something was wrong, really wrong:

"What we're telling people to do," a woman's voice was saying when he found the station again, "is to stay home with their families, to read their Bibles, and to pray. That's about all you *can* do at this point. Bob and I will be leaving the station at five o'clock to join *our* families. Until then, we're here to take your calls." She gave the number.

"Should we go down into the basement?" the next caller wanted to know.

"No, we think you should stay right in your living room. Going down to the basement's not going to help you."

Rudy switched on the lamp and sat up in bed. Another missile crisis, or worse—only this time it would be LBJ climbing into the ring with Nikita. He'd seen something about it in the *Corpus Christi Daily Herald* that he'd looked at in the diner:

U Thant Predicts WW III if US Doesn't Leave Vietnam

but he hadn't read past the header. This could be it. His last night on earth. The missiles might be in the air already: Titans, Minuteman-Is, Soviet SS-8s. NASA facilities in Houston would be a prime target. Mission Control. He thought he heard a siren, but it was only the buzzing of the neon sign. That's when he thought of Gary's letter again: *The Lord Jesus Christ is coming soon, any minute. I wonder at God's patience with humanity.* Could this be *it*? Christ himself pushing the button, all she wrote, end of story?

Rudy was wide-awake. He had to go to the bathroom, but he wanted to listen. It took him a while to figure out what Bob and Helen at KORK 101 were talking about: not a nuclear attack but the Second Coming, so he'd been right after all, in a way.

Momentarily relieved, he slipped on the Italian silk robe that his wife—same name as the woman on the radio—had ordered for him shortly before her death, and which he never wore except when he was travelling, and sat down on the edge of the bed. A former computer scientist working as a janitor at NASA, he learned from a news update, had secretly programmed the big computer—the one that was keeping Gemini 9 on course—to determine scientifically the date of the Second Coming, which was going to be tomorrow at sunrise in Jerusalem. Eleven twenty-five A.M., Texas time. Rudy went outside and got a bottle of Dr Pepper from the pop machine.

It's easy to laugh at this sort of stuff when you're sitting at the kitchen table thumbing through the evening paper, but when you're two thousand miles away from home and you've got three bowls of Texas chili from last night's supper still sloshing around in your stomach—nothing but shredded meat and jalapeño peppers, no beans, no tomato sauce—along with seven or eight bottles of Lone Star Beer, and you were brought up in the Methodist Church—even though you haven't been to church in twenty years, except for weddings and funerals—it can be pretty upsetting.

What were you supposed to do in the meantime? That's what callers wanted to know. They wanted instructions. Practical advice. Just the idea of the Second Coming was upsetting. People shouldn't be allowed to broadcast such nonsense. Rudy was annoyed. But he didn't turn off the radio.

The next caller was a woman named Marge from Hidalgo with a message for her husband: "Gene, please come home." She was on the edge of tears. "I'm sorry. If you can hear me, come back." Someone else wanted to know what Bible passages would be good to concentrate on. Helen suggested John 3:16–21, "For God so loved the world . . ."; Bob voted for the parable of the vineyard, Matthew 21:28–41. And then a mother from Kingsville followed Marge's lead by trying to reach her daughter, who'd run off with a Mexican farmworker: "Debbie, this is your mom. Your dad and I've been prayin' for you every minute of every day and every night. Won't you please call us right away, before it's too late? We love you so much." Sobbing. There was a call from somewhere in Mexico. Bob and Helen spoke to the man in Spanish. Rudy couldn't make out what they were saying, but the man started to sob too—masculine Mexican sobbing, which was different from anything he'd ever heard.

Rudy finished his Dr Pepper. The calls kept coming in: husbands and wives, moms and dads, children too, all reaching out with the same message: Come home, or if you're too far away, call us before it's too late. We want to talk to you once more before the end. We want to tell you we love you; we just want you to hear it one more time; we just want to hear your voice.

Who were these people? What were they doing up at three thirty in the morning? Then it hit him. They were people just like him, listening to the radio because they couldn't sleep, because they were lonely. Did they know something he didn't know?

He got to thinking: What if it *was* the world's last night? What would he do? If he called the station, who would be listening? His daughters? They were all too far away, and they wouldn't be listening anyway. Besides, if he wanted to call them, he'd call them at home; at least he could reach Meg at her home. But what about Helen?

It was a foolish impulse, but he yielded to it like a man yielding to a sudden and irresistible temptation. He picked up the phone, dialed 9, and then the number of the station. It rang four times and then someone answered—not Helen or Bob but an operator who was taking the calls. There were three people ahead of him, she said, could he hang on? She took his name and put him on hold and he started to hear music, a song he hadn't heard in years:

Dee-eee-ee-e-eep river,
my home lies O-O-ver Jor-do-uh-uhn.
Dee-eee-ee-e-eep river, Looord;
I want to cross over into campground.

It was a song the men's chorus used to sing at the campground in Berrien Springs, where he'd gone with his folks every summer when he was a kid. He was thinking about the campground—the wooden cabins, unpainted and sagging, and the white porcelain chamber pots, and the men's deep voices—when the operator told him he was about to go on the air, and then he was on, and Bob was saying, "Hello? Rudy? Hello? Rudy, are you there?" And Rudy, suddenly finding himself short of breath, said, "I've got a message for my wife, Helen. Helen, this is Rudy, if you can hear me, please call me. I'm in Mission, Texas. The number is"—he had to look closely at the phone to get the number—"Cyprus 3-5926. I love you. Good-bye."

He hung up the phone immediately. He'd heard his own voice on the radio just a fraction of a second or so after he spoke the words, as if someone else in the room had been repeating the words right after him, and then Bob was thanking him and taking the next call.

Rudy went to the bathroom again, tied the belt of his robe around his waist, and went out for another Dr Pepper, something to clear the cobwebs out of his throat. When he came back in he lay down on the bed and nursed the Dr Pepper as he listened to the calls that kept coming in. He could hear the phones ringing in the studio, and a couple of times, just as he was drifting off to sleep, he woke up with a start, thinking that the phone beside the bed was ringing, that someone was trying to reach him. But when he picked up the receiver, all he got was a dial tone. By the time Bob and Helen signed off and went home to wait for the Second Coming with their families, he was fast asleep.

The property Rudy had come to look at was an avocado grove about twenty miles outside of Mission. He picked up the real estate agent at an office on the edge of town and they followed the county highway to a place called Parrotville, where there was a general store and a couple of mobile homes and a fork in the road. The real estate agent, whose name was Barney, indicated the right fork, pointing with his whole arm, his hand held flat, vertical, as if he were giving himself directions. Barney was too big for the little Honda; his stomach rubbed against the dash; he had to spread out his knees and cross his feet over each other, and his head kept banging against the roof. But he didn't complain. He filled the silence with his plans for golf courses, hospitals, retirement communities, condominiums—all the things Rudy was trying to get away from. But what bothered Rudy was that Barney seemed to have an instinctive understanding of what he, Rudy himself, wanted. He expressed himself in a quasi-poetic style: "It's a great thing to live on the land," he said. "There's times of heartache and weariness, but there's times of great satisfaction too. Be your own man, your own boss. Live your own life. See the sun come up in the morning, when everything's still. Go out into the trees at night; hear them grow. See the fruit ripen. It's like you're part of nature, part of the great plan of things." He spoke without looking at Rudy, who was looking in the rearview mirror at the trail of dust they were leaving behind them.

Rudy had in fact felt some of these things, but he hadn't put them into words. The words made him uncomfortable.

Made the whole thing seem sad and pathetic, like putting a panther in a dirty little cage. Pretty soon the poor thing gets dispirited and just lies there. Something like that happened to Rudy. He was trying to recover the feeling that had led him to Texas in the first place, a feeling that he could only compare to spreading one's wings, as if one were a bird preparing to take off and leave the world behind. But it was like trying to conjure up an erection when you're tired and nervous and hungover and you ask yourself, *What am I doing here? What on earth am I doing here?* It really was pathetic, wasn't it? An old man expecting that there was still some extraordinary happiness in store for him. And foolish. He had a job, a house, family, friends. His old life began to call out to him, to present itself to his imagination in warm, rich colors. Gus Agostino had been good to him. He would miss the South Water Street Market with its big awnings, the fruit and vegetables piled up on the sloping sidewalks, the hum of the rollers, the chuffing of the big trucks, the clatter of dice in Neumann's Market Bar.

He'd miss his house too, the polished parquetry—scratched by the dogs but still beautiful—of the dining room floor, with its shadow effects created by different kinds of wood; the butcher's table in the kitchen; the eyebrow windows; the balcony; all the work he'd done—the new soil pipe, a downstairs bathroom, insulation, painting, the curved storm windows he'd built himself; Helen's bookcases with their funny arches like the curve of some Italian bridge, he could never remember which; the bricks in the patio, which Helen called a *terrazza*; the grape arbor. All these things joined together and spoke in one voice: "You'll never escape us. You're rooted in this house. We'll shelter you and your children and your children's children. Love and work, that's what we represent. Your history, your past is embedded here. This is where you belong. You can't escape us now."

The previous owner of the avocado grove had died of a heart attack six months earlier, but his widow hadn't cleaned out his office, which was at the back of the house. A window opened onto the grove, about three hundred acres. The advertisement had described the trees as "mature," and Rudy had been afraid he'd find that they were past their prime, but they were in good shape, twenty-five to thirty feet high, alternating rows of Fuerte and Hass, well spaced. Rudy sat at the dead man's desk, going over the records—irrigation, fertilization, crop production—which were kept in big cardboard boxes with orange backs with LETTERS printed on them. You sometimes see boxes like that in lawyers' offices. Each one was marked NOV. 1—OCT. 31—the avocado calendar—followed by the year, starting in 1945.

He could hear Barney talking to the widow, Mrs. Wilson, in the kitchen. They were drinking coffee, and she kept coming in to fill up his cup. Barney said she was considering several offers, but Rudy didn't believe him. She looked anxious, eager to sell.

Rudy had done his homework; he'd studied the *Avocado Grower's Handbook*, gotten advice (much of it contradictory) from growers and shippers and brokers whom he'd done business with over the years. He'd brought a checklist with him, and he went down the list item by item: PCPs in the water supply, irrigation records, fertilization history, amount of allowable tipburn caused by the nitrogen in the fertilizer, production leaf analysis, chlorides and sodium in the irrigation water, the age and quality and type of irrigation system, the dollar returns per acre, market accessibility, labor, how much water was necessary to leach the salts out of the soil. He'd gotten a soil profile and a history of low-register thermometer readings in the winter from the Soil Conservation Service of the USDA.

But neither the records of the grove nor the county agent nor the former owner's widow could tell him what he really needed to know: would he be happy here?

Out the window he could see a tractor pulling a wagon up the gentle slope of a hill; he could see the pickers on the ladders with their avocado shears; he could see the wagon silhouetted at the top of the slope. He put the boxes marked LETTERS back in order on the shelves, noticing, as he did so, a big Latin dictionary just like Helen's.

The county agent was talking to one of the pickers about halfway up the hill. He was pointing and gesturing. Rudy and Barney walked toward them, side by side. Barney was puffing. The county agent, who was collecting soil samples with a tube, was speaking in Spanish. Rudy listened. He thought he could almost make out what they were saying. But the soil samples weren't necessary; he could feel the loose loamy soil under his feet. And he'd checked out the banks by the side of the road.

He looked at his watch. Eleven seventeen. In eight minutes it would be sunrise in Jerusalem. He gave a little laugh that came out like a hiccup. He started to make a joke about the Second Coming. He wanted to tell somebody, anybody, about the letter from his nephew, about the radio program. But something stopped him, a counter-impulse. He turned and started to walk up the hill. "I got to take a leak," he said. He wanted to wait it out alone. Not that he thought anything was going to happen. Not that at all. But he wanted to think for a minute by himself.

From the top of the hill—not much of a hill, a kind of shallow bluff with a slight drop—he could see in the valley beneath him a river stretching from one horizon to another like a ribbon wrapped around the earth. A ribbon that hadn't been pulled tight or that had worked itself loose. The Rio Grande. This was the Rio Grande Valley after all. The Rio Grande was the reason he wasn't standing in the middle of a desert. But he hadn't counted on it adjoining his property. It wasn't like anything he'd ever seen. It was mud colored but shining too, a smooth surface reflecting the bright sunlight. He was so overwhelmed that he forgot for a moment that he had to take a leak. He looked at his watch again. Eleven twenty-one. If you were going to wait for the end of the world, where would you want to be? The radio hostess had advised people to stay in their living rooms, but Rudy thought he'd found a better vantage place. He unzipped his fly and watered the ground, tracing a big *R*, for Rudy. Eleven twenty-three. Two minutes. He watched the second hand on his watch, sweeping time before it, sweeping the seconds away, describing by its movement a mysterious dividing line between past and present. It was a long two minutes; it was like waiting for an egg to boil. You sometimes feel there's time to write a letter or read a novel or go out and rake the yard. Come *on*. But you can't do anything about it. *What would it be like?* he wondered. The Second Coming/nuclear holocaust. Which would be worse? He had forty seconds left to think about it. His mind suddenly started racing, traversing his whole life—his wedding day, the births of his children, the death of his wife. And that only took up two seconds. He had thirty-eight seconds to go, an eternity. He counted them: thirty-seven, thirty-six, thirty-five, but he was too impatient. He felt in his pocket for the keys to the rental car. They were there okay. His wallet was okay too, but it was too fat; there was too much junk in it. He took it out of his pocket and checked the hundred-dollar bill he'd folded up and stuck in the section behind his credit cards. Seven seconds to go. One one thousand, two one thousand, three one thousand, four one thousand, five one thousand, six one thousand, seven! Eight. Nine. Ten. Rudy waited another minute, just to make sure, before heading back down the hill.

The county agent was jotting something down with a pencil on a pad of paper. Barney was lighting a cigar. Rudy kicked a rock, and they both looked up at him, looking for a sign. He shrugged his shoulders. He didn't want them to know that he'd decided to buy the property. He didn't want them to know that in the twinkling of an eye, just like that, the old world had vanished, and a new one had been set in its place.

SNAPSHOTS OF APHRODITE

ROSALIND WAS A ROSE garden in flames, DiVita an indefatigable gardener, grafting new pleasures on the ancient stock, forcing them in the hothouse of desire to burst precociously into searing colors. The afternoon clerk at the Delta Towers pulled his thin lips back against his yellow teeth; the old men dozing in wingback chairs stirred and twitched their noses, old dogs smelling a bitch in heat, as she walked across the lobby, her sandals clicking like castanets on the parquet, her young woman's haunches swaying like long-stemmed roses in a summer breeze, her young woman's smells concentrated in an alembic of *O Glory Hallelujah*, thought DiVita, fingering the elevator button, summoning a chariot to carry them up to the gates of paradise—a room on the fifteenth floor of the Delta Towers Hotel. Fifteen dollars for the afternoon. A real bargain.

"What does she put on her cunt?" Cosmo, the bartender at the Casino on Taylor Street had asked him. "You can smell it a mile away. It would wake the dead." He'd raised his fingertips to his nose. "Wait till your pal finds out you've been dicking his wife."

Rosalind's husband, Graham, a distinguished scholar with an international reputation, DiVita's mentor and friend, was a good man—a deeply religious man, that is—who brought reason to bear upon his passions and desires. Such a man might have conversed with philosopher kings or banqueted with the blessed saints; but how could he have married his graduate assistant, an Italian girl half his age? And how could a girl like Rosalind have fallen for a man with a monk's tonsure and a game leg? Though DiVita knew that some girls were attracted to gimps.

They had been married two years, and she had just published a naughty story in *The Gargoyle*, the campus literary magazine, and Graham had threatened to paddle her if she pulled another stunt like that again; he'd put a stop to it in a mighty big hurry, he'd said. He'd threatened to put a private detective on her tail; and every morning he'd drive her across town to the Newberry Library, where she would check the footnotes for the long-awaited second volume of his *History of the Investiture Controversy*. In the evenings he'd pick her up at the front door of the library, unless he was prevented from doing so by his busy schedule. In which case he'd send DiVita.

"It's just a story, Graham," DiVita had tried to explain, but Graham taught history, not fiction.

"Just a story? Nobody could make up something like *that*."

"Graham, she's twenty-five years old."

But Graham had waved the question of age aside. "There are places in Africa where they'd put her in a sack with a chicken and a snake and a dog and toss her into the river."

DiVita didn't see the sense of it. But he was alarmed, and not without reason. Graham had bought a gun, a pistol, a .38 special snub nose with a two-inch barrel. He'd taken DiVita up to his bedroom to show him.

* * *

The fifteenth floor of the Delta Towers had originally been furnished in the style of a turn-of-the-century bordello, and some of the furnishings remained: velvet upholsteries, faded but opulent; lacquered wallpapers with erotic motifs; four-posters; and beveled cheval glasses in every room.

"Okay, Mister, this is going to be the supreme test, and if you fail . . ."

"Jesus, Rossi, where do you get this stuff?"

"I don't get it out of a book, I'll tell you that."

Did she get it from Graham? DiVita rejected the idea instinctively.

"Where do you get it?"

"Shut up," she said. "I'll do the talking. If only you could see yourself now!"

DiVita knew that it couldn't last, knew that something would happen, something as inevitable as the hour of death. He expected that Graham would discover one of the notes that DiVita left in her pockets and purse. Or someone at the Newberry would get wind of it, or someone would see them coming out of the Delta Towers. He foresaw a scandal, a storm of outrage and indignation, and, at the eye of the hurricane, jealousy—so fair, she was, laughter-loving Aphrodite. Who would not have risked Hephaestus's golden net for a turn in her bed? What actually happened, however, was totally unexpected, and failed to have the immediate result that DiVita anticipated.

What actually happened was that they were photographed in their hotel room. The door was opened with a passkey, and the security chain was snipped with a menacing tool like the beak of a large and terrible bird, though DiVita didn't really get a very good look at it. He didn't move, couldn't move, for

Rosalind had secured him to the four-poster with two pairs of Fogal dot stockings.

The men who photographed them were not professionals—they had trouble with the electronic flash, and one of them dropped the camera—but they shot an entire roll of film—twenty exposures—while Rosalind, thrusting her bare chest forward defiantly, swore at them in their own language: *"Non mi rompere le palle."*

Afterward the lovers stopped for drinks at the Palmer House. "What can he do?"

"He could do plenty," Rosalind said. Rosalind, who had taken everything very coolly, was beginning to crack. It would take more than a couple of drinks to get them through the rest of the day. DiVita pictured the two of them lying on the living room floor, pools of blood, Graham on the phone in the butler's pantry, turning himself in.

"Not if we can get past the first couple of minutes."

In the end they decided that there was nothing for it but to anticipate the arrival of the photos by making a full confession, throwing themselves on Graham's mercy.

But that sort of thing was not possible, because they neither knew what they wanted nor what they intended to do. DiVita, in fact, could not think beyond the next, say, thirty-five minutes, depending on traffic. The Marshall Field's clock said ten after five. Thirty-five minutes. It was like waiting for a bomb to explode. You couldn't know what you would do afterward, but you would do something, if you were still alive. And everything would be changed. Yes. But how? That was the question.

On Graham's doorstep—the threshold of a new life—they hesitated a moment before bearding the lion; but the lion, his face beaming, greeted them with such cordiality that they lost the initiative, if indeed they ever had it. It would have been impossible to interrupt his geniality with such a sordid tale; or perhaps it was that they had not decided how the subject should be broached, or who would do the broaching, or perhaps it was easier to sink down into the sofa cushions and let fate take its own course instead of trying to meddle with it. Such were DiVita's thoughts. And he allowed himself to entertain the possibility that the men had broken into the wrong room, and that it had all been a mistake, and that the photos wouldn't turn out anyway. Perhaps the shutter had jammed; perhaps the lens had been damaged. He tried to recall the precise sound the camera had made when it fell, listened to his memory for a crunching or cracking sound, for the small tinkle of a delicate Christmas tree ornament shattering on the carpet.

Graham poured drinks and prepared hors d'oeuvres—artichoke bottoms spread with capers and homemade mayonnaise. The *Esperanza*, he said—part of a recent bequest—had docked at the Jackson Park Yacht Club, where it would remain for a decent interval before being sold. In the meantime, the dean had invited them all for a picnic lunch on board. Graham, sitting down heavily on the sofa, put a hand on DiVita's knee. "You're in."

It was the dean who would act upon the department's recommendation regarding DiVita's tenure. Either the university would open its arms to enfold him forever, or it would suggest, politely but firmly, that he might find greater scope elsewhere for the exercise of his talents.

"Did he *say* that, Graham?"

"No, he didn't *say* it; he couldn't *say* it, *now*, not till June. But you don't think he'd invite you if he was going to give you the sack, do you?"

DiVita nodded ambiguously. He had always assumed that

Graham would remove this obstacle from his path, just as he had removed others.

They drank more wine while Graham broiled steaks on the Weber grill.

It was chilly outside, but Graham's dining room with its Baccarat crystal chandelier and oak paneling was warm and cozy, elegant and romantic. The light from the chandelier, refracted from hundreds of scalloped prisms, gathered in limpid pools on the darkened glossy varnish of the lacquer and the wainscoting. After supper Graham built a coal fire in the old-fashioned grate. He had taken off his shoes, and the faint odor of his feet, encased in nylon stockings, mingled with the scent of the kindling and the crackling coal. Something tugged at DiVita's heart like a kite on a long, long string, a string so long you couldn't make out the kite at all. Everything seemed possible. They could talk it over together, work it out. He glanced at Rosalind. Was she thinking the same thing? He wanted to speak to her alone for just a minute, had to, to coordinate their timing, their plans, signals. But when Graham went into the kitchen to make coffee, and DiVita followed her into the tiny downstairs john, she said, "Are you crazy? Are you out of your mind?" She was frightened, upset. "Get out of here," she said. "I can't pee when you're standing there watching."

Friday came and still no photographs. Walgreens, DiVita had observed, offered same-day service for an extra charge, but surely they wouldn't have them developed at Walgreens. Wasn't there a law against that sort of thing? But of course there were no doubt outfits that would develop anything overnight, no questions asked. Nonetheless, DiVita's hope was turning into a settled conviction: the photographs had not turned out. He would have to be careful not to get caught a second time. They would have to find a safer pied-à-terre, or he could buy one of those little devices that he had seen advertised in mail order catalogs that you put on a hotel door to prevent break-ins. Maybe a new life wouldn't be necessary after all.

But on Saturday morning, when Graham swung his new Oldsmobile into the back parking lot at the Jackson Park Yacht Club, where DiVita had been making small talk with the Singletons—the dean and his wife—he knew at once that he had been deceiving himself and that the grace period was over. Graham, dressed for the occasion in white duck trousers and a dark blue double-breasted serge jacket, had come alone. His face was flushed, and he seemed to be having trouble breathing. DiVita, afraid to ask where Rosalind was, waited for the Singletons to express their curiosity; but the Singletons maintained a discreet silence.

DiVita should have spoken sooner, should have broken the news over a drink. *It would have been easy enough,* he thought as he looked back and remembered how congenial the three of them had all been, drinking red wine with their porterhouse steaks. But now it seemed impossible. He had given up the initiative without a struggle. He closed his eyes and tried to picture the photographs, tried to see them through Graham's eyes. But he couldn't, and he was afraid like a child about to be spanked. But he was afraid for Graham too, afraid that there were limits to goodness and charity, and that Graham, the best and most charitable of men, was in the process of discovering those limits, discovering within himself what lay on the other side of goodness and charity. *Well, why not?* DiVita thought. He knew the territory well himself. But his limits were not Graham's limits; he didn't have to go far to reach them. But he thought of Graham's limits as lying

211

much further away, marking, like the Pillars of Hercules, the boundaries of the known moral world.

The *Esperanza*, a sixty-foot ketch that had once won the Race to Mackinac but was now rigged for cruising, rode at anchor in fifty feet of water. Graham and the dean were both avid sailors, but DiVita, who didn't know a yawl from a ketch, a sloop from a schooner, didn't care for water sports. He was pleased, however, when the dean produced not one but two wicker hampers from the trunk of his car and stowed them in the dinghy—a sturdy-looking flat-bottomed boat with short oarlocks, the stern of which had been pulled up on the beach. Perhaps, over a glass or two of good wine. Surely Graham did not intend to confront him in the presence of the dean and his wife. On the other hand, maybe that was exactly what Graham had in mind: a public humiliation, a fitting end to his career at the university. Why else wouldn't he have simply called the dean and said they couldn't come?

His immediate concern, however, was to secure a place in the dinghy so as not to be left alone with Graham. He wanted to speak to Rosalind, but where was she? What had Graham *done* with her? *To* her?

Graham, who was inflating his new canoe with a foot pump, called to the Singletons to go ahead in the dinghy. He and DiVita would paddle out in the canoe, he said. DiVita, who had already settled himself in the dinghy, rose to obey. He was getting a headache, and he had to go to the bathroom.

"Give us a push," said the dean. "Just let us get settled first."

The little boat scrunched on the sand and then floated free. The dean pulled on the oars a couple of strokes before tipping the blue-green Evinrude motor into the water and pushing the electric starter. DiVita could hardly distinguish the sound of the motor from the buzzing in his own ears.

The sand clung to DiVita's wet sneakers as he walked slowly up the beach to the spot where Graham was inflating the canoe, which had by now assumed its true form, actually that of a pointed canoe rather than the rounded rubber raft DiVita had expected.

"About got it?" he said, looking at Graham and then down again at the pulsating canoe.

Graham kept pumping.

"Want me to do that for a while?"

Graham kept pumping.

The left side of the canoe, to which the hose from the pump was connected, was as shiny and tight as the skin of a drum, but by the time Graham unscrewed the hose—the escaping air hissed like a startled snake—and screwed on the cap, it had begun to sag like the right side.

"There ought to be a better way," DiVita offered. "Did you read the instructions?"

Graham kicked the boat with his game leg. "It'll do," he said, and then he added, "Marco, I want to have a talk with you." His voice quiet but uneven.

"What's up?" It was DiVita's turn to kick the boat, which didn't look very seaworthy to him. "Aren't there any life jackets for this thing?" Even now, now that the moment was upon him, he couldn't help stalling, even if it would gain only a few seconds, even if the decent thing to do would be to speak honestly: *My intentions are honorable, Graham. I just didn't know how to break it to you; remember the woman taken in adultery? What was it again that Christ said? And the man, too. Whatever became of him?*

"They're in the car."

"I'll get them."

"Don't bother." It was an order. The imperative mood. "We won't need them. It's not that far out there."

"Isn't it against the law or something?" It was all very well for Graham, an excellent swimmer, to do without a life jacket, but DiVita felt differently. "I'm not much of a swimmer, Graham," he said.

"Odd, you know; you're such a good athlete."

"It's all right. I've got to go up to the bathroom anyway."

"You can go on the *Esperanza*."

"What about the pump? I'll run it up to the car."

"We'll take it with us. We may need it."

DiVita would have preferred to have it out on dry land, but he couldn't bring himself to speak or to give Graham an opening, so they carried the lightweight canoe down to the lip of the water. Graham was tongue-tied too, able to issue negative commands but not to say what was on his mind.

If the boat had had more air in it, it wouldn't have sat so low in the water, wouldn't have been quite so unstable. But there was nothing to be done about it now. DiVita tried to keep perfectly still as he paddled first on one side and then the other with a short-handled paddle.

"You've got to feather the blade," said Graham. "Just turn the paddle a little as you finish your stroke—and stay on one side or the other; don't keep switching back and forth. I'll do the navigating."

DiVita, kneeling in the bottom of the canoe, braced himself against a curved wooden shelf mounted on one of the struts that kept the frame rigid. He could not see Graham, nor could he hear the sound of Graham's paddle, which cut noiselessly, like the blade of a knife, into the gray-green folds of the lake, but he could feel Graham's powerful thrusts propelling them farther and farther away from the shore, and when Graham stopped paddling and the canoe began to curve to the left in response to his own splashy efforts, he imagined the thin edge of Graham's paddle descending in a clean arc, splitting his head wide open. King Mark splitting Tristan's head open with a long-handled battle axe. DiVita tried to head the boat toward the *Esperanza*, but Graham, using his own paddle as a rudder, steered them out toward the opening in the breakwater.

"Marco?"

Too far out for comfort.

"Marco, there's something I want to show you, something I want you to explain. Something I hope you can explain. Something that has upset me very much. I can't tell you how much."

"Jesus, Graham, can't it wait? I've got to take a leak in the worst way."

"You can take a leak over the side, Marco. We'll swing around to the starboard side of this little cabin cruiser here so no one can see you. Except me, of course."

"Graham, forget it. Let's just get to the *Esperanza*, for Christ's sake." But Graham with a single stroke of the paddle had given the canoe a ninety-degree turn and was thrusting forward with long smooth strokes.

They went out farther and farther, putting the cabin cruiser—the *Wait 'n' Sea*—between them and the *Esperanza*. DiVita tried to imagine someone coming out of the cabin yelling at them, offering drinks. But the boat was all trussed up like a chicken waiting to be roasted.

"You can take your leak now." Graham brought the canoe to a standstill. "Better stay down on your knees."

As he knelt sideways in the canoe, DiVita glanced at Graham, trying to read his intentions without meeting his gaze. He fumbled with his zipper and extricated himself with some difficulty from his underpants. His penis had shrunk under Graham's gaze to the size of his little finger, to the size of a carrot stick on an hors d'oeuvres tray. He waited, his knees pressing into the bottom of the boat so sharply that the front end was forced up into the air like the prow of a Viking ship. When he raised his right leg to shield himself from Graham's gaze, his left knee thrust down even harder and the side of the boat dipped under the water. He tried to shift his weight again, to pull back from the side of the canoe, but before he knew what had happened, he was tilting forward, as if the floor on which he was kneeling had suddenly given way. The lake rose up to meet him, offered only a slight resistance, a thin shock of cold which supported him for a moment, like a skin of ice, before giving way. He moved in slow motion, struggling against the heavy clothing that carried him down, his corduroy pants, his Princeton rugger shirt, his badminton sneakers. When he surfaced he threw his arms up over his head, frantically, not knowing whether, in the brief interval that had been allotted him, to take in more oxygen to prepare for the ensuing struggle, or to use up the little store that remained to let Graham know that he was drowning, that he really *could not* swim.

"Help, Graham. Help," he cried, his fear overcoming his faith that in spite of everything Graham would save him. It was embarrassing to cry out like that, humiliating; but he had to let Graham know, make him understand. He went under again, lungs bursting. When he surfaced he could see Graham sitting silently not ten feet away, like a hunter in a blind. Their eyes met for an instant—a fraction of a second, no more—during which Graham seemed to hesitate as he might have hesitated on the badminton court, waiting till the last possible moment to play a difficult shot that was probably going out anyway (but you couldn't be sure, and if you played it you'd never know).

When DiVita went under again he relaxed slightly, waiting . . . Waiting for Graham to play the shot, to return his volley. Waiting for Graham, for a chance to explain. And he thought that Graham might be waiting too, waiting for him to lose consciousness lest, in the rescue attempt, DiVita grasp him with a terrible and unbreakable grip so that he, Graham, should drown too. DiVita was unbearably tired. In his heart oxygen was rapidly being replaced by carbon dioxide. The heart itself was pumping dark venous blood into his circulatory system. The veins gorged with blood. He imagined himself dead, his corpse lifted softly by invisible currents, turning and turning in slow motion, describing passionless hyperbolas.

But he was not dead, not yet, and he made a last fierce effort to climb to the surface, as if he were scrambling up a rockfall with his pockets and boots full of stones. When he reached the summit, he gasped and started to churn the water in a ridiculous dog paddle, heading not toward Graham but toward the *Wait 'n' Sea*.

Graham started after him, pulled the canoe alongside him just as they reached the *Wait 'n' Sea*. Graham raised the paddle, and DiVita, shoving the canoe away, took a glancing blow on his shoulder.

"Oh my God, oh my God," Graham cried out, bellowing like an animal.

DiVita grabbed onto the ladder, freezing, nauseous from the water he had swallowed.

"Let me get alongside you," Graham shouted.

"Fuck off, Graham. Don't come near me."

DiVita managed to climb onto the narrow gunwale of the *Wait 'n' Sea*. He could see the *Esperanza* but couldn't raise his right arm to wave. His shoulder was numb.

Graham, below him, looked up without appearing to see him or hear him or to understand the simplest language.

"Get away, Graham. Get away."

But the rubber nose of the canoe bump-bump-bumped against the ladder as Graham thrashed the water with the paddle. DiVita, like a seasick passenger, leaned over the railing and vomited.

Within ten minutes—though it seemed like an hour—the dean had picked him up in the dinghy. Graham followed them back to the *Esperanza* in the canoe. Belowdecks DiVita stripped, slipped on the dean's lightweight parka, and wrapped himself in a wool blanket. He warmed himself with hot coffee, which the dean had cooked on a Coleman stove. He spread the contents of his billfold out on the bed: credit cards, a fifty-dollar bill, notes, addresses, telephone numbers, identification, three feet of emergency dental floss wrapped around a slip of thin cardboard. He heard Graham and Mrs. Singleton coming down the ladder and Mrs. Singleton saying, "This way." The door—the hatch—of the master stateroom at the other end of the companionway opened and closed.

The water DiVita had swallowed upset his stomach, irritated the lining, but once on deck he began to talk animatedly to the dean about his inability to swim, even though he was, as Graham had said, *such a good athlete*; and he brought the conversation around to famous people who had drowned: Edward King, Margaret Fuller, Percy Bysshe Shelley.

All this to prove . . .? That it was Graham, not he, who needed to be looked after. And it was true. "He's very upset," the dean said. And the dean demonstrated how Graham had been holding his clutched fists over his chest. "Mrs. Singleton's with him," the dean said, "down in the master stateroom."

The dean went below and returned with more coffee. Mrs. Singleton followed him up the narrow ladder, her tweed skirt hiked up around her thick hips. "Graham wants to see you," she said, settling herself in a deck chair and arranging her skirt. "He's very upset now. You could have drowned, and he thinks you blame him."

Tout comprendre, c'est tout pardonner? DiVita wasn't so sure. If he began to explain, where would he stop?

"You should have come back in the canoe with him," she continued, "instead of calling for my husband. It's as if you didn't trust him anymore."

After two cups of coffee DiVita felt somewhat recovered. Even so, in the pocket of Graham's blue blazer, which was hanging on the back of Mrs. Singleton's deck chair, he could see the outline of what must be the incriminating photographs, and he began to toy with the idea of showing them to the dean and his wife. Wouldn't *that* be something? Better (or worse) than flinging off the Pendleton blanket that concealed his lower parts? But what did he want? Simply to startle the living daylights out of these good people? Or to be seen as he really was, and to be forgiven? Or condemned?

"He'll get over it," he said, standing up and stretching.

"Don't make it hard for him. You're all right, after all. There's no reason to kick up a fuss."

DiVita smiled. "I won't." He picked up Graham's jacket, tossed it over his shoulder—the numbness was giving way to a burning sensation that was not entirely unpleasant—and went below; but before going in to see Graham he ducked into the head. He knew that the balance of power had shifted; the hunter had become the hunted. He no longer had anything to fear from Graham. But he wanted to have a look at the photos.

As he was adjusting himself on the cool seat of the commode, a line from Shelley popped into his mind: *Life, like a dome of many-colored glass / Stains the white radiance of eternity.*

Poor old Shelley, he thought. They'd burned his body on the beach at Spezzia (or was it Viareggio?); Byron had been there, and someone had snatched the heart from the flames.

The color snapshots, all twenty of them, were in a plain white envelope. DiVita turned them over, one at a time like a man playing solitaire, discarding those that were too dark, too light, too blurred, till he was down to a half dozen or so, all more or less the same: Rosalind's bare chest thrust forward like the figurehead of a ship; his own face inclined toward the camera, animated by a smile that he could not remember now. Such a smile, under the circumstances, must have been doubly provoking to Graham, proverbial insult added to injury, though it hadn't been intended that way.

Did rational human beings, he asked himself, really do such things? Risk their jobs, their careers, their friendships, the esteem of their colleagues, for such moments? Of course they did. And not infrequently, either. But what could they possibly say for themselves when brought to judgment? How could they excuse themselves? How could he have smiled like that?

Judgment. Bound in nylon fetters, DiVita awaited the judgment of the wise and the good, the philosopher kings and blessed saints whose august presences seemed at that very moment to fill the tiny room with contending vapors, with strands of hair combed carefully over bald pates, with all the cumbersome paraphernalia of wisdom and goodness—scrolls and tablets and books and hooded gowns and hair shirts and strange instruments of discipline to make the senses quiver. They exchanged reproving remarks as they passed the photos back and forth, smudging and crinkling them with eager fingers. But where was Graham? It was not Graham who interrupted the excited hum and buzz, but Apollo, the lord of music and song, the giver of prophecy, the healer of bodies, the inspirer of poets, the god of light, the eye of heaven: "Hermes, my friend, how would *you* like to be trussed up like Marco and straddled by golden Aphrodite?"

"Wouldn't I though?" the great Wayfinder replied. "Tie me to the bedposts with woolen stockings three times as strong as these flimsy nylons; invite the wise and the good to see the fun; only let me lie beneath the pale-golden one!"

DiVita stood up suddenly and shook himself. *Even the wise and the good,* he thought . . . He rewrapped himself in the blanket and flushed the photos down the head, which he had to pump vigorously, before going to see if he could do anything to make it easier for Graham.

I SPEAK A LITTLE FRENCH

IT WAS DECEMBER AND I was forty-nine years old. I tried not to let it get me down, but when my daughter wrote to say that she wouldn't be coming to Florence for the holidays, I didn't see how I could hang on in Italy for another seven months. On the other hand, I didn't see how I could go home before June without losing face. After all, hadn't I always carried on about Florence as if it were the Garden of Eden, the earthly paradise, the promised land? How would I explain? What would I say? That I was lonely? That there was no one to talk to? That I had fallen from grace?

I needed to talk; I needed to get things into words, needed to get them out into the open where I could hear them. When I was a boy I had so much energy I used to say that my legs hurt from not running. That's the way I felt. My whole being hurt from not talking. So I talked to myself, told my own story to myself as I walked along the Arno in the morning on my way to the Uffizi, or on my way from the Uffizi to the British Institute in the afternoon, using a sort of *aria parlante*; and in Italian the story of my wife's affair with, and subsequent marriage to, our family dentist took on an operatic dignity that it lacked in English. The cramp of jealousy was relaxed; the sting of humiliation drawn; the ache of incomprehension eased.

Coming back to Italy after the divorce had seemed like a good idea, but things hadn't worked out the way I'd expected. The dollar was down, rents were up, and I was on leave without pay. Instead of walking home at night through narrow streets to my own little apartment in an old palazzo—inconvenient but interesting—I found myself living in a furnished room—no cooking privileges—in the very upper left-hand corner of the map, an hour's ride from the Piazza dell'Olio, where I picked up the number twenty-three bus. I sent postcards to everyone in Italy with whom I'd ever exchanged addresses during a sabbatical year, but by the end of October I had received only two invitations. Instead of juggling a busy social schedule, I found myself eating salami sandwiches in my room. I entertained myself with the fantasy of finding an Italian wife, someone stunning and raven-haired, someone who still believed in the sanctity of family life, someone I could talk to. But no such someone materialized, and I found myself stretched out on my bed looking through the personals in *La Pulce*:

RAGAZZA 38enne, carina, colta, sensibile, estrema pulizia morale, cerca uomo stessi requisiti, per un rapporto affettivo serio ed eventuale matrimonio, gradita foto restituibile e telefono. F. P. C. F1 P.A. 281.901.1/P

But at the last minute I lost my nerve; instead of sending the photo that I'd taken of myself at one of the automatic machines outside the station, I signed up for cooking lessons in the basement of the Istituto Culturale, where I learned to prepare a number of elaborate dishes, including pumpkin soup and truffled capon, which I'd never eaten before and have never eaten since.

I'd reserved a double room for Alison—my daughter—at the small Albergo Medici on the Arno, not far from the Biblioteca Nazionale, but I put off canceling the reservation till the very last minute—till the night of her intended arrival, in fact. The night clerk, Volmaro, with whom I'd discussed her visit several times, refused to return my deposit, and we had a regular Italian argument with shouting and gesturing. Afterward, nervous and upset, I took one street and then another and soon found myself at the little Piazza San Pier Maggiore, where I had a drink at the *bettola* under the Volta di San Piero—a vaulted passageway containing part of the medieval city wall. It was one of the few places in the city where men gathered to drink in silence, as they do in American bars, though the *bettola* was so small that the patrons had to stand outside.

I drank a glass of cheap red wine, then another, and then a third. From where I was standing I could see the *friggitoria* where Bill—Bill is my son—and Alison had spent their pocket money on French fries and hamburgers; I could see the bakery where I'd bought bread every morning and the *latteria* and the *pizzicheria* and the lit windows of our old apartment. I had another glass of wine and then I had one of those revelations that come from time to time to almost everyone who drinks more than occasionally: every-thing suddenly becomes sparkling clear, like a fruit tart painted with apricot glaze; you see things as they are; you experience viscerally what you've known all along: that you should return good for evil; that material possessions aren't important; that in the light of our mortality what's really important is love.

At least that's the way it was with me that night. I was overwhelmed with love for all humankind: for my six or seven drinking companions who, like me, had their collars turned up against the cold, for distant friends, for my children, for my enemies (i.e., my wife and her husband, D.D.S.).

Spurious? Undoubtedly, but my immediate problem was that wisdom of this sort demands expression. The emotions become too big for the body and need to be released through the mouth.

Which I opened and said, not addressing anyone in particular, "That Baggio is really something, isn't he?" (Baggio was a sort of Florentine Michael Jordan; I didn't really care for soccer, but I read the sports pages in *La Repubblica* so I'd have something to talk about.) "Three goals in three minutes," I said. There were some grunts of agreement in response, but no actual words. "Against Napoli," I said. "Must be some kind of a record."

I was about to order another glass of wine when I noticed a young woman crossing the piazza dragging the largest suitcase I'd ever seen. The suitcase had wheels on it so that you could pull it down long airport corridors, but the wheels were too small for the rough paving bricks of the piazza, and the suitcase kept tipping over like a large dog that keeps flopping itself down. She wasn't able to go twenty feet without the suitcase falling, and it was so big and heavy she had trouble setting it upright again. I stepped out from under the *volta* to get a better look, and when she saw me in the light of the piazza, she cried out, *"Acqua, acqua."*

I shrugged my shoulders. After all, there were two bars in the piazza, in addition to the *bettola*. We were in the center of a modern city, not in the middle of the desert.

"Acqua, acqua."

I could hear the tears in her voice.

"Acqua Arno," she said, and it dawned on me that she was looking for the river.

"Right down Via Verdi," I said in Italian, pointing in the direction of Via Verdi and indicating that she should turn to the right.

The suitcase tipped over again and this time she left it. *"Acqua Arno,"* she repeated.

"Parla Italiano?" I asked, helping her right the suitcase.

"Acqua Arno."

"English?"

"Je suis française."

"Ahi," I said. *"Non parla italiano? O inglese?"*

"Française," she repeated. *"Je suis française."*

I'd had two years of French in college and said the first thing that popped into my head. *"Je peux parler un peu de français."*

"Dieu merci." A look of relief rose to her face. *"Je cherche l'Arno, s'il vous plaît . . ."* She kept going, but too fast for me to follow. Quite naturally she expected more, but unfortunately there was no more. To her rapid questions I could make only a single response: *"Je peux parler un peu de français"*—I can speak a little French—which I kept repeating, hoping that something would click. But nothing clicked. I was imprisoned in a single phrase. What had looked like an open door was a trompe l'oeil.

"Acqua Arno?" This time it was a tentative question. She had given up. She was a damsel in distress, and I was her knight-errant; but without the sword of language I couldn't come to her rescue, so I pointed her once again in the direction of Via Verdi, extending my arm toward the river—

acqua Arno—and watched as she crossed the piazza. As she approached Via Verdi the enormous suitcase teetered, tottered, and fell over again. She struggled to set it on its wheels, and then she disappeared around the corner and was gone.

Je peux parler un peu de français. It was ridiculous. It was maddening. *Je peux parler un peu de français.* It didn't occur to me at the time that if I'd gone on in French, in school, instead of switching to Italian I'd probably be in Paris instead of Florence, or that if she had spoken Italian, she wouldn't be in the middle of the piazza asking for *acqua Arno.* No, all I could think of was that my whole life had been leading up to this point, *and I'd studied the wrong language.*

I caught up with her in front of the Banca del Lavoro on Via Verdi. I hadn't made a decision; I'd just paid for another glass of wine, and then, without drinking it, I'd started to run after her. She hadn't gotten far because of the suitcase. Between the two of us, we managed to keep it upright—two police officers escorting a troublesome drunk—until we reached the river.

"*Pension,*" she said, looking up and down the *lungarno.*

"*Pensione,*" I said, not knowing if she had a particular *pensione* in mind or if she were looking for a *pensione,* any *pensione.* "*Indirizzo,*" I said. Address. No response. "Uhndrezz." I gave the English word a French twist, but she didn't understand.

The third week in December was not cold as we understand cold in Chicago, but it was chilly and I thought the French woman needed more clothes, warmer clothes.

The small *albergo* where I'd reserved a room for my daughter was not far away, just past the Biblioteca Nazionale.

Since I hadn't collected my deposit earlier in the evening—I'd paid in advance for two nights—I considered the room reserved.

Volmaro, with whom I had quarreled bitterly only an hour earlier, gave me a puzzled look, as if there'd been some mistake. "Professore," he said. "Your daughter has arrived after all?"

I explained the situation and Volmaro smiled. Nothing enigmatic, just a smile.

"You can put my deposit toward her bill."

"Of course, but let me remind you that the policy of the hotel . . ."

"Please." I interrupted him. "Let me help you with the suitcase and I'll be on my way."

Together we maneuvered the suitcase up a small flight of stairs to the elevator landing while the French woman watched, her image reflected ad infinitum in a pair of gilt mirrors on opposite sides of the landing. She was a woman in her mid-thirties, dressed from top to toe in the very latest fashions: a short jacket, cinched at the waist, leggings that were soft and clingy. She had forest green boots on her feet; her hair had been dyed a metallic copper color; and on her wrist she wore a bulky Russian watch. She was more fashionable than beautiful. But she was beautiful too.

Volmaro pushed a button and the elevator door clanked open and he rolled the suitcase into the elevator and my left knee began to quiver and quite suddenly I remembered another phrase in French. It came to me as a gift, rising to the surface like a cork that's been held underwater: *"Dans le fonds des forêts votre image me suis."* In the depths of the forest your image follows me. It was a line from Racine, something that had stuck in my mind, because as a young man I'd once written it on one of those little cards that florists give you when you send flowers.

She colored slightly and smiled.

"Alle undici," I said. Eleven o'clock. I held up two forefingers, side by side.

"Onze?" she said.

"Onze," I repeated. *"Qui."* I pointed at the floor, the ceiling, the four walls.

"Ici," she said, nodding her head as she stepped backward into the elevator.

In the morning I bought a shirt and a pair of corduroy pants at Raspini, across from the Baptistery. There was a jacket in the window, too, a really splendid jacket. I'd never seen such a jacket before, rich dark-chocolaty suede, soft as butter. It fit perfectly, but it wasn't really any warmer than my Windbreaker. It was totally impractical, in fact; DO NOT WASH read a tag, in English, that I pulled out of the inside pocket; DO NOT DRY-CLEAN. And the salesman admitted that it would be ruined by rain. Besides, it was outrageously expensive—I could have spent two weeks in Rome for what it cost—and when I asked, just to double-check, I found that the price in the window was incorrect. The jacket really cost a great deal more, so I settled for a green silk scarf, which I knotted around my neck like a tie.

Leaving my jeans and turtleneck at Raspini to be picked up later, I crossed Via Cavour and admired my new clothes in the window of the Mazocco bookstore, where I picked out a French–Italian dictionary that was small enough to fit into my jacket pocket and included a brief outline of French grammar. I also bought a Michelin Guide to the city, in French. Then I made my way to the *albergo,* where I found the French woman waiting in the lobby, dressed in black stockings, a short apricot-colored skirt, and a flowery silk blouse. Her makeup, minimal but skillfully applied, matched the skirt.

"Bonjour, madame," I said.

"Bonjour, monsieur."

I gave her a complete tour of Santa Croce, because it was close, and because I didn't know what else to do, and because I had the *Guide Michelin* and could read to her in French, which took her so completely by surprise that she laughed and covered her mouth with her hand, on which I noticed a ring. The more I read, the more she laughed; but when, embarrassed, I handed *her* the book, she handed it back. *"Lisez,"* she said. *"Lisez."*

It was one o'clock by the time we left the church. I ordered sandwiches—*schiacciatta* with *prosciutto arosto* and *pecorino* and *salsa di funghi*—in a bar in Piazza San Pier Maggiore, and while she ate I read aloud from the guidebook: "'The tower that dominates the piazza was built by the Donati family at the beginning of the thirteenth century. In 1308 Corso Donati, captain of the Black Guelphs and brother of Piccarda, Dante's inconstant nun, was besieged in the tower by his enemies. In an attempt to escape he was dragged to his death by his own horses on the present-day Via Pietrapiana.'"

I could understand the guidebook French because the subject matter was familiar; but I couldn't talk, couldn't put together a sentence, couldn't tell her that I myself had lived in that very tower with my family, that I used to stand in the window with a glass of Gallo Nero, waiting for my wife to come back from I Tatti, how she'd get off the bus in front of the post office looking beautiful in the red dress I'd bought for her on the Via Tornabuoni, how happy we'd been then, that my image of happiness was bound up with that tower apartment, with that piazza, with the *pizzicheria*, the *forno*, the *latteria*, and the *polleria*, even the dry cleaner with its peculiar odor; and how our neighbors and the teachers at the language school and the parents of the children's classmates and even people I met on the bus had been happy to sit at our table, to talk: food, love, philosophy, religion. But I tried, with a handful of words from my French–Italian dictionary: *famille, femme, enfants, appartement, convives, table, manger, parler*. She leaned forward so as not to drop crumbs in her lap. *"Heureux,"* I said. She looked at me thoughtfully, the way an adult would look at a child who was trying to explain a complicated dream that he didn't fully understand.

She nodded. She was a nodder, and she nodded that evening in the Trattoria Maremmana, where my wife and I, on our last night in Florence, asked if we could have the last of our *bistecca alla fiorentina* for our dog, and the waiter, after he'd taken our plates, brought us a large sack full of old bones: *femme, dernier nuit, bistecca, bourse pour les os, garçon, os pour le chien.*

That night I made a frontal assault on the French language: I studied the grammar in my dictionary, conjugated *parler, finir,* and *répondre* in the present indicative (which is all you really need), memorized a list of irregular verbs, reviewed prepositions from *à* to *vers,* tried to formulate some hypothetical phrases, and fell asleep with the dictionary in my hand.

In the morning we went to the Uffizi. Aesthetic response is my special subject, my academic raison d'être. What is aesthetic experience like? Why do we value it? How can we translate it into words? After four months it was nice to experience the real thing again—the tug of beauty like the tug of a kite on a long string. If only I could speak—if only I could tell her—but all I could do was read from the *Guide Michelin*—clichés as universal as international traffic signs: *cette Venus couchée . . . symphonie harmonieuse de coleurs . . . intense et vibrant . . . chiaroscuro doucement modelé . . . le realisme du petit chien endormi sur le lit . . .*

Her response was more physical, and when she took my arm for the first time, a French phrase rose to the surface of my imagination, one of the first things a young man learns or figures out in French 101: *Voulez-vous coucher avec moi? But surely,* I thought, vous *is the formal form. Wouldn't you ask such a question with a* tu?

At lunch I posed some of the questions I had formulated the evening before. She answered absently, paying more attention to her slippery bucatini, which sent tomato sauce splattering off in all directions, than to me. Her name was Yvonne. She was from Dijon. She was on holiday. She worked for an architectural firm . . . But I couldn't figure out what I really wanted to know: Why had she come to Florence alone? How had she landed in Piazza San Pier Maggiore with her enormous suitcase?

In the afternoon I wanted her to notice how the streets in the city center run at right angles to each other—the old Roman castrum—but she led me back to the *pensione.* Her room was dark. I opened the shutters. I needed air and light. She sat on the edge of the bed and I thumbed through my dictionary, searching for the words I needed to explain that it was perfectly all right just the way it was: to talk . . . that it wasn't necessary . . . that in all the years I'd been married I'd never . . . that I really didn't think . . . I kept on turning pages while she removed her clothes. I was still turning when she took the dictionary out of my hands and put it in the drawer of the bedside *commodino*, where it remained for the rest of her stay.

When I looked into her eyes, I saw my wife, Maggie, and I could see in Yvonne's eyes that she too was seeing someone else. And I could see not only that this was so, but that she knew it was so and knew that I knew, and knew that I knew that she knew . . .

An infinite regress? Yes and no. Maybe this mutual knowledge united us more firmly and closely than our embraces. I couldn't be sure.

In the mornings we went to the museums; in the afternoons we walked around the city or took the bus up to Fiesole or Settignano. We walked down the narrow *mulatteria* where the carriage scenes in *A Room with a View* had been shot. We paused at the field full of flowers where the young lovers meet, though the field was bare and I would never have recognized it if I hadn't in fact watched the scene being filmed. Maggie and I had been walking from Fiesole to Settignano . . . But I no longer tried to explain.

The city itself seemed brighter and sharper, like a fresco that's been recently restored. The steady hum of traffic provided a basso continuo to the ringing of bells, and the smells of roasting chestnuts and boiled tripe drew us from one street corner to another. We ate our way through the menu at Trattoria Maremmana and walked home, holding hands, to Albergo Medici, where Volmaro turned a blind eye to our comings and goings. In the darkness we came together in silence.

On Christmas morning we had the city to ourselves. Empty panettone boxes and champagne bottles were tucked into doorways. She had a ticket for the night train to Paris.

In the afternoon I stood at the window while she packed her suitcase. The clothes that she hadn't worn made me think that she'd had something else in mind. Something fancier, more high-toned.

At the station she waited at the taxi stand while I looked for a luggage cart for the suitcase. I helped her onto a second-class carriage, and then a young man helped me lift the suitcase up onto the luggage rack. I got off the train and she stayed on. I waited outside her window till the train pulled out of the station, and then I went home and cleaned up my room. We hadn't exchanged addresses.

The next day I bought the soft leather jacket I'd seen in the window at Raspini. I couldn't afford it, but I couldn't help myself. It was too beautiful. It was the sort of jacket that the archangel Gabriel would wear in a modern-dress version of the Annunciation. Walking out onto Via Cavour, I felt as conspicuous as Gabriel himself must have felt, wings spread, halo glowing. How all eyes must have turned to him.

I walked around the city center till it began to grow dark, and then I took a number thirteen bus up to Piazzale Michelangelo and walked back down. And yet no crowds gathered. No one followed me. No one even looked at me. The jacket, far from making me conspicuous, had made me invisible.

That night—and every night for a long time—I could feel her presence in the bed, beside me, on top of me, under me. For many years, whenever I looked back on that difficult time, I could summon up her presence, and she would be there.

I'd never discovered why she'd come to Italy, never understood how she'd happened to turn up in Piazza San Pier Maggiore with her huge suitcase. But my curiosity about these things no longer ran very deep. What ran deep was the memory of what she had given me. The gift of her body. No small thing, even in this age of casual affairs. But there was another gift too, more durable than the memory of her caresses—the gift of silence. Leaving behind my stories and anecdotes, I had followed her across the border into another country. Without words, at first I was afraid I wouldn't know who I was, but in the silence, I no longer needed to know.

HOW TO WRITE A MEMOIR

The goal in your memoir is to discover, for yourself and for your reader, the meaning of something important in your past. Don't worry about making a point. Just start with something—some event or issue—that you want to explore:

I went to Italy with my aunt Lydia last summer. She said that Italy would get the taste of shame and humiliation out of my mouth, like a piece of rhubarb pie.

Make a map of the scene: Imagine the place where the event or episode took place. Use your map to create a sense of place.

I've got two maps taped up over my desk in Mary Markley Residence Hall, where I live with twelve hundred other first-year students. One I ripped out of the back of the Carthage, Michigan, phone book. The other is a map of Florence, Italy, that I ripped out of my Florence guidebook. On the first I've circled our house on North Street, my aunt's apartment on

Seminary, the high school, the Franklin Funeral Home (on the corner of Oak and M60), and the gasket company (Midwest Gaskets) out on Southport Road, where my aunt works. On the map of Florence I've marked the location of the station, the Hotel Mona Lisa on Borgo Pinti; the Osteria dei Pazzi, where my aunt and I ate with Severino on our first and last nights in Florence; the Bargello (where I got all worked up about Donatello's *David*); Piazzale Michelangelo; and the bus stop by the post office in Piazza Salvemini.

Describe the people. Who are your main characters? How old are they? What do they look like? What do they say? What do they want? How do they respond to the events of the story?

My Aunt:

Technically my aunt Lydia, who's about forty, is an old maid. My mother always sighs when my aunt's marital status comes up in conversation. But Aunt Lydia is not like the other old maids in the Methodist church, who are sometimes called "maiden ladies." When she was my age she went to the General Motors Institute in Flint and now she's an executive vice president at the gasket company on the edge of town, before you get to the railroad hump yard. They used to manufacture all the gaskets for Maytag refrigerators, and when Maytag pulled out and moved to Mexico, everyone thought Carthage Gaskets was finished. But it wasn't. The parent gasket company in Italy was expanding, not retrenching, and would be sending a team of engineers to oversee a retooling process. Which is why my aunt had to go to Italy. The engineers would be coming in September.

My aunt is someone I can talk to about certain things that I can't talk to my mother about. For example, my aunt is the one I called when Howard Franklin, who's a Christian Scientist, broke our date for the senior prom so he could go with another Christian Scientist, one he met at a retreat at the Christian Science Temple in Michigan City. It was lunch hour and we were standing outside my locker. He was sorry, he said, but I didn't want to listen to his apologies. "Will she let you dry hump her," I asked him, "or do you only dry hump Methodists?" I went straight to the office and called my aunt and she told me to take a taxi out to the plant, which is what I did. She asked if I wanted to go to Italy with her, and I said I did. And later on she gave me a book about Christian Science by Mark Twain, who called Mary Baker Eddy the "queen of frauds and hypocrites."

She said she really wanted me to go with her because I'd taken four years of Spanish in high school and that would make it easy for me to understand Italian, so I could help her get around.

Stella (me):

Me, I'm a strong student. Not the valedictorian, but strong— more artsy than academic. I did all the artwork for the yearbook. I'm the youngest of four children and have two brothers and a sister. I'm the last to leave home. My parents wanted me to go to St. Joe Community College, like my brothers, because it's cheaper, but Aunt Lydia offered to pay for my tuition at U of M.

I was reasonably popular in high school. I always had a boyfriend. I'm pretty good-looking. Not much in the way of boobs, but I've been told that my legs and my butt are "shapely" and I've got a "winning" smile. I started getting serious about sex during my junior year in high school, when I was dating Howard Franklin. I wanted to go all the way, but Howard was reluctant to cross that bridge. I guess he was satisfied with dry humping. Those are the ugliest words I've ever heard. "Dry humping." I can barely write them down.

I had lots of friends, including hundreds of Facebook friends. After Howard broke our date for the prom, I unfriended him right away, and then I stopped logging on. I stopped tweeting too. I didn't want to be smothered with sympathetic tweets, which started coming in right away, along with pictures of the prom. I went cold turkey. My eyes had been opened. I could see what a terrible school Carthage High was, and what a terrible place Carthage was. No one was interested in culture or art, the important things. I couldn't wait to get out.

Severino:

Severino works for the parent company in Italy. Centro Guarnizione Italia S.p.A. "Guarnizione" means "gasket" in Italian, and it also means "garnish." Like those little sprigs of parsley you sometimes find on your plate. "S.p.A" means "Società per Azioni," which means "Society for Actions," whatever that means. It's sort of like "Inc." The company headquarters are in Sesto Fiorentino, which is close to Florence, but Severino lives in Florence. With his mother. It was his job to show my aunt around, and me too of course. To get her to meetings in Sesto, and to take us out to dinner in the evening.

There aren't any men like Severino in Carthage. His looks. His clothes—and not those silly-looking Armani suits either. He was *sooo* at home everywhere. People stopped to talk to him on the street. He was friends with the waiters in all the restaurants. Wherever we ate, the chef came out to say hello and to bring us something special. He was full of masculine energy, but not cocky. Maybe even a little uncertain, like he was on a journey of self-discovery. Like me. And there was always the hint of a smile at the corners of his mouth. There was something spiritual about him too. He was named after a saint, San Severino, who was executed by having a wet leather band tied around his head. When it dried, it crushed his skull.

And he could talk about anything. He even made gaskets interesting. Gaskets for caskets, for example. Who cared? A lot of people. I thought that in Italy they dug up the bones after a few years and threw them in a big pile at the back of the cemetery, but Severino's grandfather was buried in a special deluxe casket with a one-piece solid rubber gasket, and then a metal seal. The whole thing was soldered up tight and then put in a vault. And he could talk about all the works of art in Florence, like he studied art history all his life. Maybe he just grew up with it.

Describe the complication. The "complication" is whatever disturbs the status quo. It's the problem or challenge that you need to resolve. Your description of the complication should help you figure out what is at stake. Try breaking it up into stages.

Stage 1: The Complication (First Night)

The complication is not hard to understand. I fell in love with Severino. I couldn't get enough of him. I couldn't think about anything else. I fell in love with him the very first night when he came to the hotel to take us out to dinner. At dinner I fingered the business card he'd given me and listened while he and Aunt Lydia talked about gaskets. They talked about gasket tools, gasket materials, full-face flange gaskets, ring-type flange gaskets, rubber gaskets, gasket-making tools, standard vs. custom gaskets, gasket cutting machinery, boiler gaskets, tapes and sealants, compression packing for gaskets, markets for gaskets, demand going up worldwide by 5.5 percent, demand increasing exponentially in India and China. It was interesting at first, but after a while I wanted Severino to talk to me. I didn't know how to break into the conversation, except by asking questions about the menu, and that's how I wound up ordering risotto with squid cooked in its own ink for my first course.

"Are you sure that's what you want?" Severino asked. "Squid in its own ink?"

"Of course," I said as if I ate squid cooked in its own ink two or three times a week at home.

"That should take the taste of shame and humiliation out of your mouth," Aunt Lydia said. I tried to stop her, but she went on to tell Severino about Howard Franklin and how he broke our date for the senior prom. She had to explain what a prom was.

We were drinking wine and eating bread that didn't have any salt in it. It was the first time I'd ever drunk wine with dinner, and it was the first time I'd ever seen Aunt Lydia drink wine.

"Shame and humiliation," Severino said, refilling my glass. "And what did you learn from this experience?"

"I learned that people will believe anything," I said. "It doesn't matter how ridiculous it is, somebody will believe it." I was talking to make myself sound interesting. "Howard was a

Christian Scientist," I explained. "They believe that death and illness are illusions. And his father's a funeral director! Mark Twain called Mary Baker Eddy the 'queen of frauds and hypocrites.'"

Severino laughed. "Stella," he said—and the sound of my name on his lips made my heart flutter—"there's a Christian Science reading room in Via de' Servi. Right downtown."

"The funny thing," I said, "is that I believed it myself for a while. I went to church with Howard a couple of times, and when I smashed my thumb in the door of his car, he took me to a Christian Science reader instead of a doctor."

"And did it work?"

"My thumb got better, if that's what you mean."

"Like Christ healing the blind man at Siloam?"

"Exactly," I said. The wine was making me bold. "It was exactly like that." And I held out my thumb and stuck it in his face. He took it in his hand and examined it carefully. I thought I was going to have a heart attack.

"Perfect," he said. "No sign of previous trauma."

Stage 2: Mornings

Mornings, Aunt Lydia went to Sesto on the train with Severino. She didn't get back till after six o'clock. I was on my own. Lost at first without my cell phone. Without my old Facebook friends. No one to talk to. But I bought a couple of sexy dresses at the San Lorenzo market. I didn't bring any dresses because I didn't think I'd need them. Just jeans and tops. It was the first time I'd actually spoken Italian. *"Vorrei . . ."* I said ("I would like . . ."), and pointed at a lime green dress hanging from an overhead rack. Piece of cake. You used the conditional just like in Spanish, more or less. I *vorrei*ed a black dress too, at the stall next to the one where I bought the green dress. I took the dresses back to the hotel, which was really lovely, by the way—air-conditioned—and modeled them in front of the big mirror in the bathroom.

Severino had given me a ticket for two o'clock at the Uffizi, so I wouldn't have to stand in line. I stopped for pizza on the way. *"Vorrei due,"* I said—two slices, not two pizzas—and then farther down the street, I *vorrei*ed some ice cream.

I kept my map in my backpack, in case I got lost, but I didn't really need it. I had a pretty good idea of how to get to the Uffizi, but I practiced asking directions anyway: *"Dov'è l'Uffizi?"*

Stage 3: Going to Museums

I liked going to the museums because I'm an artist, and I like art. I know that not everyone does. No one in Carthage does, except Mr. Bronson, the art teacher at the high school. And because I like being on my own. And besides, art gave me something to talk about in the evenings. Besides gaskets.

Severino knew all about gaskets, but he knew all about art too. It seemed like I hadn't really seen anything till I'd talked to Severino at dinner and he'd started asking questions and I'd remember things like I was standing right in front of them—the haloes that look like deluxe Frisbees, the angels that go barefoot, the Virgin Mary who's got her thumb stuck in the book she's reading to keep her place while the Angel Gabriel's telling her she's preggers.

"Do you think a person can be changed by experiencing a great work of art?" I asked. I was conscious (as always) of trying to make myself interesting, but it was a real question too. I wanted to know.

I was wearing one of my new dresses, a sleeveless dress with little slits at the front and back to give it some toughness, and studded hardware for accents. Severino couldn't *not* notice.

"Imported," my aunt had said. "From China." She'd looked at the label while I was in the shower.

"Most people see what they want to see," he said. "They can interpret anything so that it fits in with what they already believe."

"But I'm not most people," I said.

"Obviously," he said. "*Your* job right now is to take chances, to open yourself to the possibility that you can be changed. It's risky."

"How about you?" I asked. "Have you ever been changed?"

"Go to the Bargello tomorrow," he said. "Look at Donatello's *David* and then tell me what you think."

Eating in an Italian restaurant gave me a sense of well-being that I'd never felt at home. I think my aunt felt it too. There was nothing like it in Carthage. There were a couple of good restaurants in Carthage, but they were so dark you could hardly see your food. The restaurants in Florence were well lit. You started with bread and wine. Then maybe an antipasto, and then your *primo,* which was like a whole meal at home, and then you sit back and relax and the waiter comes and you order your *secondo.* No more squid in its own ink for me, but all sorts of wonderful things that I'm going to leave out, because I want to get to Donatello's *David.*

There was a long line at the Bargello, but Severino had given me a ticket, so I didn't have to wait too long. I went straight to the *David* on the second floor, and right away I could feel myself changing. David looked just like Severino, but a little younger, and I thought: *this* is what he'd wanted me to *see*. All my feelings for Severino boiled up inside me. This was beyond what I'd thought of as love. I knew that the *David* was the first freestanding life-sized nude bronze of the Renaissance, and I knew that there'd never been anything else quite like it. But even so it wasn't what I had expected. I thought I'd been awakened sexually by Howard Franklin, but that was a snooze. Circling round the *David* I could feel my stomach churning. I was flooded with a desire to do all sorts of things that I'd heard about but had always found pretty disgusting. I wanted to take his penis into my mouth, his balls too. I opened my mouth as wide as I could to see if they'd fit. There was no barrier, no ropes like the ropes in movie theaters around the bronze statue. I had to restrain myself to keep from touching him, from licking him, from running my hands over his bare buttocks, from tearing his helmet off and putting it on my own head, from taking a shoe off and rolling Goliath's head back and forth under my bare foot, from imagining that Goliath's head was really my aunt Lydia's head.

So this is what it's all about, I thought. I'd always thought it was about something else.

That afternoon I wrote a letter to Severino on Hotel Mona Lisa stationery. His address was on the business card in my wallet. I told him in great detail everything that had happened and said that I'd like to talk to him about it privately. I figured that since he was an Italian, he'd be able to figure out what to do next. I wrote quickly, stuffed the letter in an envelope, and gave it to the woman at the front desk, who said she'd mail it immediately. Then I lay down in my bed and played with myself while I waited for my aunt to come back from Sesto. I'd always been able to talk to my aunt about anything, things that I couldn't talk to my mother about. But Severino was my secret.

That night, over vin santo and biscotti di Prato, I gave Severino and my aunt an edited version of my impressions of *David.* But as usual, I soon felt that I hadn't seen it at all. Where I'd seen a helmet, Severino saw a woman's hat. Where I'd seen a hard-bodied young man, Severino saw a young woman's prepubescent breasts. About the size of my own breasts, I realized when I looked at the statue in my imagination. On and on. The buttocks I'd wanted to lick were a young woman's buttocks. A young woman only five feet tall. Shorter than me. And what about the penis and balls that I'd wanted to hold in my mouth? Where had all those fantasies come from? The statue had in fact been condemned by the Church, Severino said, and Donatello was lucky he hadn't been burned at the stake. Donatello's *David* wasn't just a transvestite; it was a *donnauomo* or a *femminauomo.*

"How would you say that in English?" Severino asked, as he was paying the bill with his gasket-company credit card.

I didn't have to think too hard. "How about a 'sheman,'" I said, "or a 'shemale'?"

"Bennissimo," he said.

The event: Describe exactly what happened. What did you do? What did other characters do?

By the end of the week I was desperate. If Severino had received my letter, he gave no sign of it. I watched him like a hawk, waiting, trying to resign myself to an unspoken love that could only be expressed through meaningful glances, like the love between Rose and Jack in *Titanic,* but still competing with my aunt for Severino's attention by interjecting Italian phrases into the conversation and by introducing my observations about the works of art that I'd seen. Anything but gaskets.

On Saturday night we ate again at the Osteria dei Pazzi. We shared a *tris*, which is three different kinds of pasta served family style, and then *bistecca alla fiorentina*. It was our last night in Florence, and I couldn't bear to let go. On the way back to the hotel I said, "Let's go up to Piazzale Michelangelo again." I looked at Severino, and Severino looked at my aunt. We waited for a number thirteen bus at the stop by the post office. The first bus that came was a number twenty-three. "Let's take the number twenty-three," I said, "and ride all the way to the end of the line and then back. It will be an adventure." I was imagining myself sitting next to Severino. (I wasn't imagining Aunt Lydia at all.)

I got on the bus, punched my ticket in the ticket machine, and looked around for a good seat. The moment I sat down I realized that Aunt Lydia and Severino were not on the bus, which had already started to move. Out my window I caught a glimpse of Severino tying his shoe. Aunt Lydia was looking down at him, intently, as if she'd never seen anyone tie a shoe before.

This is sooo *stupid,* I thought.

I could have gotten off at the next stop, in front of the big Feltrinelli bookstore, but I was too annoyed. I could have gotten off at the station and found my way home easily. But by this time I was convinced that what had happened was not a stupid mistake; it was deliberate. I should have gotten off the bus and rushed back to the hotel, but something stopped me: what if they'd gone up to Piazzale Michelangelo without me?

Once we were past the station, I was in unfamiliar territory. I thought I recognized the street where the American Church was located, but I couldn't be sure. After that, everything looked the same—the same shops over and over again, the same piazzas. The same but not the same. And then we were entering a different Florence. Definitely not the Florence you see pictured in the guidebooks. We stopped in piazzas and on poorly lit streets and then we plunged into the dark. No more piazzas. Just ... factories? I couldn't be sure. It was too dark to see. Housing developments? But why weren't there any lights on? The driver kept making stops. People kept getting off. But no one was getting on. Finally I was the only one left on the bus.

I was angry now. At boiling point. How could they have done this to me? The bus was going faster and faster, not making any more stops. Even so, it was another fifteen minutes before we came to the end of the line. I was sitting by the back door, behind the ticket machine, waiting for the bus to start up again and head back into town. I think the driver didn't see me at first. When he did, he came to the back of the bus and told me I had to get off, making his meaning clear with his hands.

I didn't exactly panic, but I reverted to Spanish: *"Quiero volver,"* I said, showing him my ticket, which should have been good for an hour. And then in English: "I want to go back."

"Non torna," he said. *"Capolinea. Finito. Basta."*

"Tengo que volver," I said in Spanish. ("I have to turn back.") But he shook his head. *"Mi trovo in difficoltà,"* I said. ("I find myself in difficulty.") A useful phrase I'd learned from Severino. It was Italian, but I don't know if the driver understood me or not. He just kept shaking his head and waving me off the bus.

Suddenly I was afraid, but my fear was mixed with something else. I *wanted* something bad to happen so that my aunt would find herself in big *difficoltà* for letting me go off on my own. I got off the bus and watched as it disappeared into the darkness. There were no lights on in the buildings that lined the streets. There was only one streetlight, just enough for me to make out the sign at the bus stop. CAPOLINEA. I knew what it meant: head of the line. I'd thought I was at the *end* of the line, but I was at the beginning. I had to think about this for a while.

I thought about it, and I thought about the letter and I thought about all the stupid things I'd said at dinner, trying to make myself interesting, as if I wasn't interesting enough without jabbering on about Botticelli's *Primavera* and Piero della Francesca's *Portrait of Federico da Montefeltro* and about being changed by the Donatello *David*. I didn't know what to make of it, didn't know what to make of anything.

What to do? There was nothing there, just dark buildings and a row of parked cars. Somebody must live there, or be around somewhere. Whose cars were they? My fear was like the damp leather that they, whoever they were, had tied around the head of San Severino. The strap was starting to dry out and tighten.

I summoned up my anger to counteract my fear. I should have refused to get off the bus. I should have tried to explain to the driver. He could have called the hotel. Or a taxi.

I started to walk. I'd been walking for about ten minutes when I heard a car start up. Red taillights. Someone was backing out of a parking place. I ran toward the car and stood in the street in front of it, waving my arms. The car stopped. The driver rolled down his window.

"*Mi trovo in difficoltà,*" I said, and that was enough.

The driver was a young guy, about twenty-five. I didn't notice his girlfriend till she opened her door and got into the backseat. I tried to protest, but she just laughed and motioned me into the front seat. Neither one of them spoke English, but that was all right. I didn't really want to explain what I'd done.

"Stazione," I said. "Hotel Mona Lisa."

My fear was completely gone by now and I was trying to concentrate on my anger. I wanted to have a showdown with my aunt, but it was hard to hang on to my anger with this cheerful couple talking at me in Italian, asking questions I couldn't really understand, though I did manage to convey the basic information: I'd come to Florence with my aunt, got on the wrong bus. I didn't try to explain Severino or the gasket company in Sesto Fiorentino.

I walked back to the hotel from the station. I knew the way. It was the last time I'd be walking this way, but I didn't make any special effort to memorize the route. I didn't need to. It was already imprinted on my brain.

Severino was at the hotel. Surprise. Duh! I could see that the bed had been unmade and then loosely made up again, and suddenly everything became clear. No wonder my aunt never got back from Sesto till six o'clock; no wonder she always needed to take a nap when she did get back.

The evaluation: What did you think was happening? What did other people think was happening? Were there any misunderstandings? Did you discuss your responses to what had happened?

What did *I* think was happening? What I was thinking was that it was about as awkward a moment as there could be. I was thinking that Severino had been humping my aunt—not dry humping her either—and I was thinking that my aunt was afraid. Afraid of me, afraid that she'd broken something that couldn't be mended. I could see pleading in her eyes, and I realize now that my response at that moment would determine not only our relationship in the future, but also the kind of person I was going to become. It was like having a good angel on one shoulder and an evil angel on the other. The evil angel was telling me to wrap a wet leather strap around my aunt's head and wait for it to dry and tighten up and crush her skull. The good angel was telling me that I'd been a fool all along, from the moment I first saw Severino in the lobby of the Hotel Mona Lisa. The good angel was telling me to keep my mouth shut.

The resolution: Did you resolve the complication? What did you decide to do? If you didn't resolve the complication, how did you handle your feelings? How did you change to deal with the new status quo? How did other people change?

No. We didn't resolve the complication. What did we decide to do? Nothing. We just finished the bottle of wine that was on the table, and I gave them an edited version of my adventure, and we talked about the things we were going to do in September when Severino came to Carthage with the retooling crew. But to tell you the truth, I wasn't interested.

Actually, we did do one thing. Before he left Severino got out a copy of *TuttoCittà*, which was in a drawer with the Florence phone book. *TuttoCittà* contains detailed maps of every part of the city, and it also has a map that shows all the bus routes. Severino opened it up on the desk and traced the route of the number twenty-three bus all the way from the stop by the post office to the station, on out past the wholesale produce market into *zone industriali*, and then right off the edge of the map.

"You went out into the unknown," Severino said, putting *TuttoCittà* back in the drawer. "Beyond the boundaries of the known world. And you made it back safe and sound."

Concluding with a point: In your conclusion you should describe what you have learned and what your reader should have learned from your experience. Not the "moral" of the story, like the morals in Aesop's fables, but something that brings closure, some insight or understanding that goes beyond the obvious.

I don't know about closure or going beyond the obvious, and I'm not sure what I learned, but this is what happened. Severino never answered my letter, but he wrote to my aunt. He would not be coming with the Italian crew in September to install the new machinery and do the retooling. He was needed at the plant in Sesto Fiorentino. He asked my aunt to pass his greetings on to me.

My aunt showed me the letter. We were sitting on the large deck at the back of her second-story apartment downtown. It was August, and I was leaving for Ann Arbor at the end of the month. The deck was full of flowers—window boxes with trailing geraniums, large Italian pots with verbena and petunias; a tomato plant in one of the Italian pots was covered with yellow blossoms and tiny red grape tomatoes. We were drinking a glass of white wine, which I was not allowed to do at home, and I was glad, at that moment, that I'd held my tongue back at Hotel Mona Lisa, glad that I hadn't lashed out at my aunt. I wanted to put my arms around her and tell her how much I appreciated all the things she'd done for me over the years. I wanted to tell her what a good aunt she was.

It was six o'clock when I finished my glass of wine, which was warm by now. "I've got to go home," I said.

"Thanks for coming," she said.

"Tomorrow's Saturday," I said. "Maybe we could bike out to the forest preserve."

"I'd like that," she said.

And that's how it ended.

We'd both gone off the map, and I wasn't sure either one of us would ever make it all the way back.

THE MOUNTAIN OF LIGHTS

JULIAN DIJKSTERHUIS STOOD BY a half-opened door in the vaulted corridor, his shoulder blades pressing against the clean white wall like the runners of a sled. He wasn't in anyone's way, but he didn't belong there, and the nurses kept suggesting that he would be more comfortable in the waiting room, or sitting with his wife.

"Thanks," he said, flicking ashes off a cigarette, exhaling smoke through his nostrils, "but I think I'll wait here."

His wife, Hannah, was talking rapidly in a low voice in the room behind him. The sudden death of their six-year-old daughter, Dinah, had toppled her over the edge of sanity, and Julian hadn't been there to catch her. Perhaps he'd even given her a little push, though God knows he hadn't meant to. But she wouldn't stop talking.

Her chatter had filled their three-bedroom apartment on Chestnut Street, spilled out into the hallway, down the stairwells and elevator shafts. "Keep an eye on her," old Dr. Janacek had said, who lived just below them on the thirty-second floor. And she hadn't slept. If he'd get her to bed by midnight, she'd be up again at twelve fifteen with a steaming cup of coffee, a cigarette smoking in the ashtray on the old rolltop desk in their bedroom, where she turned pages, made notes on index cards, and dozed a little from time to time.

Julian would pretend to sleep, until he couldn't stand it any longer: "You've got to get some *sleep*. You've *got* to get some sleep."

"I can't sleep when you're nagging at me all the time."

"Lie down in bed, for Christ's sake. And don't drink so much coffee. How the hell could *any*one sleep after twenty cups of coffee?"

"I need it."

"You need rest—can't you see that?"

"Just leave me alone. I don't see how in the hell *you* can sleep so soundly."

"Lay off, will you?"

That's the way it had been between them for the last three weeks, and now he was waiting for the doctor to bring the forms that he would have to fill out before she could be admitted, involuntarily, to one of the psychiatric wards.

"An acute psychotic break," the doctor had said on the phone, and Julian wondered how he had missed it, hadn't read, so to speak, the large block capitals on the wall: ACUTE PSYCHOTIC BREAK. But over the years he had not only become accustomed to her unorthodox ways. He even took a kind of pride in them, as the English pride themselves on tolerating mild eccentricities. *Has it ever occurred to you, Dijksterhuis, that your wife isn't like other people?* Yes, it had occurred to him. Regularly, in fact. It occurred to him when he climbed into bed with her at night, and when he climbed back out again in the morning. She was terrific in the sack,

Aphrodite herself, fair ankled, soft armed, sweetly smiling, sweet smelling, quick glancing, laughter loving. Didn't restrain herself there, or anywhere else, for that matter. That was the trouble. Lack of restraint—shapeless enthusiasms thrusting upward like the columns of books on the bedroom floor—pop psychology, holistic health, the Catholic Pentecostal movement, all interspersed with her classics: Teubners, Budés, red-and-green Loebs, OCTs. A temple under construction. Or perhaps in ruins.

Julian wrote out checks to Blackwell's and Heffers and Kroch's, and to the Cudahy Library at Loyola University, where she had matriculated in classics. Her fines were astronomical.

"Finish the degree, for Christ's sake," he advised her, "and why fart around with Plato and Augustine when you could be reading Homer or Ovid and Catullus?"

But she was a seeker; she sought to understand. "I want Truth, not Entertainment," she said. "If I wanted Entertainment I'd lie in bed all day and fiddle with myself. That's what you do with your detective stories."

And she had a large heart. She brought home the lost souls who, drawn by invisible threads, sat next to her on the Howard Street L or the Michigan Avenue bus. Julian would feed them an omelet or a sandwich—and sometimes he gave them money—before sending them off into the night.

"Why do you pick up these creeps?"

"They're human beings, Julie. They need help, just like you and me."

She was specially fond of priests. Julian didn't take much notice at first, not till the appearance of Father Axelrod, the Hyde Park opera buff, who wanted Julian to accompany him while he sang arias from Verdi and Paisiello. "This is a magnificent piano," he liked to say, seating himself at the old Blüthner grand (with its eighty-five keys) that had once belonged to Julian's Aunt Hattie, "a splendid instrument."

There was an Episcopalian too who couldn't sing a note. Frog-toned Father Jack from St. Chrysostom's on Dearborn. "Smilin' Jack," as Julian called him, was a disciple of Wilhelm Reich, and for a time Hannah embraced a number of bizarre Reichian doctrines. Julian didn't have the patience to listen to her explanations—Christ as genital man, putting it to Mary Magdalene, and so on. She embraced Father Jack as well, in an orgone energy accumulator, a coffinlike contraption made of alternating layers of steel wool and rock or glass-wool encased in panels of Celotex soft board. The metal sides of the accumulator were designed to reflect and concentrate the orgone energy radiated by its occupant, causing it to repenetrate the body through the pores and through respiration.

"Cancer, head colds, psychoses—it cures everything," Father Jack claimed, "maybe even death, eventually."

Hannah got a big kick out of it.

"Why do you listen to this stuff?" Julian asked her. "Do you think I want to hear this crap? I ought to go to the bishop; I could have that frog-voiced shyster defrocked, that croaking bastard."

But the bishop had already received complaints from other sources. Father Jack decamped to Toledo, Ohio; Hannah began taking instruction from a Jesuit, Father Frank Neumiller, whom she met in the library at Loyola.

"She's absolutely safe with me," the old priest told Julian. "You can put your mind at ease."

The police had picked her up in Old Town and taken her to the Passavant Pavilion of Northwestern Memorial Hospital, between Huron and Superior, half a mile south of the Dijksterhuis apartment. "They had to put her in restraints," the doctor told him on the phone. "We can't do a thing until you get down here."

"In restraints?"

"A straitjacket."

A clutch of horror at Julian's chest.

She'd been talking gibberish on the phone when he woke up in the morning, speaking in tongues to Father Neumiller. He had gone into the bathroom and closed the door so he wouldn't have to listen to her while he shaved.

"Take it easy," he said later, lifting the filmy skirt of her silk breakfast dress and stroking her panties before he left for the Solomon Pharmacy to pick up a Sunday *Times*. "Calm down. Don't get yourself all worked up. Try to get some rest. We've got to hold ourselves together."

"'The Lord giveth, and the Lord taketh away,'" she said, "'and His will is our peace.'"

E la sua voluntade è nostra pace. She wanted it on Dinah's tombstone, and after a prolonged argument, he had given in.

"It's Italian," he explained to Mr. Stoneking at the monument company, turning over samples of different colored marble. RICHLY REWARDING—a plaque on the Formica counter—IS THE SPIRITUAL HARVEST OF A LIFE WELL LIVED. A MONUMENT SHOULD REVERENTLY AND BEAUTIFULLY EXPRESS THIS TRUTH.

"Don't worry for a thing, Mister, I got two Eye-talians working for me in the shop right now. Master craftsmen. They'll get it right if anybody can."

"I want the accent right. Look—there's one over the second *e* but not over the first."

"I understand, Mister. That's why we got these forms for

you to print on, just the way you want it. In this business it don't pay to make mistakes."

Hannah had been raised a Free Methodist; her father, the minister of a hyperactive congregation in St. Joe, Michigan, whipped her for square dancing with her classmates in the fifth grade. And she never quite got over it. Julian taught her to drink and smoke and swear, and he dressed her in European lingerie, which they ordered from special catalogs—a merry widow, silk stockings, lacy tap pants, and wispy bikinis in raspberry, blush, chocolate. Her brother, a motorcycle evangelist, wouldn't set his righteous foot in the Dijksterhuis apartment. But in spite of everything she remained, in Father Neumiller's words, a *deeply religious person*. "Her faith will sustain her," the priest said to Julian, "but what about *you*?"

But her faith hadn't sustained her, and now she was in trouble, and Julian was in trouble too. He didn't want her committed, locked up in the loony bin like his Aunt Hattie. Twenty-five years in a nuthouse on the outskirts of Kalamazoo, eating like a horse. Hannah was a good eater too, but she stayed slim on plain lettuce and broiled calves' liver that Julian bought for her at a Greek meat market on Jackson and Halsted. Twenty-five years in a nuthouse with no exercise, and she'd be as big as Aunt Hat, whose upper arms hung down over her elbows, and he'd be sixty. Too late. He had to do something now, tonight, had to explain Dinah's death to her in a language she could understand. But how could he explain it to himself? He couldn't do it in English. Greek or Latin either.

In the small waiting room at the end of the corridor he could see Father Neumiller trying to interest Sara, Dinah's older sister, in a magazine. He was turning pages, pointing with his square index finger. But Sara was boy-crazy, interested in one thing only. She spent her allowance on teen magazines and record albums that made Julian's head reel. She chewed gum to mask the odor of tobacco and powdered the hickeys on her neck. Backseat work. The son of her ninth-grade science teacher. "A Boys Town dropout," Julian said to Hannah.

He spoke to the boy's father at a school open house. "Not to worry, Mr. Dijksterhuis. They're a couple of good kids. It's the chemistry of adolescence."

But Julian worried. She had become silent and unresponsive when he read to her at night or tried to tell her a story. He was piqued. He fancied himself a regular Demodocus, a teller of tales, an old-style raconteur. "Once upon a time," his stories began, "there were two little girls named Seremonda and Duva, who lived in a village halfway between the east and the west." And what adventures they had, traveling south to the Mediterranean—Olympus, Ilium, Ithaka, Phaeacia, Uruk, Rome—and north to the halls of Hrothgar, to Heorot, to Camelot and Asgard. Thus did he keep his children from their play and his wife from her own quest for Truth, which she sought to exantlate from the deepest wells. But now there was only Sara, and Julian wished that *she* had died instead of Dinah. This thought was like a tumor pressing against the back of his brain, distorting his vision.

Sara was staring sullenly at Father Neumiller's shiny bald head, just as she stared at Julian when he tried to talk to her about her schoolwork or sex or the importance of scales and arpeggios. Her piano lessons were nonnegotiable, and despite a show of reluctance, she played well on Aunt Hattie's piano: Chopin, Schumann, Cyril Scott. And duets with Julian. They made their way through the Brahms waltzes like two people walking freely on firm ground. "It's marvelous, really," Dr. Janacek said to Julian in the elevator one day, "but don't hurry the opening measures so—*poco andante, poco andante.*"

Julian had given her lessons at home for the first four years before enrolling her at the Chicago Music Conservatory, where he himself coached would-be professionals on a lethargic Steinway B and lectured on the history of music in the late middle ages.

Father Neumiller closed the magazine and slapped it down on the table. Julian was sorry now that he had phoned the old priest, who lived in the Jesuit residence at Loyola. But he had panicked when he'd learned that Hannah had cracked up. And who else could he have called on a Sunday evening? He ground out a cigarette on the green tile floor and hitched up his beltless trousers. He'd lost weight since Dinah's death, couldn't eat though he was as empty inside as an open grave, a ravenous darkness.

"God has touched you," Father Neumiller had said to him the night before the funeral. "He's touched us all; but when we won't respond, sometimes he has to knock down our house of cards. It's the only way he can get through to us."

"Now, Frank, what in the hell is that supposed to mean?" Julian had been drunk. "This is God's way of touching me? Is that what you're getting at? We're in the hand of God, and God crumples up his fist? That's rich. God so loved little Dinah that he couldn't wait to crush her against his stony bosom, to break her little arms and legs? Christ almighty, you're out of your mind."

"You've got to open up your heart. God is knocking at the door of your heart, and you've got to open up and let him in."

"I like you, Father, but you don't know your ass from a hole in the ground. Now finish your Postum and clear out. I'll call a cab."

"You're only upsetting your*self*."

Hannah, who had been lying down in the bedroom, joined them at the old-fashioned table that was too large for the dining alcove. The smooth planes of her freckled face had been redefined by the non-Euclidian geometry of grief; parallel lines were beginning to meet around her eyes. "'The Lord giveth,'" she said, "'and the Lord taketh away.' We've got to celebrate this death just like we did Daddy's."

"Jesus Christ, your daddy was seventy-five years old."

"It's God's will, Julie." Father Neumiller held out a trembling hand to her. He was a tough old bird, a whiskey priest with a few good years left. He took pills that kept him off the sauce, some of the time anyway. The pills dried out his mouth as well as his liver, and his tongue flicked out unpredictably from between his heavy lips. Hannah had brought him home one night from the library, and the three of them had tied one on. In the middle of the night they'd gone up to the fortieth floor to have a look at the lights of the city. "The City of God," Father Neumiller had mumbled into a Waterford tumbler full of yellow whiskey. He held the tumbler close to his lips and waved his free hand vaguely in the general direction of the sky: "'Seek him who maketh the seven stars and Orion.' *Isaiah*." Together they gazed up at the great constellations wheeling above them—Canis Minor, Taurus, the great bear—monsters grazing across the Chicago sky as they had grazed over the ancient civilizations of China and Greece, imaginary configurations by which mariners still navigate, as if the universe were in fact a system of concentric spheres and not a mathematical description of a finite curve with unimaginable coordinates. They were too far gone to notice Boötes the herdsman rising over Lake Michigan.

"Dinah. Dinah. Dinah." Hannah was calling softly. Julian turned and entered the room behind him, which was windowless and small, barely wide enough to accommodate the narrow hospital gurney that she was lying on, her arms and legs restrained by canvas straps. Her face glowed with a terrible flame that illuminated Julian's inner darkness—Dinah's sparkling gray eyes peering up at him through her first pair of glasses. *"Papa, papa. I can see them. I can see the stars."*

Hannah did not look at him. "Yes, yes, yes," she said; "He will understand. If only I could make *you* understand, Julie." Her voice, slow and measured, as if she were reciting a poem in Latin, began to pick up speed, a broad river flowing into a narrow channel. "How anxious I've become. My skin is crawling, and when I look at the lamp it's like looking at the sun, but the sky around is all dark and I can see little lights, circling, counterclockwise around my heart, unwinding the center like a ball of twine, undoing everything. We must go at once before it's too late. Can't you hear her crying?"

Julian listened. A door closed. Someone *was* crying. There was a strange buzzing in his ears—life-support systems humming steadily in distant wards. Were there life-support systems for the soul? For Dinah's? For Hannah's?

She was still wearing her silk breakfast dress. She had been gone when he returned with the *Times*. The thin material of the dress had been sewn with the fabric reversed, muting constellations of pink roses. Julian pulled the hem down over her legs.

"There's no grieving in that land," she said, "but oh, Julie, I can't bear to her crying so. It's kept me awake all this time, and I'm so tired, Julie. I didn't want to tell you, but I'm so tired now."

In what land? In what land could they meet again as man

and wife, two bodies with one soul inspired? Julian did not know where to locate it on the map of the future. Confused and conflicting reports taxed his powers, just as confused and conflicting accounts of the New World once taxed the powers of Renaissance cartographers.

"It's terrible to lie there all alone. My baby, my baby, Mama hears you. Don't struggle so. I've packed your new jumper and Penrod."

The fierce jaws of Penrod, a stuffed alligator, protruded from Hannah's oversized handbag, propped against the lamp on a small table that also held a water pitcher and a box of tissues. Julian's deepest fears condensed into a shower of pain, and he struggled to find his way through the pain to a place of shelter beyond the present moment. But wherever he turned he was met by Dinah running to greet him, her thin arms outstretched, her glasses slipping down her nose. In his eagerness to embrace her he started forward, but like a dream she slipped through his arms, and he stumbled, more desolate than before. He was falling from a high place, and Father Neumiller was waiting to catch him. But Father Neumiller was falling too. Julian had caught his arm just in time to prevent him from stumbling down the steps at the funeral parlor.

Hannah began to struggle against the canvas restraints. She thrashed about like someone who has been thrown overboard, bound hand and foot. What bold swimmer would plunge in and rescue her? Those seas were too heavy for Julian; she was too far from shore. He was about to call for help when the doctor entered. He was too large for the little room and for the white hospital jacket that lay on his huge frame like snow on the sloping sides of a mountain. Julian, unable to conceal his relief, smiled stupidly at the yellow papers that the doctor waved at him, as if the papers contained whatever explanation was necessary.

Hannah's name had already been typed in capital letters at the top of the form, which the doctor placed on the table next to the handbag containing Penrod. The table was slightly damp and the papers stuck to it. Julian waved aside the doctor's ballpoint and with his own broad-nibbed Italic pen began to check a series of boxes affirming that he was an interested person, eighteen or older, seeking the respondent's admission in order to prevent him/her from inflicting serious physical harm upon himself/herself or others in the near future and that he had no financial interest in this matter and that he was not involved in litigation with the respondent. At the bottom of the second page he signed his name, Julian R. Dijksterhuis—a ripple of anxiety on the calm surface of the official document.

Hannah, he learned, had been searching for Dinah at the Old Town School of Folk Music on Armitage Avenue when she was picked up by the police.

"I take it," said the doctor, "that you attended a program at the Old Town School on the afternoon of your daughter's death?"

"Yes."

They had gone to see Maurice Jenkins's popular one-man enactment of the Pied Piper of Hamelin. Jenkins, one of Julian's colleagues at the Conservatory, was a versatile and accomplished musician who'd charmed the children in the audience onto the stage, hopping and skipping like Danny Kaye and brandishing a fourteen-string German lute. Dinah had been the first to join in. And even Sara, who considered herself too grown-up for such antics, couldn't resist the pull of the strange medieval sonorities, consecutive fifths and octaves, both melancholy and gay. She'd danced with the rest, three times around the rows of folding chairs, bringing up the rear. And when the children disappeared through a narrow curtain at the back of the hall, it was she who had reappeared to explain that the others had gone to live under the mountain and would not be coming back.

After the program was over, children had exploded into the hall; but Julian had to fetch Dinah, who had wandered up the back staircase and had been drinking a Coca-Cola with Jenkins himself. She was having trouble breathing.

"Get her to a doctor, for Christ's sake," Maurice had said to him.

"It's her asthma," said Julian. "And she's allergic to a million things. We've just got to live with it."

She died that night—asthma complicated by a sudden bacterial pneumonia. Massive doses of sulfadiazine had been administered, but too late to check the flow of pneumococci that had cascaded over the mucus secretions and cilia that line the respiratory tract, on into the air sacs of the lungs, drowning her in her own inflammatory exudate.

Hannah began to murmur in a low voice. Familiar biblical phrases bobbed up and down on a tumbling stream of nonsense.

"Glossolalia," Julian explained. "She gets it from the priest. He's a charismatic. A drunk, too."

The doctor's eyes moved from Julian to Hannah and back again. "The human mind," he said, "is absolutely astonishing—a biochemical maze more intricate and ingeniously constructed than any other cubic half-foot in the universe. Our crude analogies—the telephone exchange, the binary computer—don't begin to suggest the complexities." He waved his hand in front of his face, as if to brush aside the complexities. "But for all that we're groping our way to the inner chambers. Like the King Tut people, eh?"

Julian handed him the yellow form. "What do you expect to find when you get there?"

"Perhaps the self-reflections of our own thought processes, perhaps nothing."

"What do you mean, 'nothing'? There's got to be *some*thing."

"That remains to be seen."

"And in the meantime?"

"In the meantime we have at our disposal a powerful pharmacopoeia, not just a series of isolated medications, but whole families of drugs that take effect along quite different neurological pathways. The first step is to isolate one that will silence the voices she's been hallucinating." The doctor looked down at Hannah.

"It's the little girl's death that causes them," explained Julian.

"More likely a lithium deficiency or an excess of tryptophan amines in the bloodstream."

"It came at a bad time."

"I've gathered as much, Mr. Dijksterhuis; but one time is much like another, especially in the case of a child, which can't be reconciled with *any* metaphysical system, much less your wife's. The strain has precipitated an acute psychotic break, a chemical imbalance that will have to be redressed."

Better a chemical imbalance, thought Julian, *than the hand of God.* But he did not want the doctor to have it all his own way either. "Surely, a metaphysical system is like a cup," he said; "it may be larger or smaller, but it will hold some truth." He was repeating something he had heard from Father Neumiller.

The doctor frowned. "If I may alter the metaphor," he said,

"I should say that a metaphysical system is like a sieve; however large or small it is, it won't hold water."

"But you can't get on without *some* metaphysical assumptions, whether you articulate them or not."

"Well, perhaps so, but at least you can abandon the claim to occupy a privileged position, one outside the natural order of things. That's where the mischief begins. How presumptuous we are. It's astonishing, really. We shut ourselves up in our studies and imagine existences that transcend the writhing life of the planet, when in fact we are firmly embedded in nature. The oxidative energy that enables the profoundest metaphysician to lift his pen is released in the cells by mitochondria which are themselves derived from migrant prokaryotes—primitive bacteria. These in turn . . . But why go on? It's our most persistent illusion. A shooting star on the horizon"—the doctor gazed upward at an imaginary shooting star—"inflames our imaginations, and we envision a bright land beyond the world's end. But in the struggle to maintain the vision, even the strongest natures are exhausted and lose their hold on reality."

Julian raised his hand, like the doctor's profound metaphysician, and laid it on Hannah's forehead, a simple gesture that filled him with wonder. His arm tingled. He thought of himself as a colony of cells, colonies within colonies of microorganisms pursuing their appointed tasks independent of his will, links in a chain that bound him to foxes and wolves in distant forests, on the slopes of distant mountains, and to the forests themselves, the whole kingdom of becoming.

"When I went out this morning," Hannah said loudly and clearly, "I heard someone say, 'It's the handmaiden of the Lord,' but I couldn't see who it was."

"Try to keep her quiet," the doctor said.

"I have to tell you something." Her forehead crinkled under Julian's hand. "There were people at the bus stop, and I thought that one of them had mistaken me for someone else. I couldn't be sure, so I got on the bus, and then I heard it again."

"Mrs. Dijksterhuis, I'm going to give you something that will help you sleep."

"You'll have to let me go first."

"Just try to relax now."

"I have to go to the toilet. I've had to go for a long time."

The doctor turned to leave. "I'll be back in a jiffy," he said. "Don't undo her whatever you do or we'll have the devil to pay. I want to give her a sedative and a dose of Thorazine. Keep her quiet—that's the main thing. Talk to her; tell her a story; anything."

The doctor's broad back filled the doorway.

"What have I done?" she wailed. "What have I done? Everyone on the bus stared at me as if I were drunk, but I *wasn't* drunk. I was in great trouble and I had to pour out my soul before the Lord."

"Why don't I tell you a story?"

"Yes, Julie, but I have to tinkle. Badly."

"Is that all?"

"I think so."

Julian closed the door.

"Once upon a time," he began as he loosened the straps on the near side of the cart, "there were two little girls named Seremonda and Duva."

"They told me," Hannah interrupted, "that the children had gone away."

"You have to listen."

"I *am* listening."

Hannah swung her legs down over the side of the cart and stood up unsteadily. Julian helped her squat over the wastebasket, casting about in his mind for a suitable adventure, adding familiar landmarks one by one as he did so—the schoolhouse, the churchyard, the baker's great stone oven, and of course, the great highways that bound east and west, north and south. The north–south highway was the geographical axis of the children's adventures; invariably they set out north to the mountains or south to the sea. It was bisected, in the center of the village, by the east–west highway, which provided a sort of metaphysical axis, though this was never defined very precisely. The westward road, which led through rolling meadows and fertile valleys to the ancient city where the king held his court, was kept in good repair, and every now and then some of the villagers, either to seek their fortunes or to escape from sickness and trouble, would pack up their belongings and set out for the city, never to be seen again. But the highway that led to the east disappeared into a dense forest and was said to be impassible.

Hannah let loose a noisy stream of urine. "A river bordered the kingdom on the east," continued Julian. "Hardly a trace remained of the bridge that had once spanned it; few of the villagers cared to venture even that far into the forest, and no one ventured any farther." Not even Julian.

"But where did the children *go*?" asked Hannah.

"Are you through?"

"Not yet."

"Are you listening?"

"Yes, I'm listening. They were under the mountain, don't you remember? Tell me about it, Julie. They wouldn't let me go there. They shoved so and held my arms."

"You couldn't see the mountain from the village itself, because of the forest, but you could see it from the church-yard, which was on a high hill. It was cold and white even in summer, and on holy days at night you could see little lights, like fireflies, just where the top of the mountain should have been."

"I saw them too, Julie, dancing round the lamp. What are they?"

Julian wasn't sure, but the schoolmaster said they were only shooting stars in the sky beyond the mountain, and the priest said they were fairy lights dancing on the mountain itself. The villagers were divided, but there was no way of settling the questions because there were no longer any travelers on the eastern highway.

Someone will have to set out eastwards, thought Julian. *Tonight.*

The door opened and Hannah stood up suddenly, her skirt concealing the wastebasket. Sara ran to her mother. Father Neumiller was silhouetted in the doorway, his briefcase in one hand.

"Papa's telling a story about Seremonda and Duva." Hannah kissed Sara's teary face.

"Are you all right, Mama?"

"Of course I'm all right. You must come and listen. But didn't you bring Dinah?"

"No, Mama."

"You mustn't leave her all alone."

"Mama, she's dead—don't you remember?"

"Then we must fetch her."

Hannah stepped out of her underpants and looked around, as if to see who was going to accompany her. No one moved. A look of pain swept across her face and her knees buckled.

Julian caught her and with Father Neumiller's help lifted her back onto the gurney.

Julian poured some water from the pitcher into the wastebasket. He raised his arm again, renewing the strange sense of wonder that had come over him earlier, and let his hand rest on the side of his wife's face.

"No one ever ventured eastwards. Never even thought of it." Sara looked up at him.

"Except." Julian took the plunge. "No one ever ventured eastwards *except* the wandering minstrels and jongleurs who came out of the forest in the fall, dressed like wild animals, bound for the west."

"Why did they dress like wild animals?" asked Hannah.

"The animals were their totems."

"Oh. What did they do in the west?"

"They spent the dark winter months entertaining the king and his court."

"Where did they come from?"

"Listen to the story and you'll see. You're worse than the children."

But her question prompted him.

"Did they come from the Mountain of Lights?"

"Well, they told stories about it; they said that although the side of the mountain you could see from the churchyard was always covered with snow, on the far side it was always summer; and that spring lay to the north, and autumn to the south."

"Shouldn't it be the other way round?"

"That's the way it was."

"Did the villagers like the minstrels?"

"Yes and no. They didn't trust them, but they gathered on the green to watch the juggling and tumbling and to listen to talk of life at the king's court and songs of faraway lands."

Julian waited for another question. He looked at Sara. "Well, what happened?"

Not much to go on. "One of the minstrels . . ." He trailed off, but then continued. "One of the minstrels was the favorite of Seremonda and Duva. His name was Joachim, and he was more reckless and gay than the rest. He was the last to arrive in the fall, dressed as a she-wolf, and he was the first to disappear into the forest in the spring. 'Ich am of Faerielonde,' he sang to the villagers, plucking a lute made of seven different kinds of polished wood and strung with gold and silver strings that glistened in the firelight.

"Ich am of Faerielonde
And of the holy londe
of Faerielonde.
Good sirs, pray ich thee,
Come and dance with me
in Faerielonde."

Julian half sang, half chanted, improvising a melody. He summoned the villagers into a ring, children, parents, grandparents. They danced to Joachim's music, some of them, like the schoolmaster, against their will. Seremonda waited for the schoolmaster's son, the first love of her heart; but Duva, who lay close to Julian's heart, was the first to join the magic circle. And when the dancing was over, and Joachim disappeared into the darkness, Duva went with him; and Julian knew that wherever her road led her that night, he could never call her back.

"By the time they reached the edge of the forest they could hear the villagers calling after them; but soon their cries became indistinguishable from the cries of the waterbirds nesting along the banks of the river."

"What about Seremonda?" Sara asked. "Doesn't she go too?"

It was her story too, of course; but she didn't suit Julian's present purpose.

"Just listen, will you? You always want to know everything in advance. They stopped to rest for a while—okay?—when they got to the river. They could hear the alarm bell tolling in the distance, but Joachim knew that the villagers wouldn't pursue them into the forest at night. Pretty soon, though, they heard footsteps; not the clatter of heavy boots on the cracked paving stones, but the slap of small shoes."

"Oh, Papa."

Hannah smiled. She was lying on her side, one hand on Julian's. Father Neumiller grunted in the back of the room and began to fiddle with his briefcase.

"Was it Seremonda?"

"Of course. But do you know what? Joachim was very angry with her. He said that she was too old to come with them, that she would be unhappy; but she wouldn't go home, so they slept on beds of leaves and pine needles and break-fasted on nuts and berries before setting off through the forest, following the course of the river as it curved toward the east."

Father Neumiller's scowling face emerged into the light. He offered a hip flask to Julian. Julian took a swallow and gave the bottle to Hannah. Cheap brandy. He wanted her to sleep before the doctor returned. She dribbled the brandy down her front. Julian dabbed at it with a Kleenex, and then he brought the minstrel and the children to the far side of the forest, where there was a great gate and gatekeeper who thrust his lantern in their faces. "'What have we here?' growled the gatekeeper when he saw Seremonda. 'You minstrels have no mercy.' But he gave them chunks of bread, which they toasted at an open fire, and cups of hot wine, which they stirred with cinnamon sticks. On the far side of the river rose the Mountain of Lights.

"The children clapped their hands," said Julian, clapping his own, "and watched in wonder as the lights that gave the mountain its name began to appear, blue-white and amber, flickering like candle flames, whole constellations of lights dancing in the dark as if the stars themselves were dancing in the deep dome of heaven."

He added a song, which Joachim sang as he escorted the children over a bridge spanning a steep chasm:

> *"Love of a distant country,*
> *My whole heart aches for you;*
> *O children, more beautiful than the stars,*
> *Lights on the mountain,*
> *The fields are harvested, the woods are hewn,*
> *By those who never return."*

The mountain itself seemed to take up the song with a thousand echoing voices.

"No one grew older in that land, and the four seasons were at the command of the children, who swam in summer, and sprang in spring, and fell in fall, tumbling down the mountain like rockslides."

Where am I now? wondered Julian. *Given enough time,* he thought, *it would be possible to work out the metaphysical details, to reconcile discrepancies.* But there was no time. Tears had begun to sparkle in the corners of Hannah's eyes; Sara was shuffling her feet; Father Neumiller would soon be drunk and loquacious. And in the doorway stood the doctor, gently squeezing a hypodermic needle in his huge hand. A drop of clear liquid ran down the silver shaft of the needle and caught the lamplight as it fell, like a tear, or a star.

"On the west slope," said Julian, turning back to Hannah, "the children wondered about the wide world beyond the forest, which they could see from the very top of the mountain, where they danced on holy days at night, carrying little torches." *So much for the lights.*

Father Neumiller's hand reached out of the darkness and caught the doctor's arm. "Let him finish."

"I told you not to undo her," said the doctor, but his voice was tired rather than angry.

Julian held up his hand, palm out, motioning the doctor to be silent. Hannah was lying perfectly still. Julian filled the high halls that honeycombed the mountain with the music of sackbuts and shams, rebels and krumhorns, lutes and tournebouts. He set Duva a-dancing in courtyards overlooking orchards and vineyards and green gardens laid out in neat rows and watered by mountain springs like the garden of Alcinöos. But he hung the songs of the minstrels like heavy weights on the heart of Seremonda. He was clearing a path for her return.

"She grew pale and did not dance with the rest but sat apart in inglenooks, in silence and shadow, in fire and fleet and candlelight. Joachim did what he could to comfort her with counsel and cheer, marvels and magic, pranks and presents. He brought her a pear-shaped lute with seven pairs of gold and silver strings and taught her to play, to bind sadness in song; and soon she was strumming stately sarabands, plucking proud pavanes. The other children gathered round her, and Duva led the dancing. Seremonda's heart grew whole, but she did not forget the wide world in the west, her heart's

THE TRUTH ABOUT DEATH

home, and the schoolmaster's son, the first love of her heart, and a terrible longing seized her, the same longing that sent the minstrels migrating like birds back to the wide world and beyond. When they began to gather in groups, talking of travel to faraway lands, she asked Joachim if she and Duva might not go too.

"'You shall come with me,' he said, 'for love calls you back to the things of the world.'"

Alas, thought Julian, *for Duva must stay behind;* "But Joachim said, 'Duva will not wish to leave the mountain.'" And indeed nothing would persuade her to return. Seremonda became quite cross with her, but to no avail.

It suddenly occurred to Julian that she might travel farther east. They might all meet at the king's court in the west. The world is round, after all. But he let the opportunity slip through his fingers. Duva remained on the mountain. Joachim and Seremonda departed, dressed as wild animals, keeping the river on their right.

"Seremonda forgot the sharp pain of parting as she drew nearer and nearer to her old home, which they reached on the third day at nightfall. They drew the villagers into a circle. 'Ich am of Faerielonde,' Joachim sang, and Seremonda plucked the gold and silver strings of her pear-shaped lute. One by one the children joined the dance, followed by their parents. Seremonda's mother and father joined hands with the rest, and the schoolmaster's son too, the first love of her heart. The priest blessed them reluctantly before stepping into the magic circle. Only the schoolmaster remained in the darkness. But Seremonda joined her voice, high and clear, with Joachim's till the schoolmaster too stepped forward into the warm glow of the firelight.

"Only a few embers were glowing in the dark when the

dancers, released at last from the spell of the music, looked round at one another, astonished at the fullness of their hearts, while above them, turning on the silent axletree of Heaven, Boötes the herdsman followed his flocks across the pastures of the sky." *Enough, enough.* Julian looked around him at the circle of listeners.

Sara was the first to break the silence. "Is that all?"

"That's all."

The doctor stepped forward.

"She's asleep," said Julian. "What do we do now?"

Father Neumiller offered the flask, nearly empty, to the doctor. "Have a drink of this."

"Thanks."

The doctor finished the brandy. He pointed the hypodermic into the air and squeezed firmly. A fine spray hung in the light for a moment over the lamp, like the Milky Way, and then went out.

"Amen," said the priest.

"Papa?"

"Yes?"

"What about Duva?"

"Oh for heaven's sake."

"It's just a story, isn't it?"

"Yes, it's just a story."

POCKETS OF SILENCE

S HORTLY BEFORE SHE DIED my mother made a tape for us, several tapes. She had some things she wanted to say, big things, little things. It was kind of a mystery. I mean, I don't think she had any big secret sins to confess—her sins always rose to the surface right away—so what could she possibly have to say that she hadn't said, or couldn't say to our faces? After all, we weren't one of those families that couldn't talk to each other or express our emotions. If anything, we were at the other end of the spectrum.

"I just want to be able to say things as they occur to me. I don't want to have to call you. So many things come to me during the day, and at night too, especially at night; so many happy memories—some unhappy ones too—but mostly happy. I want you to have a record of that. So many things to say to each one of you, and all of you."

So Papa set up a tape recorder by the bed. An amateur musician, he had lots of recording equipment and made quite a production out of it.

"Why don't you just get me one of those little cassette

recorders?" Mama asked; but Papa had to do things in a big way. He set up his four-track tape recorder on the stand next to the bed where Mama kept her medication. He bought two new low-impedance microphones and tried out every possible permutation of microphone locations and settings on the tape recorder. It was his way of working off some of his frustration.

"Testing, one two three four testing. Now *you* do it."

But Mama didn't want to do it. "I feel like I'm onstage, on the radio." One mike was on a boom that swung over the bed. "I want this to be private."

"Testing, one two three four testing."

And the tape recorder would repeat, "Testing, one two three four testing."

The finishing touch was a remote punch in/out switch that Mama could keep on the bed beside her so she wouldn't have to twist around to start and stop the recorder. All she had to do was punch a button.

"I've always wanted one of these anyway," Papa said. "That's how professionals correct their mistakes. If you've got a sour note, you just play along with the tape, and when you get to the sour note, you punch in and then out and it records right over it."

Once Papa had everything in place Mama felt better. She had an object in her life, what remained of it. A mission. Something to be accomplished. Something that could not have been accomplished under any other circumstances: the recording of a happy and productive and sometimes turbulent life under the pressure of death. Death was a lens that would reveal things as they really were: what was important would assume its true importance; what was unimportant would recede into the shadows.

Mama kept the tapes right on the bed. She didn't want us to listen to them while she was still alive. But during the long summer afternoons we could hear the tape recorder clicking on and off. Sometimes, if I got up to go to the bathroom in the middle of the night, I'd hear the familiar click and put my ear to her door, but I couldn't make out what she was saying, only the faint murmur of her weakened voice.

She filled up half a dozen seven-inch tapes. Seven hours. And when she'd said what she had to say, she stopped talking. A week later she died, and ever since her death the house has seemed strangely silent, even when Papa was playing his guitar and we were all singing.

It was over three years before we worked up the courage to listen to the tapes, which had been stored on a shelf in the dining room closet next to the Waterford crystal that we never used anymore. When I say "courage" I don't mean that we were afraid of what we might hear; I mean we were afraid we wouldn't be able to bear it, especially during the holidays. But we'd had a wonderful Christmas, and we were feeling strong. Papa had suffered some business losses, but things were looking up; I was a senior at Kenwood High School and would be following my sisters to the U of C, which everyone said was just as good as Harvard and (more important) close to home. Molly was in graduate school at the University of Michigan, Mama's alma mater. Meg had married and was expecting, and her husband, Dan, was just perfect. Handsome, romantic, practical, talented. Papa had been teaching him to play the harmonica and he learned so quickly that they'd made a tape together—Papa on the guitar, Dan on the harp, Meg and Molly singing the blues songs that had embarrassed us as children, and that still embarrassed me:

THE TRUTH ABOUT DEATH

Mr. Jelly Roll Baker
let me be your slave
when Gabriel blows his trumpet
you know I'll rise from my grave
for some of your jelly
some of your good jelly roll
you know it's doin' me good
way down deep in my soul.

It was New Year's Day. Meg and Dan would be driving back to Milwaukee that afternoon. Molly would be at home with Papa and me for another couple of days before going back to school. It just seemed like the right time, and I don't think anyone was surprised when Meg brought one of the tapes into the living room, holding it tight against her big swelling belly.

Papa got up and without a word began to thread the tape; Meg poked a couple sticks of kindling under the smoldering logs in the fireplace and then sat down next to Dan at the piano and filled up the silence with a chorus of "Fum, Fum, Fum," Mama's favorite carol: *A venti-cinq de dicembre, fum fum fum.* Molly and I were sitting at opposite ends of the couch, the bottoms of our bare feet pressed together.

Papa switched on the tape recorder and there was a moment of silence so intense that the dogs, snoozing in front of the fire, perked up their ears. (If Mama had been there she'd have made them lie down on their own rug under the piano.) Papa hurried across the room and into his chair.

I suppose we each brought different questions to that moment, even Dan, who had never met Mama, but who'd heard enough about her, and maybe we *were* in fact a little apprehensive. What was going to emerge as truly important? What was going to recede into the shadows?

I didn't know what the others were thinking, but I was wondering about the Italian novelist—a visiting writer at the University—that Mama'd had an affair with. *I* knew that Mama had misbehaved, but no one had ever explained to me exactly what had happened, and I was still curious because I couldn't fit it into the picture I had of our family. Papa and Mama had had plenty of differences, which they never bothered to conceal from us; but on the whole our family life had been shaped by the love they'd felt for each other and expressed, physically, all the time. Neither one had been able to walk by the other without giving a little pat on the backside, and they had always taken naps when they couldn't possibly have been tired. So where did Alessandro Postiglione fit into the picture? Was he one of those things that was going to assume its true importance? Or was he going to recede into the shadows? I didn't know why it seemed so important; but it did.

We waited, and then waited some more. Papa got out of his chair and made some adjustments. Still no sound. He ran the tape forward for a few seconds and tried again. Still nothing. The big reels turned in silence. Papa ran the tape forward again. Nothing. He turned it over and tried the other side. Still nothing. Meg got up and brought the rest of the tapes from the dining room closet. They were all clearly labeled: HELEN'S TAPE-AUGUST 15–16, 1968. HELEN'S TAPE-AUGUST 17–18, 1968. HELEN'S TAPE-AUGUST 19–22, 1968. And so on. Papa tried one after another, but there was no sound.

I'd never seen Papa—or any adult for that matter—really lose control before. It didn't happen all at once, but you could hear it coming. He spent the rest of the day at the tape recorder,

trying this and then that. If you've ever hooked up a sophisti-
cated stereo system you'll know that in cases like this there's
usually some button that needs to be pushed, or a knob that
needs to be turned, or a patch cord that's plugged into the
wrong hole. It's as simple as that. But Papa exhausted all the
possibilities. The rest of us, sitting in the kitchen, could hear
him cursing softly, nonstop. Occasionally there was a blast of
sound as he tried some other tape, or turned on the tuner, but
he couldn't coax any sound out of Mama's tapes, and finally he
cracked. He didn't break anything; he just started screaming—
shouting, swearing as loud as he could—and then he started
to cry, really cry, huge rattling sobs as he stumbled up the
stairs.

Meg and Dan left for Milwaukee at about three. Dan had to
go back to work the next morning. Molly and I emptied the
dishwasher and filled it again and washed the dishes that
wouldn't fit in the second load. We put the turkey carcass in
the stockpot and covered it with water. Molly scrubbed down
the butcher's table with bleach, the way Mama used to do,
while I put the spices back in alphabetical order. And then we
took all the jars and lids out of the closet in the butler's pantry
and matched them up. It was like trying to match up socks;
there were a lot of odd jars and a lot of odd lids left over.

Finally, when there was nothing more to be done, we went
upstairs. I'd never been afraid to approach my father before,
even when he was angry. But I was afraid now, afraid of what
we'd find. We tiptoed through Mama's study and pushed open
the bedroom door. Papa was lying facedown on the bed. The
late-afternoon sun, caught by the beveled edges of small
windowpanes, covered the bed with tiny rainbows. Papa's pale
hair—once carrot red—was flecked with light.

Papa always slept on his stomach so I thought he might be asleep, but when Molly tiptoed around the bed, he looked up at her.

"Papa? Are you all right?"

I could see him shake his head: no.

He kept the register closed, and the bedroom was very cold. Molly turned back the comforter and crawled in next to Papa. I did the same on the other side. There were still two comforters on the bed; I pulled the second one over me, and we lay like that while the sun went down, watching the little rainbows gradually grow together and then fade away completely.

About four or five times a year Ann Landers prints a letter from someone advising readers to tell their loved ones that they love them—before it's too late. Whenever I read one of those letters I think of Mama and her tapes. But the analogy is imperfect; the moral is not the same. Mama *was* trying to tell us.

But then what *is* the moral?

Check *all* your equipment? Well, of course. The problem, it turned out, was with the new remote punch in/out switch, which had been activating the tape recorder without engaging the recording heads. Papa hadn't used it in the three years since Mama's death, so he'd never discovered that it hadn't been working properly. He sent the tapes to the Ampex Laboratory in Schenectady, New York, to have them analyzed on the off chance that a weak signal had gotten through, but there was nothing to be recovered. The tapes were virginal.

So, by all means, check all your equipment. Yes. But that's a moral for the head, not the heart. What can I say about the heart?

I suppose the real question is: Why does it matter so intensely? What could Mama have said that would have altered the course of our lives?

I think about this question a lot—not all the time, but often enough—without coming any closer to an answer. All I know is that my life is filled with little pockets of silence. When I put a record on the turntable, for example, there's a little interval—between the time the needle touches down on the record and the time the music actually starts—during which my heart refuses to beat. All I know is that between the rings of the telephone, between the touch of a button and the sound of the radio coming on, between the dimming of the lights at the cinema and the start of the film, between the lightning and the thunder, between the shout and the echo, between the lifting of a baton and the opening bars of a symphony, between the dropping of a stone and the plunk that comes back from the bottom of a well, between the ringing of the doorbell and the barking of the dogs I sometimes catch myself, involuntarily, listening for the sound of my mother's voice, still waiting for the tape to begin.

ACKNOWLEDGMENTS

I would like to thank my first three readers for their continued support and encouragement: Virginia (my wife); Henry Dunow (my agent), and Nancy Miller (my editor). And I'd like to thank Gleni Bartels (my production editor) for stitching these stories together.

Special thanks to the following for helping me to expand my frame of reference to include: New York City (John Sheedy and Marilyn Webb), Vietnam (Richard Stout), embalming (Christopher Hroziencik), museum exhibits (Sheri Lindquist), cartooning (Bob Mankoff), French food (Anne Steinbeck), all things Italian (Vincenzina Cipriani, Janet Smith, and Rita Severi), the Guardia Medica in Rome (Marina Frontani), Stearmans in Italy (Piero Angiolillo), and Texas avocados (Noe Torres and Medardo Riojas).

And to the following for supplying just the right words when I needed them: Susan Erickson, "Renaissance angels balancing effortlessly on stepping-stone clouds" (p. 136)— adapted from "Angels Italiano" (*The Art of Departure*, Egress Studio Press, Bellingham, WA 2003); Michel McFee, "How hard to take the trail as it comes" (p. 105)—from "Plain Air" (*Plain Air*, University Press of Florida, Gainesville, FL 1983); and Peter Burian, translation of Leopardi's "Il passero solitario" (p. 53).

PUBLICATION INFORMATION:

Published stories included in *The Truth About Death and Other Stories*:

"The Removal," *Printers Row Fiction* (April, 2016).
"A Christmas Letter," *Ploughshares* (Spring 2014), 112–133. Selected for online publication by *Electric Literature*'s "Recommended Reading," http://recommendedreading.tumblr.com/.
"FOR SALE," *Black Warrior Review* 23 (Spring/Summer 1997), 1–13.
"I Speak a Little French," *Crazyhorse* 43 (Winter 1992), 82–91.
"Pockets of Silence," *The Chicago Tribune*, Magazine Section, 29 January 1989, 18–20. Later incorporated into *The Sixteen Pleasures* (1994).
"Snapshots of Aphrodite," *StoryQuarterly* 38 (2002), 478–488.
"The Mountain of Lights," *The California Quarterly* 21 (1982), 93–112. Reprinted in *Best Short Stories from the California Quarterly, 1971–1985*.
"The Second Coming," *Mississippi Valley Review* 23 (Fall 1992), 63–79.

A NOTE ON THE AUTHOR

Robert Hellenga was educated at the University of Michigan, the Queen's University of Belfast, and Princeton University. He is a professor emeritus at Knox College in Galesburg, Illinois, and the author of the novels *The Confessions of Frances Godwin*, *Snakewoman of Little Egypt*, *The Sixteen Pleasures*, *The Fall of a Sparrow*, *Blues Lessons*, *Philosophy Made Simple*, and *The Italian Lover*. He lives in Galesburg, Illinois.